The Dead Donkey

&

The Guillotined Woman

THE GOTHIC SOCIETY at *The Gargoyle's Head Press*

The Gothic Society publishes books and studies in the field of the morbid, the macabre and the darkly romantic. There is also a society magazine six times a year, which covers the same field, and which is renowned for its illustrations and individual style.

For further details contact the publisher at the address overleaf.

THE
DEAD DONKEY
and
THE
GUILLOTINED WOMAN

By Jules Janin

Preface & Afterword by Terry Hale

THE GOTHIC SOCIETY
at The Gargoyle's Head Press

THE GOTHIC SOCIETY
Chatham House
Gosshill Road
Chislehurst
Kent BR7 5NS
© Copyright Preface & Afterword: Terry Hale 1993

Printed in Great Britain by Antony Rowe Ltd
ISBN 1-874100-05-5

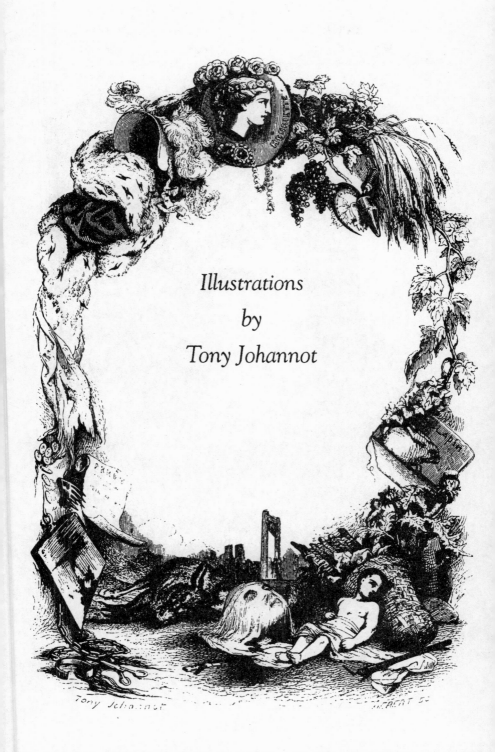

Illustrations

by

Tony Johannot

Jules Janin

Contents

Vignette by Tony Johannot for
Paul Lacroix's "La Danse macabre, histoire fantastique du XVe siècle"
(Paris: Renduel, 1832)

Preface

Writing in 1927, Michael Sadler asked the following question: "It remains to inquire where, when its great days were over, the Gothic romance took refuge."[1] One answer to this question was that it migrated to France. However, although the English Gothic novel was almost as popular in France during the years of the French Revolution and its aftermath, by the time Jules Janin's *L'Ane mort et la femme guillotinée* (The Dead Donkey and the Guillotined Woman) was published in 1829, the French horror novel (or the *roman frénétique* as it was rapidly christened — had already largely evolved into an authentically French genre in which most signs of foreign influences had been effaced.

In her memoirs, published towards the end of the last century, Countess Dash — a close friend and occasional collaborator of Alexandre Dumas *père* (a couple of her works even carry his name) — provides not only an indication of the enthusiasm that the horror novel was capable of generating in the France of the 1820s and the first half of the 1830s but also a brief survey of the most memorable works in the genre. "Everybody was reading *Le Solitaire* then," she remarks à propos the early 1820s, "a novel by the vicomte d'Arlincourt [...]. There must have been at least five or six plays on the subject. It even gave rise to a colour. The name of the heroine likewise. [...] This was the novel that was responsible for the craze for the Gothic and the Middle Ages which obsessed us all for so many years. One cannot say that it exerted a very profound literary or moral influence, but it exercised a tremendous fascination over our imaginations, over our thoughts on death, and in France that counts for much."[2]

Although Arlincourt's novel is all but forgotten nowadays, the success of some horror novels was less ephemeral: "Victor Hugo's *Han d'Islande* had us all trembling and stopped me from sleeping for two or three weeks. How in love we were with the hero! We were all mad over Ordener. When I was asked to become the god-mother of a young cousin, I wanted to have him christened Ordener. If he hadn't died fifteen days later, I dread to think what he would have thought of his name which nowadays seems absolutely ridiculous."[3]

Towards the end of the decade, she informs us, Jules Janin's *L'Ane mort et la femme guillotinée* created another sensation: "We all wept over that poor donkey, and" — she adds wryly — "it was so prettily written."[4] These years represent perhaps the apogee of the French horror writing. "It was as if books and writers were bursting out at the seams: Eugène Süe with *Plik et Plok*, Jules Janin with *Barnave*, Paul Lacroix with *Le Roi des Ribauds*, and many others too. We read all day long and all night long — and not because we were bored or in order to instruct ourselves, but compulsively, because we were unable to stop."[5]

When she managed to drag herself away from the latest best-seller in order to attend the theatre, more often than not it was a melodrama which left the most vivid impression. She recalls *Le Vampire* at the Porte-Saint-Martin in 1820, and shortly afterwards two plays based on the lives of eighteenth-century criminals — *Mandrin*, also at the Porte-Saint-Martin, and *Cartouche* at the Ambigu.[6] On the evidence of Countess Dash's memoirs, horror and crime would appear to be the predominant defining characteristics of the entire literature and theatre of the epoch.

Théophile Gautier, in his preface to *Mademoiselle de Maupin* (1835), paints a similar picture of the reading habits of his time, even if he implies a clearer distinction between works with a historical setting and the horror novel than was perhaps the case:[7]

At a very remote epoch, which is lost in the mist of ages, very nearly three weeks ago, the romance of the Middle Ages flourished principally in Paris and the suburbs. The coat-of-arms was held in great honour; head-dresses, *à la* Hennin, were not despised, parti-coloured trousers were esteemed; the dagger was beyond all price; the pointed shoe was worshipped like a fetich. [...]

The critic had not waited for the second romance in order to begin his work of deprecation. No sooner had the first appeared than he had wrapped himself up in his cloth of camel hair, poured a bushel of ashes on his head, and then, assuming that loud and doleful tone of his, begun to cry out:—

"Still the Middle Ages, always the Middle Ages! who will deliver me from the Middle Ages, from the Middle Ages that are not the Middle Ages?" [...]

By the side of the romance of the Middle Ages sprouted the romance of the charnel house, a very agreeable kind, largely consumed by nervous women of fashion and *blasé* cooks.

The journalists very soon scented it out. [...] What did they not say? what did they not write? Literature of the morgue or the galleys, nightmare of the hangman, hallucination of drunken butchers and hot-fevered convict-keepers! They benignly gave us to understand that the authors were assassins and vampires, that they had contracted the vicious habit of killing their fathers and mothers, that they drank blood in skulls, used tibias instead of forks, and cut their bread with a guillotine.

It was in this latter tradition of what Gautier styled "the romance of the charnel house" that Jules Janin's *L'Ane mort et la femme guillotinée* was conceived and written. Unlike previous attempts at the genre, however, if we discount the works of Sade, it provided horror in a far more concentrated form. One recent French commentator has described it as no less than "a journey to the country of Horror."[8] Indeed, although the author himself later dismissed it as "one of my little jests",[9] Janin's novel played a central role in defining the aesthetics of the French horror story for the next few years.

Almost overnight it made its author — hitherto an obscure journalist — into a celebrity, if not by name (as with Hugo's *Le Dernier jour d'un condamné*, which had appeared earlier in the year, Janin's novel was published anonymously) then by reputation. In just over a decade, it went through some seven different editions (by 1876 the figure had risen to seventeen), an astonishing number for the epoch. Not a few of these, moreover, were relatively luxurious publications. Even the first edition contained two vignettes by Eugène Dévéria, already widely recognised as a rising Romantic artist. As if to seal its success, Balzac even wrote a short comically macabre continuation of the novel, translated here for the first time since it appeared in *Le Voleur* on Feb. 5, 1830, in which he follows the novel's heroine into the dissection-room.[10]

The English Gothic horror-romance — a category whichperhaps excludes "shudder novels" such as Lewis's *The Monk* — was written in the main by women and, if not exclusively for women, then at least with women readers in mind. As Chris Baldick has pointed out in his recent introduction to the *Oxford Book of Gothic Tales*, the typical Gothic theme of incarceration may easily be read as an analogy of some feminine lives.[11] The *roman frénétique*, on the other hand, was written almost exclusively by men and far from exploring the feminine predicament expresses what one commentator — in a somewhat different context — has referred to as male anxieties about women invading the public place.[12]

Let there be no doubt: *L'Ane mort et la femme guillotinée* is a profoundly misogynistic novel — though whether the author himself is a misogynist or whether he is satirising Romantic misogyny I shall leave readers to decide for themselves. This theme of the fear of women finds expression in the *roman frénétique* not only in the portrayal of women who are powerful, seductive and egoistical, traditional attributes of the *femme fatale*, but also in the portrayal of women who are merely economically independent. Foedora, in Balzac's *La Peau de chagrin* of 1831 (now generally known in English as *The Wild Ass's Skin*) is a good example of the former; Henrietta, the heroine of *L'Ane mort et la femme guillotinée*, an excellent example of the latter. In both cases, the *femme fatale* is defined with reference to a thoroughly "effeminized" male protagonist. These disintegrating gender boundaries would have been an an equally powerful source of horror for contemporary readers of Janin's novel as the author's almost paranoiac description of a society in which everyone is engaged in some capacity or another in the judicial machinery of death.

There is, by now, a substantial literature dealing with various aspects of the theme of the *femme fatale* in literature. For many commentators such an archetype is perceived as a legacy of the Christian tradition. Margaret Hallissy, for example, in a recent study of the female poisoner in literature, succinctly expresses the point in the following terms: "Their situation and that of the man who loves them invites analysis of the complex factors affecting attribution of moral guilt in sexual matters. In the religious traditions that influence Western literature, the female body is viewed as an enticement into sin. Even if she is *virgo intacta*, virtuous as can be, she is never really innocent; she is always sin incarnate."[13]

If this is the case, Janin's recourse to the figure of the *femme fatale* in *L'Ane mort et la femme guillotinée* (and Henrietta, whose fall from virtue to prostitution provides one of the central themes of the work, is far from being sexually innocent) is linked not only to the process of industrialisation (and the different relationship between the sexes that are entailed by changing work practices) but also to the religious revival which swept France in the 1820s and 30s. This, too, is referred to by Gautier in *Mademoiselle de Maupin*. "It is the fashion now to be virtuous and Christian," he remarks, "people have taken a turn for it. They affect Saint Jerome as formerly they affected Don Juan; they are pale and macerated, they wear their hair apostle-wise, they walk with clasped hands and with eyes fixed on the ground; they have a Bible open on the mantelpiece, and a crucifix and some consecrated box-wood by the bed; they swear no longer, smoke little, and scarcely chew at all."[14]

No doubt there is an element of exaggeration in all this, but it should not be forgotten that the most successful book of the period was not, as we might think, Victor Hugo's *Notre-Dame de Paris* but the abbé Lamennais's work of popular (one might say revolutionary) Christianity, *Paroles d'un croyant* (1834). The real roots of Romantic misogyny, however, or so we shall argue in the Afterword, are not to be found solely in this religious revival but in the curious coupling of religion with radical left-wing politics. This again is hinted at by Gautier in *Mademoiselle de Maupin* when he speaks of those writers of the early 1830s who "infuse a little Republicanism into their religion" and who "couple Robespierre and Jesus Christ in the most jovial fashion, and, with a seriousness worthy of praise, amalgamate the Acts of the Apostles with the decrees of the *holy* Convention."[15] By the holy Convention, Gautier intended to designate the system of government which resulted in the execution of some 40,000 people mainly in the course of those three fearful years from 1792 to 1795. The sort of writers he had in mind would have been Pétrus Borel, the self-styled "Lycanthrope" (and leader of the young Romantics), and Charles Lassailly, who died insane after writing one tremendous novel of pessimism and disgust. He was, no doubt, not altogether wrong in his claim that such writers were "by no means the least curious" representatives of his epoch. Gautier, however, was at one time a close friend of Borel's and could speak of him with amused irony. Janin, a staunch royalist, had far less sympathy with views which tended to confuse notions of Christian virtue with revolutionary *vertu*.

Finally, a word is necessary about the present edition. Although the

roman frénétique enjoyed tremendous popularity in France, only a few of
these works made their way into English. Indeed, one can almost list on
one hand the novels which managed to complete the journey. Arlincourt's
Le Solitaire, which Countess Dash read with such enjoyment in her teens,
was the first to be translated. It was brought out under the title of *The
Recluse* the same year as the French edition (London: H. Colburn & Co.,
2 vol.,1821). There was even a sixpenny chapbook version of this work
issued under the slightly more melodramatic title of *Charles the Bold; or,
The Recluse of the Wild Mountain. A Tale of the Fifteenth Century* (London,1823). The following year, a translation of Arlincourt's *Le Renégat*
was also published, as *The Renegade*. In 1825, the same publisher (J. Robbins
& Co) brought out Victor Hugo's spectacularly lugubrious *Han of Iceland*,
complete with all its morgues, monsters, and public executioners.

Other works mentioned by Countess Dash as depriving her of her sleep,
such as Eugène Süe's *Plik et Plok* of 1830 (the somewhat obscure title
conceals two utterly cynical, not to mention extremely violent, pirate
tales of a distinctly *frénétique* hue) have never been translated, though a
number of the author's other works from the same period were eventually
brought out in English during the 1840s after he achieved European fame
with his serial novel *Les Mystères de Paris*.

It was, however, works such as these that Balzac had in mind — for the
frénétique was a genre broad enough to accommodate pirate stories,
historical works, and novels, such as *L'Ane mort et la femme guillotinée*, with
contemporary settings — when he penned the following oblique remark
to be found in his preface to *La Peau de chagrin*: "From all sides may be
heard voices raised up in protest against the violent nature of modern
writing. Cruelty, torture, people being thrown into the sea, hangings,
gibbets, condemned men, atrocious deeds committed in hot blood and in
cold, everything has become farcical!"[16]

L'Ane mort et la femme guillotinée, however, did eventually manage to
find its way into English, and was published in *The Illustrated Literature of
all Nations* in 1851. The translation followed the slightly revised French
edition of 1842. From a bibliophile's standpoint, including as it did the
illustrations by Tony Johannot, this was the most remarkable edition to
date and has long been considered one of the high points of Romantic
book production. Although Johannot's illustrations, many of which are
reproduced in the present edition, are more 'finished' in appearance than
the numerous frontispieces he designed in the early years of the previous
decade for a host of novels and plays, they nonetheless capture the
atmosphere of the novel with a rare fidelity.

Janin did not change the underlying structure of the novel for the 1842
edition, he merely amplified or occasionally moderated certain of the
underlying themes. One difference between this edition and that of 1829,
however, was that the author had by now suppressed the second half of
the title, so that the work became simply *L'Ane mort*. In other words, and
for whatever reason, it would seem that Janin no longer wished to draw
attention to the image of the guillotine with all its concomitant asso-

ciations not only with capital punishment but also, of course, with the
Terror of the French Revolution. This may have been simply because
over the course of the years the spectre of revolution had faded. The
English edition, on the other hand, gave preference to the second half of
the title and the work now became *The Guillotined Woman*. Apart from
modernising a few spellings and correcting one or two obvious mistakes,
it is this (anonymous) 1851 translation which is reprinted here.

This raises one final question. Why was it necessary to wait so long —
twenty two years from the date of the novel's first publication in 1829,
and nine from that of the illustrated edition of 1842 — for the work to be
translated into English?

There are, I think, two answers to this question. Firstly, throughout the
1840s and 1850s the French serial novel, or *roman feuilleton*, had a major
impact on British publishing. A stream of French sensation fiction,
written by instalment and with every instalment ending on a note of
suspense, filled the pages of publications such as *The London Journal* and
The Family Herald. The French serial novel undoubtedly helped prepare
the ground for the translation of other French works.[17]

Secondly, I suggest, Janin's novel anticipated by some decades Victo-
rian fears of sexual danger. First and foremost amongst these new sources
of anxiety was perhaps the image of that "quintessessential female figure
of the urban scene" (as one recent feminist commentator has called her)
— the prostitute. "For men as well as women," writes Judith Walkowitz,
"the prostitute was a central spectacle in a set of urban encounters and
fantasies. Repudiated and desired, degraded and threatening, the prostitute attracted the attention of a range of urban male explorers from the
1840s to the 1880s."[18] Walkowitz could well be describing the plot of
L'Ane mort et la femme guillotinée here, though in fact, as she makes abun-
dantly clear, what she had in mind was the "nocturnal wanderings in
search of conversation with 'women of the streets' which figure in the
lives of men like Gladstone."[19]

Although the rhetoric of the English middle-classes rarely attained the
power of the orators of the French Revolution or the minor Romantic
writers of the 1830s, there are enough similarities between their respec-
tive notions of virtue to have made Janin's novel comprehensible to an
English audience of the early 1850s. Some readers, no doubt, would have
sympathised with the much persecuted heroine; others identified with
attitudes of the anonymous narrator.

— *Terry Hale*

Notes

1. *Cited by Devendra Varma, The Gothic Flame, London, The Scarecrow Press, 1987, p. 173.*

2. *Comtesse Dash, Mémoires des Autres, Paris, La Librairie Illustrée, 1897-98, Vol. 1, p. 180-181. Comtesse Dash, incidentally, was a pseudonym for the Marquise de Saint-Mars. She only turned to the pen after the death of her husband, a high-ranking cavalry officer, left her in straightened circumstances. Most of her work belongs to what we now think of as the "silver fork" school — high society novels. Her pseudonym, however, was not intended as a literary pun on the convention by which the authors of such fictions could imply some real-life conterpart for their characters by the strategic use of blanks (e.g. Countess ——). It was, in fact, suggested to her by a Russian princess who had a lapdog called Dash.*

3. *Ibid, Vol. 2, p. 78.*

4. *Ibid, Vol. 3, p. 207.*

5. *Ibid, Vol. 4, p. 224.*

6. *Ibid, Vol. 2, pp. 229 — 231.*

7. Mademoiselle de Maupin. A Romance of Love and Passion. *London, Gibbings, 1909, pp. 20-22. The original (anonymous) translation has been slightly modified.*

8. *Pierre Castex, "Frénésie romantique", in* Cahiers du Sud, No. spécial: Les Petits Romantiques Français, *p. 34.*

9. Journal des Débats, *May 17, 1852.*

10. *The French title of this piece was:* Le Couteau à papier.

11. The Oxford Book of Gothic Tales, O.U.P., 1992, p. xxii.

12. Lynn Hunt, "The Many Bodies of Marie-Antoinette: Political Pornography and the Problem of the Feminine in the French Revolution", in Lynn Hunt (ed.), Eroticism and the Body Politic, Baltimore, Johns Hopkins University Press, 1991, p. 123.

13. Margaret Hallissey, Fear of the Female in Literature, New York, Greenwood Press 1987, p. 11.

14. *Op. cit., pp. 11-12.*

15. *Op cit., p. 12.*

16. La Peau de chagrin, *Pierre Barbéris (ed.), Paris, Le Livre de Poche, 1984, p. 12. My translation.*

17. *See on this subject Louis James,* Fiction for the Working Man, 1830-1850, *London, O.U.P., 1963, pp. 136-145.*

18. Judith R. Walkowitz, City of Dreadful Delight. Narratives of Sexual Danger in Late-Victorian London, London, Virago Press, 1992, p. 21.

19. *Ibid.*

Acknowledgements
The writer would like to thank Barbara Cresswell for her invaluable help in preparing this edition.

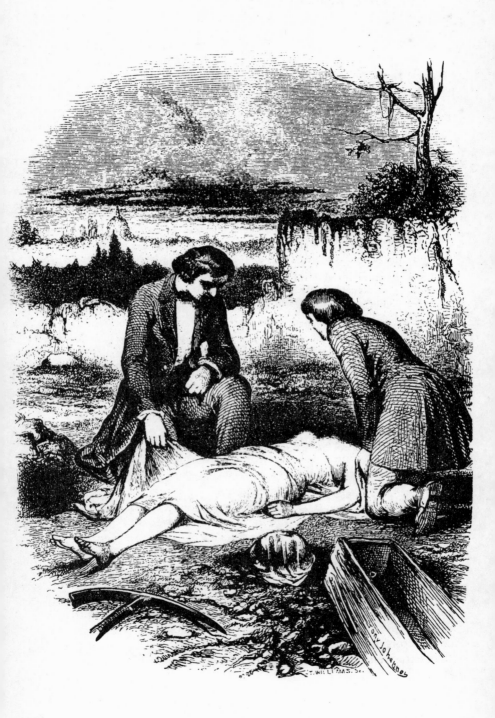

THE DEAD DONKEY AND THE GUILLOTINED WOMAN

CHAPTER I ◦§ ◦§ ◦§
The Barrière du Combat

There was a time when Sterne's "Dead Ass," and the touching funeral oration of the old peasant, brought the tears into one's eyes. I, also, am about to write the history of an ass, but, believe me, I shall not, for very good reasons, confine myself to the simplicity of the *Sentimental Journey*. In the first place, such a style would, in these days, be found insipid: it is too difficult of access for a writer, acquainted with his business, to lose time in trying to attain it, when he knows that, after all, he will only succeed in becoming both irksome and ridiculous. Give me, on the contrary, something terrible, dark and bloody; this can be depicted — this easily excites the passions! Courage, then! Wine has no longer the power to make your head swim, so swallow this tumbler of brandy. We have even gone beyond brandy; we have taken to spirits of wine; it only remains for us to turn drinkers of ether; but let us take care lest, by going from excess to excess, we may be enticed to imbibe opium.

Again, what is even the cup of Rodogune, with the Aristotelian poison that fills it to the brim, when compared with streams of dark blood, that leave an indelible track along the ground, while Christians, enveloped in pitch and sulphur, are burnt to death around the Roman circus, in order to light up its nocturnal combats? What, when the athletic champion, overthrown, and attempting, with his dying eye, to view once more the clear sky of Argolis, perceives but the greedy look of the young Roman virgin, whose white and delicate hand condemns him to die? The hero of this strange fête then arranges his death: he tries to render his last gasp harmonious — to merit once more the applause of the satisfied multitude.

We have not yet a circus, where, as among the Romans, we can devour one another, but, alas! we have already the *barrière du Combat*.

This is a wretched, dilapidated place, with large ill-shaped gates, and an extensive yard. Around this yard are stationed numerous fighting dogs, both young and old; their eyes are red, and their mouths foaming with a whitish froth that oozes slowly through their livid lips. Among the four-footed actors of this canine theatre, if I may so term it, there was, above all, one that remained silent in his corner. He was a horrible creature —

a bristling giant! Old age, and numerous combats, however, had deprived him of his teeth. You would have taken him for the elder brother of some Sultan cast out of the society of men, or for an ancient king of the Franks, with his head shaved. This veteran dog was frightful to look at; as frightful as Bajazet in his cage, with something of Cardinal de la Balue in his. Proud and cringing, powerless and snarling, savage and fawning, equally as ready to lick or bite you, he was an actor worthy of such a stage. In a corner of this infectious den were to be seen bits of horse-flesh, half-gnawed heads, bleeding legs, mangled entrails and pieces of liver placed aside for the bitches in litter. These horrible remains came direct from Montfaucon. It is at this *knackery* that all the horses of Paris go to die. They arrive, tied to one another's tails, looking sad, hollow-flanked, old, weak, and worn out, in fact, with work and ill-treatment. As soon as they have passed the gate and lodge of the old portress, who, with her eye fixed on the victims, watches them defile with such a wrinkled smile as would frighten the dead, they are placed in the middle of the yard, opposite a violet-coloured pond covered with coagulated blood. The massacre then begins. A man, with bare arms, strikes them one after the other with a knife. They fall, and die in silence. When all is over, every particle of them is sold; the skin, the hair, the hoofs, the maggots for the king's pheasants, and the flesh for the voracious actors of the *barrière du Combat*.

Well — I was one day at the *barrière du Combat*, at the entrance even of the theatre, but, unfortunately, there was no performance. The barking of the dogs had attracted the manager of the canine establishment. He was a short, spare, harsh-looking man, with scanty, red hair, and plenty of importance. A solemn tone of voice, several obsequious wrinkles, a very supple knee, and a back considerably bent, represented an agreeable medium between a superannuated courtier and a sour-faced, attenuated pew-opener. This man was, however, very polite to me. "I cannot," said he, "show you all my company today: my white bear is ill, the other is resting; my bull-dog would tear us both to pieces: they are milking my wild bull; but I can, however, have an ass baited for you, if you like." "Be it so," said I to the *Impresario*, and I entered the place with the same air as if they were about to represent *Norma* or *Semiramide*.

I took my place in the silent theatre, without even having near me an honest butcher to give free course to his feelings of admiration. I was enveloped in an atmosphere of egotism difficult to describe. The door at length slowly opened, and there entered — a poor ass.

He had once been proud and robust; he was now sad and infirm, and standing but on three legs. His left fore-leg had been broken by a hired tilbury. It was with difficulty that the poor creature had been able to drag itself to this arena.

I assure you that it was a lamentable spectacle. The first thing the poor ass did was to try and maintain his equilibrium: he made one step forward, and then another, after which he advanced his right fore-leg as much as possible, let fall his head, and waited — ready for anything. At the same time, four frightfully savage dogs rushed into the arena; they flew towards him, then drew back and hesitated; they soon became bolder, however, and threw themselves on the poor animal. Resistance was impossible; the ass could but die. The dogs lascerated his body, and pierced it with their pointed teeth. The champion remained calm and motionless; he gave not one single kick, for had he done so, he would have fallen; but, like, Marcus-Aurelius, resolved to die standing. Blood soon flowed; tears ran down the poor thing's face, and a dull, hollow sound escaped from its breast. And I was alone. At length the ass fell, and then, wretch that I was, I uttered a piercing cry — in this vanquished hero I had recognised a friend!

Yes, it was he

It was Charlot! There was his long head, his calm look, his grey coat! yes, it was himself, indeed! Poor creature! He had played too important a part of my life for the least accident that happened to him not to remain preserved in my memory. Good Charlot! — and it was I who was destined to be the cause, pretext, and impossible witness of thy death! There he lay, gasping on the blood-stained ground, he whom my hand had once so often stroked! And his mistress, his young mistress, where is she at present? Thus agitated, I ran into the arena, to escape the quicker. On passing Charlot, I saw that he was struggling with the throes of death; I even received, in one of his convulsive starts, a slight blow from his broken leg; the blow was harmless, resembling a mild and tender reproach, or the last, sad farewell of a friend you have offended, and who forgives you.

I left this fatal place nearly stifled with grief. "Charlot, Charlot!" I cried, "is it then you, Charlot? you, dead! dead for a quarter of an hour's amusement for me! You, formerly so nimble and so frolicsome!" And then, in spite of myself, I called to mind all the deceitful happiness, all the innocent allurement, all the youthful and charming grace that I one day experienced while trotting on the back of this poor ass! It is a touching and melancholy history. Here are two heroes, very different in character, no doubt, but notwithstanding that inseparable in my recollection and my tears. One was named Charlot, as you already know, and the other Henrietta. I will relate their history, first for my own satisfaction, and then, if you like, for yours.

Poor Charlot! Unfortunate Henrietta! yet I, who have lost them both, am still more to be pitied than either!

CHAPTER II ❦ ❦ ❦
The Tavern of the "Bon Lapin"

Two years ago, come the second of May, I was on the road leading to Vanves, which is situated on a bare mountain within sight of Paris, and is the equivocal haunt of washerwomen, millers, street ballad-singers, and all the other poets of the Pont-Neuf. I had entirely given myself up that day to the pleasure of existing, of breathing, of being young, of inhaling the pure and genial air, and, like a child, I stopped to admire every flower, as it slowly opened, and spent many a quarter of an hour in viewing, with magisterial gravity, the white sails of the windmills going round and round, just at the turn of this road, so badly kept, so narrow, so flinty, and yet so greatly liked; just where it leads, I say, to the tavern of the *Bon Lapin*, I suddenly perceived a young girl on an ass that had run away. Oh, the charming sight! I could have remained there all my life. She was rosy, and full of youth, and just budding into womanhood. In her terror she had lost her straw hat; her hair was in disorder, and she was crying with a loud voice, "Stop! stop!" The stupid ass, however, still went on, and I let him do so. The young girl was in no danger from being a little frightened. I was as happy to have her at my mercy. I, chance, and my dog, alone were there to help her. At last, I said to Roustan: "Stop him, Roustan." Roustan immediately flew straight at the ass; the ass stopped suddenly, the young girl fell, we simultaneously uttered a cry, I hastened up, and she was mine. The ass ran away across the fields.

I had hardly clasped her in my arms, already comtemplating her as if she belonged to me, when she unexpectedly started up, and began to run after her ass, crying out, "Charlot! Charlot!" My dog also pursued, loudly barking; Charlot, however, ran all the faster: it was useless for me to try to keep up with a dog that was running, with an ass that was galloping, and, above all, with a young girl that did not care a straw about me.

Consequently, I went back and picked up the hat of my pretty donkey-rider; it was a common straw one, trimmed with a faded ribbon, and a shabby blue flower; and yet withal it was something that revealed a good and benevolent nature. The young girl was far, very far from me, then. "Charlot! Charlot!" cried she. Roustan, however, like an intelligent animal, continued to run after the ass; he brought him back to me by the shortest way — by the spot where the hat had fallen. There was a well-defined curve between the ass, his young mistress, and me. I stopped the ass at the side of the road, behind a large bush, and while the young girl was crying out "Charlot! Charlot!" I mounted him, and, with the straw hat on my head, entered a little wood.

As she still continued to exclaim "Charlot! Charlot!" I made Charlot's bell sound rather loudly, while I tried to find out some large tree, behind which I might hide myself, and await her approach. She was then at the entrance of the wood, more rosy than ever, and breathless from anxiety. When, at length, she saw us — the ass and me — she threw herself on the former, embracing and calling him a thousand different names. "So, here you are, Charlot!" she exclaimed, clasping his large head with her tiny hands. The animal allowed himself to be caressed, while I, still on his back, would have given my life for one of those fragrant kisses that the young girl was lavishing on Charlot. Charlot absorbed all her thoughts.

At length she raised her head: "Ah! here is my hat," she exclaimed joyfully; after which, she looked at me with large, black, and limpid eyes, and as I still remained in possession of her courser, she sat down on the grass, facing me and the ass, and began to arrange her luxuriant hair. When she had wiped her forehead with her hand, she put on her hat, and sighing from fatigue, rose on her two little feet with an air that seemed to say "Get off there!" She appeared determined not to let me keep Charlot any longer.

I got down, therefore, and she jumped on his back. A jerk with the bridle, a kick with her feet, and my vision fled. I had never seen a more seductive, a more smilingly blooming young creature. She had, however, neither a look nor a smile for me. As to me, my whole soul was in my looks, but I had nothing to say to her. What could I have said? She was so much taken up with Charlot and her straw hat. No, no; I am not one of those immoral persons who fancy that there is but one way to take an interest in a woman; I, for myself, know a thousand innocent ways. Is it not, I ask, unspeakable happiness to have perceived her so animated in her terror, and to have heard her harmonious cry, half joyful, half affrighted? How she ran, too, and stopped! How graceful she was, seated on the grass, and how she started up with a single spring! And how she cried "Charlot! Charlot!" Besides, did I not get on her ass? Did I not there sit in the same place as she? True, she did not see me, but what matters? I have worn her straw hat, passed across my chin the ribbon that had touched hers, and I leant on her when she embraced Charlot, and it was I who nearly received the tender kiss! Thus reflecting, I arrived at the hospitable tavern of the *Bon Lapin*, entirely absorbed by my morning's happiness.

I like the *Bon Lapin*. You will find it, as I have already said, at the foot of the mountain of Vanves, with a mill behind it, and hospitality situated between a yard and a garden. The yard is shaded with trees, and, when necessary, protected from the heat by a thick tent, under which the customers are sheltered. This yard generally serves as a dining room to all the female gossips of Paris, who, not caring to be seen themselves, like to watch those passing along the highway. Towards this yard you continually see carried indifferent wines, brown bread, shoulders of mutton, and roast beef. The garden lends its shade to less carnivorous gastronomists. There, you see young girls and young men, young girls and old men, young girls and soldiers, young girls and lawyers. I am indeed astonished that there are so many young girls in the world; they must multiply awfully to suffice for so many things. They are like the jugged hare, at the tavern of the *Bon Lapin*.

I went and sat down in a corner of the garden, quite alone, without a young girl, but, in reality, absolute master of all those who were present, and who, in the bottom of their hearts, would have wished to be anywhere but there. I do not yet understand the noisy pleasures of a tavern. It is not love, that makes the fortune of a public-house; love hides itself; intoxication, on the contrary, seeks publicity. Is it less disgraceful to lose one's reason through a woman, than to leave it at the bottom of a glass? Let him who can, explain the problem. I only met with two happy people at the *Bon Lapin*. In the furthest arbour a youth and his cousin had taken refuge; each of them were seventeen. Their whole repast consisted of an apple and some bread; but they ate both gaily and heartily, vigorously digging their teeth into their simple viands, and interchanging bits at nearly every mouthful. One never makes such a meal twice in one's life.

The recollection of the young girl and Charlot still continued to fill my mind. How sleek and comely was the latter! How full of life, how nimble, how bold, how light, and how beautiful was the former! How animated, how alluring, how venturesome, how sylph-like! I was in love with both. How well, too, they understood each other! The name of Charlot came from her mouth so naturally. Oh, happy couple!

I turned to go home, and took the shortest way, looking neither at the growing corn, nor the mills, nor at anything of the fine landscape that had so enchanted me in the morning; I was as melancholy and morose as a man astonished at finding himself alone. An unforeseen circumstance soon drew me from my reverie. I was passing by a heavy-looking peasant

— a boor, in the full force of the word — when he cried out to a wretched ass, laden with dung, and which he was beating unmercifully, "Charlot! Charlot!" I turned round to look: it was he; the unfortunate ass, weighed down under his infectious load; he who, but a few hours before, was cantering under so ideal a form. What an abrupt transition — what an unexpected metamorphosis! I passed in front of Charlot, casting towards the poor animal a look of compassion that he returned as well as he was able. This incident made me unhappy for a week. Heavens! thus to pass from so beautiful a creature to so vile a burden; from such tender caresses to those heavy blows; from that seductive voice which said "Charlot" so sweetly; to that hoarse and brutal one that swears and blasphemes! Oh, it was too much joy and misery combined; too much even for Charlot.

It was in vain that I have since continued my melancholy walks to Vanves and the *Bon Lapin*; in vain that I have often gone and sat down at the foot of the thicket where I saw Hentietta fall. I have met, it is true, on my way, with many an ass and many a young girl, but alas! with neither Henrietta nor Charlot.

CHAPTER III ◄§ ◄§ ◄§
Social Systems

From that day forth I became melancholy, or rather, I am afraid, forced myself to become so. The time, I must own, was well selected for thus willingly renouncing all the pleasures attendant on the age of twenty — innocent and youthful pleasures that awaited my every morning on awakening, and never failed to promote my laughter, mirth, and happiness, until the hours of rest. But, unknown to me, a great revolution had already taken place in the old French gaiety. Every mind was filled with the new school of poetry just introduced, and I don't know what dark reflection of a passion *à la Werther* seized suddenly on me also, but I was no longer the same. I, who was once the soul of mirth and laughter, and ever ready with the convivial song, who loved to find myself at table beside a female form, and furtively to press that fair form's tiny foot, while soft looks gave encouragement; I, who was once so full of life and gaiety, became melancholy, apathetic, and morose. Adieu, then, all my innocent pleasures and merry songs! The drama has usurped the place of the latter,

[24]

and Heaven knows what dramas. I have constructed some terrible ones:
you would have taken their first act for the sixth act of the seventh day, or
rather of the seventh year, such was the quantity of blood spilt. I have
made some extraordinary discoveries in this branch, and found a new
incentive to grief. I have reared an Olympus of a fatal style of architecture,
heaping vice on crime, and physical infection on moral baseness. The
better to perceive this, I have played Nature, so that the bare corse, when
deprived of a skin as white and delicate as that which lies beneath the
sweet carnation and soft down of the peach, might reveal to me all the
mysteries of its blood and arteries, of its lungs, its tendons, and its viscera.
I have subjected poetry to a severe autopsy: a man, strong and young, is
stretched along a large, black stone, while two skilful executioners strip
off his warm and bleeding skin, as one does a hare's, without leaving a
single shred on his quivering flesh. Such was the manner in which Nature
had been portrayed by others, and such was the manner that I adopted,
because I had to meet again with Charlot and Henrietta!

Unfortunately, one cannot obtain so perfect a result all at once. It
requires time and study, and constant attention to be directed to the soul
and heart, to the mind and senses, in order thus to pervert one's better
feelings, and entirely to banish that innocent *naiveté* of the soul, modesty
— a thing so difficult to lose. I, in particular, who was young, and loved to
read Fontenelle and Segrais, was compelled to undergo great suffering
before attaining this poetical perfection. Alas! how well I recollect what
hours of ecstacy I was procured by shepherds in cambric shirts, shepherdesses in hoop petticoats, powdered sheep, crooks decked with rose-
coloured ribbons, pastures laid out like sofas, suns that could not scorch,
and skies without a cloud. I took great delight also in the "Galaetea" of
Virgil, and the "Two Fishermen" of Theocritus, as well as in that delicious
comedy, the "Two Athenian Women." But I must crave pardon, for my
judgement was then false. Truth! truth before everything! Do not abandon truth, even though it should cost you your life. What, after all, is a
shepherd in reality? An unhappy wretch, clothed in rags, and dying of
hunger, who gets sixpence a-day for driving a few scabby sheep along the
road. What is a *real* shepherdess? A heavy mass of badly formed flesh, with
a red face, red hands, a greasy head, and smelling of onions and butter
milk. Theocritus and Virgil have certainly lied. Why do they speak to us
of husbandmen? The husbandman is nothing but a tradesman, who
speculates in cattle as the keeper of a chandler's shop speculates in sugar
and cinnamon. Courage, then! and since it is necessary, let us give the

[25]

kiss of peace to this skinless corse we have made of Nature.

With respect to *bonnes fortunes*, everything depends on knowing how to act; a seasonable pressure of the hand, a look given in proper time and place, and a sigh skilfully managed, often go a great way in a love intrigue. The first time that I shook hands with true Nature was at the Morgue, and, as you may imagine, I had paid a long courtship before attaining such temerity.

In the first place, I had renounced the country, flowers, Vanves, the *Bon Lapin*, and that monotonous route of peace of mind, and enthusiasm for fine actions, and fine works, along which I was walking, as happy as a prince, without perceiving that my happiness was as old-fashioned as the world's first spring. As soon as I had quite overcome my ridiculous simplicity, I began to consider Nature under an entirely different aspect: I reversed my glass, and, by its magnifying discovered the most horrible things. Thus, when I placed myself every morning at my window, with my head enveloped in a comfortable night-cap with a flowing tassel, and my eyes still heavy with that quiet sleep which has long since fled, my limpid and indulgent look perceived but innocence and peace in the first movements of the town awakening from its slumbers: I dived into the stately mansion opposite, ere its shutters were scarcely open; I raised, in imagination, its rich and double curtains; I fancied I saw a pair of pretty yellow slippers on a splendid Persian carpet, a handsome shawl thrown upon the sofa, and in a sumptuous bed some young smiling duchess of the court of Charles X, buried in the deepest sleep, which seemed to take pleasure in prolonging the shortness of her summer's night dream. Five stories higher up, in a garret — that is, in the clouds — was a young girl, the fruit of love and accident — in a word, a *grisette*. She arose as gay as the lark, and without even putting on a petticoat — nobody *need* look — used to begin her toilet at the window. When her innocent ablutions were over, she took a broken horn comb, and, with a laughing face — a *grisette* does nothing without laughing — fastened her long hair; she then placed a round cap on her head, and, after having once more saluted her beauty in a broken piece of looking glass, departed gaily to her work. In the street was seen the old bachelor, who, bent through age and his former mode of life, glided silently along, with a cracked basin in his hand, to fetch his daily breakfast. How his little grey eye glistened at the mere sight of the pretty *femme de chambre*, a charitable coquet, who, as she passed, cast on him a glance! Then there was the old milk-woman, with her little cart and large dog, and in great suspense as to which of the customers that surrounded her she should serve first. Afterwards came a beggar, still young, who, by cajoling every cook, and reassuring with his good looks those whom his doleful voice might have rendered sad, reaped an abundant harvest. Further on was perceived the offspring of chance and pleasure, who, pale, haggard, and ruined, with her dress in disorder returned to her comfortless abode, to deplore the fatal game she had played the night before — a game of which she was the dupe — for she had staked in it more than the kisses of her lips. Every morning I enjoyed an hour of this insipid happiness; after which I watered my pinks, trimmed my roses, set my garden in order, embellished my estate, and lopped the lofty forest in my window-sill, while reading some old *chef-d'oeuvre* of bygone times. You see how imperfect and unpoetical a man I should have been, if not entirely a lost one, had I not perceived my mistake in time, and had I not met Henrietta on her ass, and, an instant afterwards, that same ass loaded with dung.

On how little do things in general depend! When, after many violent combats with myself, I had given up my innocent pleasures of the morning, that is, my hour at the window, my roses, my pinks, my ingenuous contemplation, and the *chefs-d'oeuvre* of great times, when I had fully persuaded myself that immorality lurked in the sumptous dwelling before me; that the *grisette* opposite abandoned herself to the first stranger who offered to take her to a ball at the Casino; that the old bachelor with the cracked basin had never been anything but a cold, calculating egotist, whose politeness was only the silent baseness; that the *femme de chambre*, who had been brought up by her mistress, had estranged the affections of that mistress's husband, and corrupted her youngest son; and when I saw that all the miserable dealers around me only got up early to adulterate still more their already adulterated goods, and that they were never charitable but through ostentation or superstition, I began to seek for something that might supply the place of my morning reverie, and so betook myself to the Law Courts at twelve, the best time for going there. One advocate is ascending and another is descending the long flight of steps: beardless orators, with a busy air and nothing to do, are passing to and fro; magistrates are presiding wearily in the different courts; noters are screaming at the top of their shrill voices, and, in the yard below, are heavy vans, filled with prisoners — poor wretches, who stake their life or liberty on the eloquence of the first advocate they meet with. I saw so much, that all I admired in the sanctuary of justice was at the gate, which is constructed of iron gilt. While standing before this gate, I pictured to

myself some young smith placed in the degrading pillory for having stolen
a piece of iron; alas! he would doubtless think that if he had possessed a
piece of the iron gate before him, he should still be happy and free in the
midst of his young family. The poor wretch is suddenly stopped in his
reflections by a cold thrill in the shoulder, followed by a burning pain and
eternal infamy! I once liked the *Quai aux Fleurs*. It is a perfect garland,
which connects the two sides of the Seine by a chain of pinks, myrtles and
roses; it is the rendezvous of all those who like to admire Nature at little
expense: there you can buy, without contract or notary, an orchard or a
garden, which you can carry triumphantly away under your arm: there are
ranunculusses, laurels, plain blue flowers with no smell, white daisies with
yellow corols, and pinks with card behind them — what a support for this
handsome flower a playing card! one of those infernal powers of whist and
ecarte that soon send a man to the hulks or an untimely grave. Now that
I have examined it more closely, the *Quai aux Fleurs* makes me melancholy. It is but at a stone's throw from the gibbet on the *Place de la Grève*,
is in front of the *Gazette des Tribunaux*, and is surrounded by sheriff's officers, bailiffs, attorneys, and notaries, without reckoning the lime put at
the bottom of each rose-pot, in order to make the flower more beautiful,
and by which that flower is killed. Thus the rose itself is made to lie.

Such is the manner in which the nature of everything is changed,
thanks to the general mania of appearing true. Truth, which is so far
sought by our poetry-mongers, is a frightful thing: I compare it to those
large mirrors at the Observatory. You approach with the greatest of
confidence, and are already smiling gracefully at yourself, when you
suddenly draw back with fright at the aspect of bloodshot eyes, coarse and
wrinkled skin, teeth covered with tartar, and lips all full of cracks: this
horrible thing, which bears the stamp of old age, is, however, your own
fine, florid face. Let this teach you not to examine your youthful features
too closely.

The frightful progress I made in truth had been too rapid: all things
soon appeared deformed to me. I was inexorable towards everything I
analysed, and boldly tore asunder the best-cut garments, untied the
smallest lace, and exposed, as the fancy seized me, the most secret
infirmities; and I maliciously rejoiced at finding so many exceptions to
the beautiful. "Really," exclaimed I to myself, "do you believe that there
is anything true and beautiful in the world? There is plenty of depravity
and falsehood, I allow, yet even they are of modern discovery." Thus
reflecting, I went to the *Quinze-Vingts*, and the music of the blind there

made me stop up my ears. I repaired to the *Sourds-Muets*, but was forced to turn away from the gestures of the dumb. I hurried to the Orthopedic Hospital, and there I saw, with something of regret, that all those vertebral deformities would soon be concealed sufficiently to deceive the world, and myself among the rest. Then I pictured to myself what would be my astonishment and horror, if, on wishing to embrace the wife I had just led home, I felt her body fall to pieces beneath my trembling hand, and, in the place of what appeared all elegance and beauty, nothing remained but deformed and shrunken limbs.

Among other specimens of deformity, I gave my attention, one *conscription* day, to the defenders of our country. They had been stripped of all their clothes, and were vying with one another in exhibiting, and boasting of, their secret infirmities, in order to escape glory. Some wore dirty shirts, others ragged ones; a few — these were the best looking — wore none at all. How unsightly were their persons! How wretched their looks! A man was examining them with less care than he would have showed for a cab-horse. Poor lost race! First deprived of soul, and afterwards of body. Yet glory must rest contented with such scare-crows.

When evening came, I still satisfied my atrocious inclinations. I went out alone, and watched poor wretches disputing for a place at the doors of our low theatres, to go and applaud a poisoner or a devil, a parricide or a leper, an incendiary or a vampire; on the stage I saw men whose occupation it was to personify in succession brigands, gendarmes, peasants, noblemen, Greeks, Turks, white bears, black bears, and, in fact, everything else besides. These men also exposed to the public gaze their wives, their little children, and their old grandfathers, and were still proud and full of vanity. A dramatic performance, supported by such characters, disgusted me; but it formed part of my system to observe the ignoble in the midst of their amusements, laughing and enjoying themselves at their own theatres, supplied with actors and actresses trained expressly for them, and provided with authors capable of distilling for them vice and horror.

After this, I perambulated the magnificent boulevards from one end to the other: they begin at a ruin, the Bastille, and terminate at another ruin, an unfinished church. I surveyed Parisian immorality in all its phases. At the Bastille it seems as if it were trying its strength; it is still timid there, and on a small scale, beginning with some young girl, who sings an obscene song to divert the men from the wharfs and wharehouses. On advancing, you will perceive that the venal woman changes her appearance. She now wears a black apron, white stockings, and a cap without ribbons; her look is modest, her step slow and unsteady, and she keeps so close to the wall, that you would think she was avoiding a person infected with the plague. Further on, the lady is gaudily attired; she is half naked, following the fashion you tolerate in your ballrooms, but reprobate elsewhere, and wears no cap; she sings snatches of songs out of tune, and with a hoarse voice, and leaves behind her a strong smell of musk and amber: this is vice, as patronised by the most refined amateurs. A degree higher, you meet with the costly cashmere shawl, and a penchant for riding in broughams. Hire a box at the theatre, and for four and twenty hours you will have at your command both the cashmere shawl and a beauty of thirty-six years standing, but you will probably regret the conquest for the next three months.

But silence: we have now to do with a sort of grand lady, whom it will be difficult to vanquish, so keep strict watch over your heart. You see those sumptuous rooms; they are filled with rich presents, treachery, billets-doux, and tender sighs, and belong to the mistress of a nobleman. This woman, who has had great experience, is young and handsome, seductive and extravagant; in a word she is either a dancer at the opera, or some artless innocent from one of the theatres. Truly, she would not be so much courted if she did not change her dress and features every evening, and were not constantly mixed up with every kind of lying passion, and, above all, if the breathless public did not incessantly repeat — "I love you!" And then, in his pride, this woman's lover says to the public — "Love her, but it is I whom *she* loves!" Madman! as if an actress could ever love anything but the public! Hurra! it is seven o'clock in the evening, and vice is now mistress of the town. At the corner of the street an old woman exposes her daughter for sale. Look up! whence comes all this noise and light? From the houses devoted to gambling and debauchery. In a cellar beneath this house a man is coining false money; in that dark recess a woman is murdering her husband, and a son robbing his father. But, listen: what frightful noise was that? A heavy weight has just fallen from the parapet of the bridge into the Seine. Oh, horror! it was perhaps a young man! Go your way, and do not trouble yourself; nothing lies long hidden beneath the dark and rolling waters.

It was thus that my imperfect sensations and dread of falsehood unfortunately led me on to seek for truth, so horrible in its nakedness, and which, like a drop of oil upon the surface of the waters, increased as I viewed it.

CHAPTER IV ৽ ৽ ৽
The Morgue

It was in vain that I gave myself up, body and soul, to these morbid pleasures; in vain that I mercilessly disfigured all that came in my way; in vain that I turned beauty into deformity, virtue into vice, and day into night: the more I progressed in the horrible, the more discouraged and wretched I became. There still remained, at the bottom of my heart, a sort of feeling of regret, if not of remorse. The new mode of life that I had adopted wanted an object — a heroine: it wanted the young girl I had met at Vanves. Unfortunately for me, I once unexpectedly came across her at the corner of the Rue Taraunce, near the fountain, where she was watching the water flow. She no longer wore her faded straw hat; the colour of her cheeks was fled, and her arms had lost their appearance of health and ruddiness. Yet this was the same young girl I had seen at Vanves. The metropolis had worked a change, and she was now attired in dirty gloves, old shoes, a new bonnet, a scanty dress, and a small plaited collar, presenting altogether an appearance of wealth and misery combined. She walked with formed dignity; and though she stopped at all the milliners' shops, and wherever there was anything to look at, she seemed as if she were desirous of making haste; but the gratification of the present moment was stronger than her will. Her chaste look, modest bearing, and the rather affected reserve visible in all her person, made me think that vice had for ever claimed her as its own.

I followed her: now she walked rapidly, now her pace was slackened; at times she stared at others, and then was, in her turn, stared at, but without being either astonished or ashamed. In this manner she arrived at the end of the Rue Saint-Jacques. There was a crowd round the door of a wretched-looking house in which an invasion had just taken place by virtue of the law: every room was full of speculators. Each side of the street was lined, as usual, with hawkers and their rubbishing wares — new mirrors, old prayer-books, and the commonest and dirtiest household utensils, with pictures without frames, and frames without pictures. A poor wretch had been arrested for debt, and they were now selling all his furniture; that furniture which was, in itself, of as little worth, but yet so valuable to him, whose *all* it formed; his bed; his deal table on which he wrote his books; his old arm-chair in which his grandmother died; the portrait he drew of his beloved wife before she ran away with her wealthy corrupting paramour to Brussels; his choice engravings that were hung against the walls, all were in the hands of the law! The law was represented by one shrill voice and several husky ones, that cried up the goods. Everything was sold, even the little canary which was held up to view in the cage: the poor debtor's dog was the only thing that nobody would bid for: his dog and child remained in a corner, without attracting the notice of the law. It only took an hour to strip this unfortunate man of all he had. No one thought of his misery and loneliness, or of the grated windows of the debtor's prison, or of his weary incarceration, at the end of which he would be restored to liberty, without a halfpenny, and to his child, without a home — no one, not even Henrietta. I had been observing her for some time: her curiosity was unintelligent and pitiless: I could discover no signs of kindness or compassion in her looks. She left this abode of misery, adjusting her dress with as much unconcern as one exhibits on leaving a gratuitous exhibition of "Punch". At about twenty paces further on she stopped again before the Police Court, where a couple of men were dragging along a mendicant for begging without license.

Till this fatal day he had been the happiest of mortals, having lived by begging all his life: in fact, his great grandfather, grandfather, father, and all his ancestors, both paternal and maternal, were sons and grandsons, either legitimate or illegitimate, of mendicants. Mendicity was the entailed domain of this family of ragamuffins.

Our present hero, when he was but a fortnight old, appealed, while at his mother's breast, to public generosity. Two years afterwards, while squatting on the Pont-Neuf, between a dog-stealer and a vendor of republican tracts, he stretched forth his tiny hand to receive the alms of the passers-by. When grown up his talent enabled him to deform himself enough to escape the military glory of the empire: he then begged in the name of lost royalty and the misfortunes of our old nobility. When royalty was restored, he became a mutilated soldier of Austerlitz and Arcole, and solicited charity in the name of French glory and our reverses at Waterloo: in this manner public pity had never failed him. Contemporary history was, for him, an unexhaustible source of charity and kindly-bestowed alms. When his daily impost was levied, he remained motionless in some public place or other, inwardly laughing at the hurried gait of so many people, breathlessly hastening towards some unknown object, in the hope of finding that happiness which he had so easily found by always remaining on the same spot. He was as proud of his life as a scholar of the fifteenth century; and he really acted like a wise man, for he was content with that happiness which was within his reach. He was also a firm supporter of the State, and enriched his country by large contributions to the indirect taxes. In the morning he indulged in long libations, which were doubtless highly gratifying to the Excise. At twelve, when the sun was shining, and the air calm and clear, he loved to enjoy the intoxicating fumes that were exhaled from his short pipe, and to surround himself with pleasing images of undulating smoke, so profitable to the revenue: and as he ate nothing but salt viands, he maintained rightly that he was the most useful of citizens, since he was one of those who consumed the most liquor, the most tobacco, and the most salt, the three most profitable articles in a representative government. This was pretty good reasoning.

Consequently, he was thunderstruck when informed that hence forth he would be lodged, boarded, supplied with firing, and washed for, without being obliged to beg.

We saw him pass as he went to the Union; his face was still serene, his attire calm, but a noble melancholy sat upon his features. As, after all, he was about to lose his liberty, I gave him my pity. Henrietta turned from him with indifference, and continued her way: I followed her, and she stopped at the Morgue.

The Morgue is a small square building, placed as if on *vedet* opposite a hospital: the roof forms a dome covered with weeds and some plants, that are always green, which produce a charming effect. The Morgue is perceived from a great way off: the water that flows beneath it is black, and full of filth. You can freely enter this place, alive or dead, at any hour of the night or day: the door is always open: the walls are damp with the moisture that trickles down them. On four or five large, black slabs — the only furniture in this cavern — are generally stretched as many corpses; sometimes, when it is very hot weather, for instance, or when any exciting melodrama is produced, there are two corpses on each slab. On the day we are speaking of there were but three in all: the first was an old journeyman-mason, who had broken his neck through falling from a third story, just as he was leaving for work to go for his scanty pay. It was evident that age and hard labour had rendered this poor fellow too weak for his laborious calling: the women who were gossipping in the place — which they looked upon as a delightful rendezvous — were telling one another that, out of the three sons the old man had brought up, not one would own his father, for fear of having to pay for his burial. Next to this poor mason was a little school-boy, who had been run over by the carriage of a countess; he was half hidden by a black sticky leather, thrown over

[33]

him to cover his frightful wound; you would have said that the poor child was asleep. Over his head were hung his cap, book, embroidered blouse, soiled with dust and blood, and the little basket containing his dinner. On the middle stone, between the child and the old mason, lay the body of a fine young man, over which was already spread death's violet tinge. Henrietta stepped before this stone, and, without changing colour said to herself in a low voice:— "It's he!"

Poor, unfortunate man! Would you believe it? He had killed himself for this woman. He had been her beauty's first plaything, which she had trampled under foot, as a child tramples on the plaything that tomorrow will replace. In the life of every woman there is always some unhappy being whom she deceives without pity or remorse, and who, in general, is the man that loves her most. Such had been the case with this unfortunate suicide. He had met this woman, and had immediately loved her far too truly, considering how people love at present. For her he had forgotten his Gothic mansion, his fine estate, his brilliant prospects in the House of Lords in England, and even his name, which America never pronounces but with respect. He, too, as well as I, had seen her on Charlot! He had seen her in all her virgin beauty, and had fancied he should find a heart beneath her lovely form. She had no heart, and he soon died. She said nothing but these words — "It's he;" and being at length quite sure that she was delivered from his burning love and unlimited devotedness, she seemed to breathe more at her ease. Thank Heaven! she will never again be loved by him. As she was about to leave the Morgue, two men, still young, entered; the first looked like one of those starched valets you see in rich houses. He was, however, nothing less than a precocious *savant*. The other might have been taken for a gentleman; he was the drowned man's servant.

The latter recognised his master immediately; they had had, if not the same mother, at least the same nurse, and had spent together their infancy and their youth; they had expected to die on the same day — they were firmly attached to each other, and the valet would have refused to be the master, so fond was he of his foster brother. He went and placed himself at the feet of the body, gradually abandoning himself to his grief, while the stupid crowd — that stupid crowd which composed for a time the French nation — seemed not to understand his silent despair.

That day was the patronymic *fête* of the keeper of the Morgue; his family and friends were assembled together at table; they were singing him songs written expressly for the occasion, and he had wholly abandoned himself to the common joy. From time to time, however, he raised the red curtain of his dining room, as if to see that no one came to rob him of his corpses.

The first of the new comers approached the Englishman. "Would you like to see your master alive again?" said he. "My master alive! see my master alive again!" exclaimed he. "Yes your master himself, full of life, and with a smile on his lips and fire in his eye." On hearing this, the features of the affrighted Englishman bore such an expression of uneasy incredulity, that you would have taken him also for an inhabitant of the other world.

"This evening," continued the stranger, "bring me your master's body at nine o'clock, and I swear to you I will keep my word." The Englishman took the stranger's card with a trembling hand, as if persuaded by so much assurance and the solemn promise that had been given him; he answered — "I will be there." The stranger, Henrietta, and myself left the Morgue at the same time, as if we all three acted in concert. As soon as I was in the street, I approached the worker of miracles; I had no longer a thought for Henrietta, but was entirely absorbed by the reflections I made respecting this corpse which was to be brought to life again, that very evening. "Sir," said I, with assurance to the stranger, "might I beg you to allow me to be present at the resurrection you have just promised to perform this evening?" "Certainly, sir," replied he; and as he thought that Henrietta was with me, he turned round and invited her also; but Heaven knows in what manner his enviable invitation was worded! As to me, that bare idea of what I was about to see made my hair stand on end. "But courage!" cried I; "you are now about to trifle with the dead!" This was certainly progressing with the horrible.

CHAPTER V ⋅⋅⋅
The Medical Soirée

I called to my aid all the courage I possessed. Evening came: the sun had set rapidly, and in a threatening manner; I was cold, afraid, ashamed. The approaching perpetration of a crime could not have troubled me more. I have formed a theory respecting criminal subjects which might furnish material for a folio volume. I fancy that if men could live in spacious apartments, they would be much less inclined to vice, and much more given to remorse. The present age has contracted everything. A man buries himself in a space of four yards long by three yards wide, which he calls his house, he lessens this space, already so small, with pictures, dusty books, and statues after the antique; he smothers himself beneath luxury and productions of art, so that he may have something new to look at every time he turns his head. Thus surrounded, how can he have a thought of virtue or of terror? Give me a large and lofty chamber, wainscoted with black oak, and into which the day-light scarcely penetrates. There everything is solemn; there the faithful echo repeats the slightest throbbing of your heart; there you really feel your solitude and weakness, the weakness of a being who does not suffice to fill the abode he occupies; there silence even has a language of its own, and offers you instruction. I was well acquainted with all this littleness, but how could I, as a devoted partisan of the terrible, refuse to profit by the promised initiation? It was impossible! How could one understand Greek, and not read the "Iliad?" So, as nine o'clock struck, I set out.

My horse went at a brisk pace; yet the drive appeared very long to me. When I arrived at the door, however, I regretted that I had not to go further. The house was a highly respectable one. I entered. In a well-lighted apartment were six or seven good-humoured, gentlemanly men: the master of the house gave me a cordial welcome; but, heavens! who is that woman reclining of the sofa? It is Henrietta! She here! Why, one would imagine that she had been the mistress of the house for the last week.

The conversation was animated and gay; they talked of everything with great facility; you would have fancied yourself at one of our fashionable *soirées*, and that they were only waiting for *the* Grisi or little Litz, when suddenly we heard a heavy footstep on the staircase, a rustling noise outside the room, the folding-doors of which were presently thrown open, and the young man we had met at the Morgue entered. He bore his master's body on his shoulder: when he saw that nothing had been prepared on which to place the corpse, he frowned, and laid it on the sofa where Henrietta was reclining; the drowned man's head rested on the same cushion as hers; beside the head of the woman for whom and by whom he had met his death.

A table was prepared, but as this table was loaded with newspapers, prints, and music, it took some time to get it ready. The Englishman turned towards the sofa, and, while the preparations were going on, never took his eyes off the ungrateful woman sitting there.

When all was ready the corpse was laid up on the table, the limb that was wanting was attached to the trunk, and art began to operate.

The corpse moved, the teeth chattered, the broken thigh fell heavily on the floor, and to the dull and flabby noise it made the piano responded by a plaintive sound, and all was over.

The Englishman was unable to contain himself. On first seeing this deceptive and horrible appearance of life he uttered a cry of but, alas! joy; all signs of resuscitation were gone in a minute. He threw himself on the insulted corpse: he seized its hand, but that hand was cold, and then he rubbed his eyes, as if he were tormented by some horrid dream, and rushed from the room. I followed, and supported him. When he had passed the door he turned round, and said to the master of the house, with a menacing look, "I will return tomorrow night at eight, sir; till then keep this woman from the corpse, both out of pity and respect."

I dragged him from the dreadful sight; and, as we went down stairs, we nearly overturned a bowl of flaming punch that a footman was carrying up to the company.

CHAPTER VI ⋵ ⋵ ⋵
The Lady Patroness

I began to think that the progress I was making in the horrible was really too rapid.

The old masters did not picture suffering in this manner; Oedipus on Mount Citheron, Hecuba, Andromache, Dido, the death of Hector, and old Priam at the knees of Achilles, ought to have sufficed me. Besides, is not moral suffering much better adapted to excite emotion than physical suffering? I therefore resolved to be a little more like other people, until the day when lithotomy should obtain the honour of being dramatised or sung in an epic poem.

But, alas! in spite of all my endeavours, I soon returned to my favorite study: truth and the horrible, the horrible and truth. We were living in times too egotistical to be touched by the misfortunes of others, consequently, pity for the imaginary ills appears revolting to us; to be satisfied with the passions of the old poetical universe was to cut one's self off from the inhabitants of a world which, tired of the heroes of history, has found

nothing better to admire than convicts and hangmen. I always returned to my first calculation.

"Thanks to all this intense suffering, I shall not weep." said I to myself. Mad and haughty that I was! Not weep! a fine thing to boast of! To play at stoicism, and keep at the bottom of my heart tears that will burst it! To renounce, so young, the sweet pleasure of weeping, and then to boast of it as of a virtuous action! Such, however, was the miserable quackery to which the new poetical art had brought me. I was like a man dying of thirst, with a bottle of wholesome water in his hand; for this bottle, which he had raised too hastily to his lips, yields not one drop of water; it is too full.

Moreover, I was determined, cost what it might, to know what would become of the heroine of my story, and to find out the meaning of the enigma she presented, as if I were fully persuaded that it had a meaning.

Poor woman! she had experienced the lot of all unfortunate woman who occupy, at one time, the highest, and at another time, the lowest station; are clothed today in silks, and tomorrow are draggling in the street; and who pass from misery to opulence, and from opulence to misery, until their beauty fades, when they fall too low ever to rise again. As Henrietta turned her youth and beauty every day to better account, she became, at last, a sort of grand lady, that is, she nearly became a respectable woman. There are positions in vice which are honoured almost as much as virtue; to a certain extent vice ceases to be an object of contempt; it is, at most, an object of scandal: contempt remains; scandal, on the contrary, gradually wears itself away. Henrietta, on finding herself thus placed in an elevated station, under the protection of a lover bearing a distinguished name, who himself owed his position to a woman's caprice, turned *dame de charité*, in order to be something else besides the mistress of a gentleman of the king's bedchamber. She had mixed a grain of holy incense with the perfumes of her toilet-table; had humbly knelt at church in all her profane beauty; and had, in consequence, arisen more elegant than ever. At that time, beauty, even when profane, gave you as good a right as did nobility and fortune to be well received in the house of the Lord. Henrietta soon possessed the privilege to enter the church at any hour, and was provided with an official seat. The beadle doffed his hat, and made the brass ferule of his staff ring, as he preceded her along the aisles. The voice in which she asked you for alms was so sweet, and the hand she stretched out so small. I still see her as she used to be at all the grand *fêtes*, carrying a violet-coloured velvet bag in her hand covered with diamonds, and imploring, with a smile, the ostentatious charity of the men, and with a curtsey the scanty charity of the women. One day she came to my house to obtain my name for a subscription; I was alone.

It was two o'clock in the afternoon; the day was intensely hot; the shutters were closed, and there was a beautiful bouquet of roses on my table; my apartment was cool and pleasant, and a single sunbeam, blue and white like the curtains, indiscreetly overcoming every obstacle, sported on a lovely Madonna's head, which you would take for the production of Raphael's pencil. So the beautiful Henrietta, now become so dashing, was in my house, breathing alone with me the perfumed air of my apartment. She was fashionable dressed, and I thought I perceived on her animated countenance something of a pale reflection of the deep carnation I had seen there when first we met. I was polite, attentive, and even kind. She who had paid no attention to me, unknown as I then was, now came to my house at as improper an hour as would have been any hour of the night. Yet she was there, seated before me, looking at me, speaking to me, imploring, in a word, my alms. For an instant I forgot her present life, and only thought of the young girl and Charlot's happy days.

"So you are come at last to see me, my dear Henrietta," said I, handing her a chair, as if I were speaking to an old acquaintance, or to a person with whom there was no need of ceremony.

"Henrietta! my dear Henrietta!" exclaimed she, nearly indignant; "but how is it you know my name, sir?"

"Where is Charlot, Henrietta? What has become of Charlot?"

"Charlot!" said she, looking at me with surprise, and as if she were trying to remember whether she had ever seen me, or as if she had really forgotten Charlot.

This forgetfulness of the ungrateful girl pierced my heart. "Yes, poor Charlot," continued I, much moved, "pretty Charlot, whom you loved so much, and embraced with rapture: Charlot, sprightly Charlot, on whose back you galloped so joyfully in the plain at Vanves; the fantastic Charlot, through whom you one day lost the steam-boat; laborious Charlot, who groaned beneath the weight of dung heaped on him by your father; unfortunate Charlot, whom I saw — Alas! if you did but know, Henrietta, where I saw him!"

Here she drew out an embroidered handkerchief a small morocco memorandum book, with gold mountings, and, without answering me, said, "We are raising a subscription for the Foundling Hospital, what shall I put you down for, sir?" "I shall give you nothing, Madam." "Oh! sir, pray give the poor children something for my sake; at the last subscription I collected twenty pounds more than the countess —, and I should be much hurt if I collected less than her this time." "Do you know what a foundling is?" exclaimed I, vehemently. "No, not yet," replied she. "Then, Madam, go and learn; and when you know what misery is, when you are poor, old, ill, and ugly, and covered with shame and scorn, come back here, ask for my servant, talk to him of Charlot, and, for Charlot's sake, I will bestow on your child an alms."

She rose, but did not forget to arrange the folds of her silk dress in the most graceful style. She left my room slowly, looking at her purse with regret, and casting a glance of satisfaction on the mirror; then she cast another glance on me, which she tried to render expressive of contempt, but it did not even bear the stamp of anger; anger is the last of those virtues which require to be supported by some feeling.

When she was gone, I regretted having so received her on her first visit. What a harsh refusal to her first demand! To be able to touch her hand while placing in it a piece of gold, and yet to repel so brutally that supplicating hand! Still, I did well to be cruel; this woman, handsome as she was, did not deserve an alms. There was too much affectation in her request, too much vanity in her benevolence; besides, she said not one single word of Charlot; nor had one thought for him who was the simple Pegasus of my young poetical days. "Yet," said I to myself, "I will see your end; I will follow you like your shadow, and never leave you throughout your life, which will not be a long one. Unfortunate creature, already sufficiently despised to be made rich in so short a time! But your fortune will not last long. A man has enriched you by caprice; by caprice he will also plunge you into misery, and trample you in the dust." And I repassed in my mind the history of the greater part of those young girls, whom their lot has placed in an humble sphere, to become the playthings of the rich, who trifle with their feelings, and then get rid of them, as they do of any other animal.

The most unfortunate creature of all creatures, made or not made in the image of their Maker, is woman. Her childhood is languishing, and consumed in trivial occupations; her girlhood is a promise or a threat, and her twentieth year is an illusion. After having been deceived by a coxcomb, she ruins a fool; her mature age is a hell upon earth. She passes from hand to hand, leaving something of her being with every new master — her innocence, her modesty, her youth, her beauty and, finally, her last tooth — the poor thing that deems herself lucky if, after having gone through every grade of misery, she can keep an apple-stall, get into a hospital, or is allowed to sell oranges and play-bills at the door of some theatre. I have seen woman, who had once been beautiful, earn their living by having paving stones broken to pieces on their stomachs; others have married thieves. I know one who became the wife of a censor, of a vile and literary censor, whose thumb and forefinger were still red with the mark left by the scissors used in his work of infamy! What, I ask, was the good of all their beauty? Yet, beauty is a priceless gift. What happiness and love, what obedience and respect does this one word command! But woe! woe to this divine and mortal covering, when beneath it there lies no heart.

CHAPTER VII ᷽ ᷽ ᷽
Virtue

I was become more morose than ever; I trembled for myself, as I was not sure whether, after all, in spite of my contempt, I was not in love with Henrietta. In order to divert my attention and somewhat release myself from my uneasiness, I gave up, for a time, my poetical speculations, and dived into the dark and mysterious labyrinth of metaphysics. According to my custom, I reduced them to a science unconnected with any other — to a realised abstract, to a musical and sonorous jargon; but all my efforts were useless; I remained incomprehensible. I sought after the cause of virtues and vices, and reflected much on happiness and pleasure. One just escaped from Bedlam could not have improved on me. "Where is happiness to be met with?" asked I of myself, and I turned toward the passers-by; every one of them was running after something that he called happiness, but no two were going in the same direction. "Let me remain stationary;" said I to myself, "and see what will befall me."

I was seated under a tree that formed a perfect parasol, by the side of the parched and dusty road, when, in the midst of my reverie, I was accosted by a wayfarer, whom, by his piteous voice more than his wallet and knotty stick, I recognised as a tramping vagabond, a sort of knight-errant, who never fails to be mild and obsequious as long as daylight lasts. As it was then broad daylight, he addressed me politely, begging me to let him partake of the shade afforded by the tree, after which, and without waiting for an answer, he sat down by my side, and, having drawn from his wallet some bread and a leathern bottle full of beer, began to eat and drink slowly: from time to time he heaved a deep sigh, as if to keep himself in practice. I imagined that, in my present inquiry, this man might be of great use to me. "My friend," said I to him with an air of interest, "do you know what happiness is?" He stared at me, took a bite at his bread, and then said "Happiness? what sort of happiness do you mean?"

I did not expect this question: it embarrassed me; and, in order to evade it, I replied by another question: "you think, then, there are several kinds of happiness?"

"Without doubt. Since I have been born I have known a thousand kinds of happiness. When I was a child I had the happiness to possess a mother, while so many others are without both mother and father. When I was a young man I had the happiness to have but one of my ears cut off, though I deserved to lose them both; and when I grew older I had the happiness to travel at the expense of the public, and to become acquainted with the manners and customs of every people: you see that there are many kinds of happiness."

"But my fine fellow, all these are but fractions of happiness; different species of the same family. How do you understand happiness in general?"

"As there are no vagabonds in general, I cannot answer you. In the course of my life I have, however, observed that, for a man in good health, happiness consisted of a glass of wine, and a piece of bacon; and that for one who was ill, it consisted of a bed, all to himself, at a hospital."

"During your life of privation and loneliness, you must have been tormented by different passions."

"I have had some terrible ones," said he in a low voice, and drawing near me. "In the first place, I had a raging passion for fruit-trees and grapevines; then I adored public-houses and taverns. I have committed a thousand foolish things for a little money. I recollect that I once sat up four long winter nights to wait for a miserable velvet coat with metal buttons, and I was near being transported for having broken open the stable of a mule. At present I have done with all these passions," added he, drawing my handkerchief from my pocket, as I was listening to him with admiration.

"I don't ask you if you have known grief," continued I, much moved, and in a doleful tone of voice.

"For me there is not grief but what a game at cards will dispel," replied he, with a smile, and on the point of proposing that we should play a game.

"Have you ever had any friends, good and worthy man?"

"When I was nineteen I had a friend, whose head I split open for a tap-house serving wench. I had another friend, whom I got hanged, from whom I won his wallet of victuals. I have had friends all my life, and shall continue to have them as long as I like," added he.

"As you have travelled much, tell me what most astonished you in your travels."

"In England I saw the cord of a gibbet break beneath the weight of the culprit; in Spain I saw an Inquisitor refuse to burn a Jew; at Paris I saw a spy fall asleep at the door of a conspirator; and at Rome I bought a loaf that weighed an ounce too much. That is all."

"You who know so well what happiness is, could perhaps tell me what virtue is."

"Of that I know nothing," replied he.

"I am sorry for it; I should have greatly prized your definition;" and I again assumed my anxious air.

Here the mendicant rose, and placed himself before me: with one hand he clasped his stick, while with the other he made a solemn gesture.

"Sir," said he, "why do you despair? Though neither you nor I know what virtue is, there are others perhaps who do. I will question them, if you wish it, and if you think that the police will let me."

"Question them," said I, "and fear nothing. To ask a man what virtue is, is not to ask him for his purse. It is only the latter demand which would be indiscreet."

The vagrant advanced into the middle of the road with the boldness of a rogue who feels that he is supported by an honest man. His step was firm, his head erect, his eye fixed, and his mouth wide enough open to show a set of at least thirty-two enormous teeth.

Two men passed: one was a usurer, and the other his victim.

"What is virtue?" asked the vagrant of them, in a voice of thunder.

"Money at twenty five percent," answered the first.

"A journey over the frontier," replied the second; and they continued their way.

The mendicant turned towards me to know whether he was to continue. I signed to him to do so. Shortly, another traveller passed.

This was the old tenant of the hulks, who had just served out his term, and who had still thirty-two shilling and eightpence to keep himself free and honest with. Nevertheless, he was gay and lively — in a word, an experienced hand. The mendicant addressed him with singular kindness. "A pleasant journey to you, mate; but, before you go on, just tell me what virtue is."

"Virtue, my boy, is a court of assizes, a trial, ten year's transportation, a convict-keeper's lash, and two letters branded on the shoulder, all which you take care never to get twice. That is what virtue is."

"Well spoken," said the interrogator; "if you like to turn traveller also, we will do business together. You know too well what virtue is for me to part from a companion like you."

They were setting off together, when a *gen-d'arme*, coming up at full gallop, cried out to them, "Stop!"

"What is virtue?" exclaimed they.

"Virtue?" replied the *gen-d'arme*; "why, good handcuffs, a good straightjacket, with a good barred cell, secured by a good triple lock;" and he drove them on before him.

That is how I obtained several definitions for the one I was seeking.

Consequently, I remained as little advanced in my researches as Cato of Utica himself, who likewise has given us his definition of virtue.

CHAPTER VIII ◄§ ◄§ ◄§
A Treatise on Moral Deformity

I had, however, learned that the leprosy of the heart was as loathsome as every other kind of leprosy. and that as I was seeking for the horrible by every means in my power, I should be wise not to stop at physical infirmities. Between the deformity of the body and the deformity of the mind must, I said, necessarily lie the solution of the problem that I had proposed to myself, namely, the science of the ugly and the deformed. How I was to be pitied! This science cost me much; it cost me my gaiety, my repose, my happiness; at first, it turned a nearly literary question into a question of love, and then into a question of criminal prosecutions. I had, however, advanced too far to turn back; I was like a man who had begun forming a collection of insects, and who, in order to complete it, is obliged to admit the most hideous ones.

This melancholy and heart-rending study would, however, as I thought, lead me to a better knowledge of men than the books of all the moralists in the world. Many treatises have been written on the sublime and the beautiful, and on moral philosophy, but they prove nothing; their authors have been satisfied with superficial appearances, whereas they ought to have dug to the root. What do I care about the drawing-room manners of that society which could not exist a day without spies, gaolers, hangman, lotteries and dens of debauchery, pot-houses, and cut-throat theatres! It formed part of my plan to become acquainted with the principal agents of social activity, and the more so as I should thus escape, at least for a time, from those tortures of the outward world, which, till then, I had made my study.

I, therefore, turned my attention towards our police spies, which miserable heroes were destined to have a place in my history. I have seen some of all kinds, and seen them everywhere, in our houses, our public buildings, and our streets; and I was never more surprised than when I heard that they were fathers of families, they they smiled on their wives, embraced their children, and had friends who came to dine with them. I once thought that, in order to do all this, it was necessary to be at least an honest citizen.

One day I saw a man enter a mean wine shop in the Rue Sainte Anne; he was in rags, and frightful to look at; his beard was long, his hair was in disorder, and his whole person a mass of filth. Whence could he come? From what haunt of crime? From what cavern? How many thieves had he denounced that very morning? A few minutes after I saw this same man come out nicely dressed, with the crosses of two orders of honour on his breast — Monsieur le Comte was going to dine at a magistrate's.

This sudden transformation made me tremble; I thought that it was perhaps thus that the two extremes met.

Another time, late at night, or rather early in the morning, I saw a subordinate employee at a gambling-house going home; for ten long hours he had contemplated, with an unmoistened eye, the ruin and despair of several families, and yet he threw his cloak to a beggar, who crouched, benumbed with cold, before his door.

This *juste-milieu* between vice and virtue, between cruel indifference and sudden pity; alarmed me still more than the change I had witnessed at the Rue Sainte Anne.

I have seen a woman seated in a lottery office; she was young and handsome, and by her side was a fine young man, to whose protestations of love she tranquilly listened, while, with an air of utter indifference, she was selling worthless lists of paper to poor workmen, who would be inevitably reduced to misery by their purchases.

Love, thus paraded in presence of a wheel of fortune, made me sick.

I have seen a literary censor sit down at his scalping board, and mercilessly strike out a noble thought from the book he was dissecting, as if he were only cutting off a human head; a drunken, ignoble man, who fought against an opinion as a soldier would against his enemy.

The most hideous thing I ever met with in all these social turpitudes was a censor.

CHAPTER IX ◄§ ◄§ ◄§
The Inventory

When I returned home, I still found myself besieged by these horrible sights. The physical world, on being viewed closely, had made me unhappy; the moral world, when looked at through my glass, had rendered me wretched. It was through my poetical visions that I had detested mankind; and the reality, I thought, ought to make me detest life itself. I was fallen very low, I, who once was walking so happily through life, and who, at every step I took, and at every pulsation of my heart, returned thanks to the Almighty for having created youth! My hopes were blighted my whole existence changed. I was entangled without knowing it, in an inextricable drama, from which I was determined to escape at any cost, but I did not know how to bring about the catastrophe. A vague idea of suicide passed through my brain, and then went onward to my heart. The poetical melancholy arising from frequent intercourse with tombs and the dead is frightful, inasmuch as it soon reconciles you even to your own corpse. By dint of harbouring every dark idea, there is no extravagance which you are not capable of committing. What! kill myself, while yet so young, so happy, so free, so much beloved! while my head is so full! while my noble-minded father, good old aunt, and still young mother are yet alive! Kill myself without cause, without a motive, merely because it has pleased a few madmen to change the language, manners, and *chefs-d'oeuvres* of my country! Well! that is the very reason why such a death appeared so sublime and poetical to me. I therefore set about arranging, not my affairs, for there was no need of that, but my papers, of which I had a great number. I opened mechanically a heavy ebony bureau, inlaid with yellowish, mother-of-pearl. An entire poem was scattered in its different drawers. I made a melancholy review of it, which review was as pleasing to me as a souvenir that has been bestowed but yesterday, but which souvenir will, if you like become a hope.

In the first place was to be seen, in the middle of the bureau, a considerable mass of papers already grown yellow from time. Among them were the poetical efforts of youth, plans for dramas, beginnings of books, the whole, in fact, forming a complete abortion — an edifice that has been but half finished, and which is already falling to pieces. Not one of those thoughts, which once had made me thrill, had ever seen the light, not one of those dreams had ever had a chance of being realised, no one had ever given them a moment's consideration. In the imaginative arts, to think is not the most difficult thing; there is something still more difficult, which is to bring your thought before the world, to render it complete enought to command attention, and to dress it in an attractive form. Though I was young and strong, I had wanted courage; like an idle or unskilful abigail, I had left my goddess half-dressed, not, however, in that decent and graceful nudity which is the perfection of art, but in that ungainly nudity which shocks the beholder: a stocking all loose, and fastened by a worn-out garter, stays of which all the work is visible, an ungraceful petticoat, and a mass of slovenly undergarments, will well represent what was in the first drawer.

The second drawer was nearly empty; it contained a few papers relating to family affairs, some title deeds, two or three government securities, procured by the sweat of my father's brow, and my will, which was contained in two lines, in a work, all my independence, my sweet and much-prized independence, was in those scraps of paper. Burn this drawer, and tomorrow I should again be lost in the crowd — tomorrow I should be but a mercenary, a trader in witticisms, for want of something better to do; a bird on the wing, trembling, from the very beginning of summer, at the thought that winter was to follow. Yet this drawer, which so necessary to my existence, was the only one that was not locked; to make up for this, the drawer next it was secured by two locks: the open drawer contained but my fortune, while the other held my heart.

I am not one of those who laugh over lost affections. I have found by experience that one love cannot be replaced by another. The second wrongs the third, and third the fourth; they become abated, like an echo, or like the transitory circle that ruffles the water when agitated by a stone which a child has cast into it. Above all, the first woman we meet with can never be replaced: but it is the second one only that we love.

I have a quantity of sweet relics, carefully arranged in chronological order, in the strong box provided for the souvenirs I possess. There are placed letters written in large text hands, or else in such small ones, that, when love has fled, it would require a magnifying-glass to read them; locks of black and brown hair, still smelling slightly of perfume; gold or silver rings, on which are marked an hour or a day — an incomplete date; but how is it ever possible to believe that we shall forget even the year of these eternal amours! — effaced portraits, broken bracelets, withered flowers, all sorts of frivolities and excuses, of lies and vows, of happiness, of promises, and of every other kind of vanity!

Yet so vivid are the recollections of early love, that, if I chose, I could resuscitate all the happiness and joy, all the ecstacy and smiles, all the terror, tears, and feverish nights, all the despair and reproaches that are shut up in this box, as well as forgotten phrenzy and evaporated perfumes, by saying, as Christ did to the dead man, "Arise!" Yes, you still recall my young and burning passions; portraits, hair, letters, ribbons, and faded flowers, I know your names and colours — I can recognise your voices and your whispers. You are the smiling phantoms of my former passions. Even at night I could, by their form or perfume, alone distinguish them one from another, and, by instinct, single them out of this pell-mell. Here is the first violet that Anna gathered for me on the banks of our favourite stream; here is the ribbon that Juliet gave me on the day of her marriage, poor woman! Hortense presented me this embroidered handkerchief the first time that I took her hand. These long black tresses were Spanish; they adorned a haughty and imperious head. When I was but still a child, in spite of the most tender words, I dared not look into those dark and brilliant eyes; her love terrified me; I trampled on it; thus beginning the education of my heart with violence.

Look at these amiable epistles, written on coarse paper, in long mis-shapen strokes, and in a language, *sui generis*, intelligible only to him who is loved. I left all my grand amours for a *grisette*, a young and gentle girl, who owed everything to me, and on whom I doted. She used to come of a morning and place herself, with a smiling face, on the carpet at my feet, and there, half asleep and half awake, sometimes quietly looking at me work, and some times getting a little impatient, she would sit for hours, and wait for the moment when I could take her, proud of my protection and her own beauty, to a *fête* or theatre, or anywhere else where, in order to be well received, it suffices to be young and pretty.

[49]

There is, also, in my treasure, a bracelet of exquisite workmanship; this I religiously preserve; it was given to me in a moment of rapturous passion, when the hand contracts in order to clasp the better; when gold slips along the arms as it does on ivory; when a woman forgets everything, even her lace and pearls. Thus she gave me at the same time her bracelet and her love. But where is now her love? Of all the gold the poor girl ever had this is perhaps all that remains. May heaven at least secure her, when she is thirty, an abode either at Bedlam or the Magdalen, as to the one or the other she must, sooner or later, come.

But shall I tell you all my riches? Here is the ring of Gustave's betrothed; she swore to me that she would prove false to him, and she has kept her word, the honest girl. Her ring — the ring which the priest had blessed — was scarcely on her finger when she exchanged it with me for a mysterious one, on which our initials were inscribed. Carry to your lips this little glove of the beautiful Anna, which she threw in my face, in a fit of bad humour, because I had danced with Julia. Do not touch this poniard, the handle of which is so capriciously carved; it defended Louisa, who could not defend her virtue. Jenny, when she left France for England, where an old husband was expecting her, gave me this porcelain cup, in which she used to keep the whiteness and brilliancy of her complexion. "Take it," said she, "I have no further need to deceive any one." Suzanne sent me this waist-ribbon the day she first felt she was a mother. Here we have the mystery of her slender form explained. For this rose, which fell from Augustine's light hair, two young students of twenty fought a duel, and I was Ernest's second: the rose is still dyed with his blood, poor fellow! I had said that mad Lucy had a large foot; the next day she sent me this black slipper, which Cinderella herself could not have worn with ease; I could never even get the fellow to it. Ah! there you are, my pretty little faded green veil; you have covered the freshest, prettiest, liveliest little face that ever smiled on youth. The following is its history:—

Madame de ——, being ill, said to me one day, "Go from me to the top of the Faubourg Saint Honore, and fetch my daughter home from school; I wish to see her; you can tell her that if she is a good girl she shall never leave me again." I went to fetch the child. She and the rest of her schoolfellows had been just let out into the garden. It did one good to watch and listen to them. They were like a lot of joyful birds that have just been set at liberty. From this crowd of ruddy faces I soon singled out Pauline, already pensive, by her floridness. I triumphantly led her away, without even giving her time to say "good bye" to her young companions.

When we arrived at her mother's door, I said to her, "What will you give me if I tell you some good news? I wish you joy, Mademoiselle Pauline, you will always remain with your mother, if you are good; school is no longer the place for you." Then Pauline, undoing her veil, said, "Here, this is what I give you for your good news;" and she immediately ran off to embrace her mother.

My pretty little veil! Chaste token! Thou art, it is true, but a piece of common gauze, and a southern sun has made thy colour fade; thy only perfume is that delicious perfume which a childhood of fifteen years leaves behind it — the perfume of innocence — and yet, pretty artless veil, thou that hadst nothing to conceal, thou art the most precious of all my treasures — thou art the honest and holy part of this touching story. Thy fifteen years, thy purity and filial love, and thy happy ignorance of everything, have risen high above all the ecstacy and prestige represented by these bits of gold and strips of silk; pardon me for having thus mixed thee with all these souvenirs of profane amours; but was not all thy innocence required to cleanse them of their impurity?

For thee, Henrietta, I would have given all these — all my treasure. And, O profanation! O madness! O ingratitude! I would have — no, not given — but for thee, Henrietta, I would have even burnt my pretty veil.

CHAPTER X ◄§ ◄§ ◄§
Poetry

As I terminated this pleasing and melancholy inventory, I placed my hand on a packet carefully sealed up; the seal was unbroken, and the address in my own hand; this package seemed to have remained there as a sacred trust that I could not violate without a crime. Yet, I know not by what innocent curiosity, I opened the mysterious packet; it contained a silk handkerchief, the colour of which evidently belonged to bygone times; in the handkerchief was a letter, carefully sealed, and still impregnated with an agreeable, though faint perfume, sweet precursor of a love letter. I opened this letter; it was written in so elegant a hand, that at first I could not believe it was my writing: it was not without emotion that I read the following verses, long since forgotten:—

Thou ask'dst for this kerchief; dear girl it is thine,
And if, e're thy couch thy sweet body shall bear,
Thou deign'st with the long silken mesh to entwine
Thy soft auburn hair;

And if o'er thy coquetry sleep shall hold sway,
And thy frank open smile be steeped in repose,
While nought but thy fair youthful beauty shall play
Round thy two lips of rose;

If milder than e're was the love, true till death,
Of Helen's twin brothers, thy eyes' lustrous light
Shall be dimmed, and if nought save the sound of thy breath
Shall disturb the still night;

Then, like the sweet song of a spirit of air,
Who follows some fairy, he waves for his mate,
And rests his bright wings on a rose that will bear,
Without bending, their weight;

A low plaintiff voice shall breathe in thine ear,
With accents so soft they shall cause no alarm,
There is one who keeps guard, slumber on without fear,
He will shield thee from harm;

He will ask from the night for the lore of past days,
For stories of pity, for words that can move,
For the conqueror's loud, joyful paeans of praise,
And for verses of love.

For thee will he seek, with a laurel to wreathe
His temples, like those of some king on his throne,
And kneeling, will say: 'Tis for thee that I breathe,
All my fame is thine own.'

And if with great deeds I would build up a name,
That the sharp scythe of time should for ever defy,
'Tis only that with it, dear maiden, thy fame
May be n'er doomed to die.

Through long future ages thy love, ever young,
By each sighing swain to his nymph shall be told,
And talked of more fondly than Delia's sung
By Tibullus of old.

But if, when the folds of this kerchief clasp tight
Thy long wavy locks thou should'st e're prove untrue,
Though Mystery's self should conceal from my sight
The wrong that you do;

If e'er, while thy lips, mad with phrenzy, replied
To those of some rival, with passion's warm glow,
His kiss this poor kerchief should e'er push aside
From thy forehead of snow;

A voice more shrill than the horrible scream,
Of the ill-omen'd owl, and with terror more rife,
More sad than the warning, which oft stays the gleam
Of the murderer's knife;

This voice will cry, 'Perjured maiden beware!
Tomorrow, perhaps, shame and sorrow may bring;
Thy lover knows all, and such injuries bear
Certain death on their wing.'

Or if to another thou e'er couldst display
My gift but to mock it, oh quick from it part;
Oh! quick in the flames let it smoulder away
Lost, lost, like my heart."

I shut the drawer violently, and seized my pistols from off the shelf; I amused myself for a time by contemplating them, and admiring the boar's head engraved on the lock-plate; my blood began to warm, my pulse to beat with force; I was revelling in the most cruel and bitter happiness, when, Heaven be thanked! I heard a gentle knock at my door. "Come in, my dear," I exclaimed. The door opened — and I was saved!

CHAPTER XI ◆§ ◆§ ◆§
Jenny

As Jenny advanced into the room, the pistol that I had raised to my forehead gradually lowered itself; at the last step the young girl made the fatal arm returned to its customary place. "What good news do you bring me, Jenny?" said I tranquilly; "Have you lost any more of my things, or scorched my best shirt?"

"Some very good news, sir; I am to be married tomorrow," answered Jenny.

I was thunderstruck; for the last six years I had treated her like a child, and that very morning I had put by for her some sweetmeats, when she, the little Jenny, a mere child, as I thought, was to be married the next day. I looked at her, and soon perceived that there was no reason why her marriage should appear at all strange. I fetched a deep sigh, and, rising in a rage, exclaimed:—

"Cursed be the sham poet, who, for his profit, first took it into his head to create the terrible! Cursed be the new poetical school, with its assassins and phantoms! they have driven me mad; by dint of forcing me to study the moral world in its most mysterious influence, they have prevented my remarking that Jenny was no longer a child."

"Excuse me, my dear Jenny," said I, drawing near her; "you have grown up to the age of eighteen without my perceiving it. But then, you see, I am become such a great philosopher."

At these words, Jenny, who was ready to cry, began to laugh, and then, offering me her plump cheek, said:—

"Won't you embrace little Jenny today?"

"I respectfully embrace you as another's bride," said I, bowing.

"As little Jenny," added she.

"Well, then, as little Jenny;" and I could not restrain a heavy sigh.

"You will come to the wedding, won't you?" said Jenny, playing with my coat; "we shall expect you tomorrow."

"With pleasure."

On hearing this, she ran off as fast as she could. I looked out of the window, and, an instant afterwards, saw her get into a heavy washer-woman's cart, drawn by a big Norman horse; she guided this cumbersome machine with as much ease as a coachman of the Faubourg Saint Germain displays when driving his noble mistress to the Church of Saint Sulpice.

The Dead Donkey

The next day I directed my steps to the outskirts of the city, where the wedding was to take place; the company was numerous; when I arrived, they were setting out for the church. Jenny led the procession; her kind, calm face breathed the greatest serenity; she was dressed in white, and her head was covered with ribbons; an enormous bouquet of orange-blossoms, which she wore on her right side, nearly made me blush. Her husband, a jovial young fellow, remarkably stupid to look at, followed her; then came the usual train, a mother in tears, a father, proud of his new coat, all the gossips of the place, and a strong culinary odour, mixing itself with the notes of a screeching violin. I followed Jenny to the altar; one would have thought that she had been accustomed to this sort of thing all her life. She said "yes" in a firm and decided tone, and, having murmured a prayer, rose to leave the church. I went to meet her, and gravely offered her the holy water; strange to say, I, who for six years had regularly embraced her twice a week, felt happy when her finger came in contact with my own; she was a child of mine that another had taken from me and kidnapped. He who had done this was a blockhead, but he was a good man; he was her husband. Still driven on, however, by my morbid taste for analysing everything, I did my best to spoil Jenny's happiness; I compared her days of rest to her days of labour, and I already fancied that this, her wedding day, and the happiest moment of her life, bore the monotonous appearance of an ordinary day; in fact, I almost imagined that I heard her, a prey, on a truckle-bed, to all the pangs of child-birth, ten months before her time. I mercilessly dissected all their joyous mirth, and distilled drop by drop the wine they drank so gaily. I said to myself that there were many hurtful things in it. My stupid philosophy was so akin to envy that I was either to be pitied or feared; notwithstanding, Jenny was happy; she was also in such a hurry to contemplate her husband at her ease, that she bid me adieu without even giving me a look. I left her, and I felt convinced, in spite of myself, that she was pretty — pretty because she was happy — and I fetched a deep sigh, which was nothing less than the sigh of a resigned man. "Can it be possible" exclaimed I, "for love not to be perceived from the very first? Could one fall in love with a woman without knowing it?" At this thought I involuntarily shuddered. Unhappy man that I was; it was not Jenny who caused my wretchedness; no, I was not the sport of a love without name or purpose; I knew too well to what a wretched and unworthy thing I had devoted my life. Infamous and degrading love! What! love such a woman! follow her, step by step, in her dreadful wake of vice and corruption of every kind, and see her hasten to her ruin, without being able to say stop, for she does not understand the language that I speak — have nothing to ask of her, for she could give me nothing but what she bestows on everyone — have nothing to say to her, for she is a woman without intelligence, as she is a woman without a heart. Thus silently and impassively to witness the rapid degradation of so beautiful a being, and yet to love her — to love but her in the whole world — to forget all for her — to give up for her even my happiness, my pleasures, the innocent amusements of my youth! Fatality! But, as the Eastern nations still say:— "Henrietta is Henrietta, and I am in love with Henrietta."

CHAPTER XII ⊸§ ⊸§ ⊸§
The Model Man

Just outside the barrière I found myself face to face with a man of mature age, with remarkably handsome features and a long black beard; I looked at him attentively.

"If you want to see me," said he, "pay me; I am a living model of the most perfect productions of nature; you shall judge for yourself. Speak! what shall I personify?"

"Apollo," answered I, leaning against a tree, "and be grand, if you wish to be paid."

The man drew himself up to his full height, pushed his beard under his chin, threw back his feet, raised his eyes upwards, and then, inflating his nostrils to their utmost extent, let fall his arm in full freedom. "A magnificent man, certainly!" said I to myself, with a touch of envy. "Now, show me a Roman slave, who is about to be whipped for having stolen some figs."

The man immediately fell on his knees; he bent his back, lowered his head, supported himself on his two trembling hands, and, dragging himself along the ground to where I stood, he look at me with the mild and fearful air of a dog that has lost its master. Thus humbled, the man was, however, scarcely a dog — a worm — a god! says Bossuet. I longed to drag this god from his abjectness. "Vile slave," said I to him, "revolt, revolt! you are now Spartacus."

Then he rose up slowly, like a man who is revolting by degrees, and who takes his time; he knelt down on one knee only, and, pretending to seize with both hands a man just killed, opened his large mouth, and, with his eye half shut, and his ear erect, he appeared to enjoy through every sense the pleasures of vengeance; I was afraid of him. "Could you now show me a man dead drunk?" asked I.

"I never take off drunkenness, out of respect," replied he, rising; "If you give me anything handsome, you will see me this evening really and truly dead drunk at the corner of the street, and, what is more, you will be able to see me gratis."

I threw him some money. As soon as Apollo, the slave, the god and the worm were become a vulgar man again, all four of them put together could muster nothing better to thank me with than a stupid grin and a look without expression. How beautiful and how insignificant a being! What an intelligent comedian! What a senseless mendicant! Yet all was contained in the same look, the same mind, the same flesh. Certainly, there was an opportunity furnished me for a fine philosophical tirade, but accident made me laugh, and, faith! I felt merry — at being still so merry.

A little Savoyard, idle, thoughtless and sauntering, like every gay *Bohemien* in the streets of Paris, thinking, no doubt, that I was a good chance, began to run after me. "Give me something your Honour!" His Honour remained dumb. "Your Lordship!" His Lordship still went on. "Your Highness!" His Highness heeded not. "Your Majesty!" Your Majesty! I was about to give him something, but I thought of Monsieur Royer-Collard and Monsieur de Lafayette, of Monsieur Sebastiani and Monsieur Odilon-Barrot, or Monsieur Manguin, of Monsieur Lafitte, of the *Constitutionnel* and all the opposition. Your Majesty! fie on it! you shall have not a farthing mendicant. The poor little fellow was at the end of his honorary titles; he stopped, and was stationary and so greatly embarrassed, I turned back. "You little donkey," said I in a passion, "you have gone so far, I suppose you will deify me next." Joining his hands, he again asked me to give him something, and I threw him the wherewithal to pass the *Pont des Arts*.

CHAPTER XIII ◆§ ◆§ ◆§
Father and Mother

A day so gaily passed was followed by a delightful night, full of the
sweetest dreams. When I awoke in the morning, I was surprised to find my
spirits so buoyant, and my thoughts so free. Softly stretched on my bed, I
gave myself up to the enjoyment of my reflections, with the same zest that
a connoisseur sips the last glens of a bottle of old wine. By Heaven!
sadness is a fine thing; but then gaiety, soft slumbers, and smiling dreams
are sweet. How cool is my bed, how light my heart, how roving my
thoughts, how animated my look! One would think that some charitable
fairy had placed her hand over the agitation of my heart. I breathe, I see,
I think; and all these sweet sensations are mine, because I gave myself up
yesterday to rambling, and forgot that I was a mad pedantic philosopher,
a poet and a thinker. Come, then! who will know it? Be a plain, simple
man for one whole day. Oh! Dr Faust! Oh! my master, how many times
hast thou not left thy books, thy furnaces, and thy alembics, to go and
walk beneath the casement of thy Marguerite!

Still thinking of the philosopher's stone, I began to dress; I decked
myself out, and became cheerful, and hummed an air that a street organ
was playing in the courtyard. I left the house, fully determined not to
take my morose philosophy with me, and, by a irresistable attraction, I
directed my steps towards Vanves. When I arrived at the *Bon Lapin*, I
stopped suddenly; yet it was there that my happiness had been disturbed,
without my knowing it! It was there that I conceived the mad idea of
becoming the impassive and constant witness of all the phases of a young
girl's life; who, though, was this girl? A peasant of the environs of Paris. I
entered, however, the gardens of the tavern; it was hot; the yellow and
faded foliage was of little use in protecting me from the close and
oppressive heat of an autumn sun. I sat down at my old table; I had
formerly cut my initials in it, artistically entwined in gothic L.; they were
still there, but half effaced; other letters sculptured later, but as easy to be
destroyed, surrounded mine. What happy moments I had spent at that
table. How calm had been my contemplations here! How many times had
I not seen from that very place, bright ribbons, and pretty bonnets,
swinging, with their owners, on those now still branches! What a crowd
of beauty filled this place but a few days back! but on that day the *Bon Lapin*
was nearly deserted. The spring had carried off with it the shade and

amours of the little garden. There were but two persons in it, who were seated at the further end of a bower half deprived of leaves. The first was a woman richly dressed, disdainful and *comme il faut*. A lady, in fact. The other was a handsome young man, who appeared to be speaking to her ardently, and to whom she was mechanically listening with an air of disdain.

The listless attitude of this woman attracted my attention. Her elegant figure inspired me with a desire to see her face; I don't know what vague presentiment seemed to say that I should recognise her, but I looked in vain; she never changed her position. Presently, a poor, infirm old man, supported by his wife, who herself was tottering on a stick, entered the garden through the gate, left half open; they came to beg. The old man's face was still fine and serene, his appearance decent, and his voice had nothing doleful about it; I was moved to pity. When he had put what I gave him into his wife's pocket, he went and held out his hand to the lady in the bower; but the lady grew impatient, and repelled him with a harsh and imperious gesture: the old man easily discouraged, was humbly retiring, when looking at this pitiless lady more attentively, he said to his wife, — "Wife, does not that lady look very much like our child?" On hearing her husband say this, the poor woman fetched a deep sigh; from the very first she had recognised their daughter. At the sight of Henrietta, her old forsaken father wanted to embrace his daughter and forgive her; but she turned from him with disgust. "In the name of your old father, my child, own us again, and dry the bitter tears we have shed for you!" exclaimed he; but she turned away. "In the name of Heaven!" said her mother, "own us and we will forgive you." The daughter still was silent. I could contain myself no longer. I rose from my seat, exclaiming— "In the name of Charlot, look on your old father at your feet." The two old people held out their arms; but, at the name of Charlot, she rose and without casting a look of pity on the shrivelled hands that were stretched forth to embrace her, hurried from the garden. The young man, who followed her appeared to be in the greatest consternation.

The last fold of her white dress had scarcely disappeared through the gate, when the old man, sitting down by my side, said, with nearly a gay air, — "Did you know Charlot, then?" "Know him, my friend, I more than knew him; I have ridden on him and, without harming any one, I can attest that he was an excellent donkey."

"Ah! yes, he was," exclaimed the old man; "he could carry twenty loads of dung a day," he added, emptying his daughter's glass, and eating the

bread she had left.

"How was it that you lost such a worthy beast, my man?" "Alas! sir, my wife often let our Henrietta have him to ride on; we loved our child so much, that I have often carried Charlot's load so that he might carry our girl. Well, one fine day — I shall recollect it all my life — Charlot and my daughter left home and never came back again; my wife wept after Henrietta, and I after Henrietta and Charlot; our child gave us courage, the ass procured us our daily bread; we lost both on the same day, and are now reduced to beggary."

"Poor, poor Henrietta," exclaimed the old woman.

"Yes, poor Henrietta, and poor Charlot," added the old man, "for I somehow fancy he made a melancholy end."

"Alas, yes, it was a melancholy one," said I, "I saw him die in order to give me a moment's amusement, they had him torn to pieces by a pack of dogs."

The two old people drew back as if they had seen a wild beast.

It was in vain that I tried to convince, and detain them, they would not listen to me; they went away more shocked at my barbarity than their daughter's.

After all, what right had I, who had neither been suckled at the old woman's breast, nor fed at that old man's table, to cause them such horrible grief?

CHAPTER XIV ⋘ ⋘ ⋘
The Memoirs of a Man who had been Hanged

Man appoints and God disappoints. In spite of myself, I again returned to my philosophy; the sight of these two old people scattered to the wind all the fine projects I had formed in the morning. I quitted the *Bon Lapin*, never to return, and I was wending my way back, vainly seeking for all the happiness I had promised myself, when, in the middle of the road, I met a traveller marching on to Paris, as if he were a triumphant army; this traveller was a jolly companion, a thoughtless lover of good wine and good living; he appeared to have no object in view, and did not seem particularly uneasy as to where he should sleep that night, or procure a repast for the next day; his face was frank and open, and his general appearance announced that he had no other guide but chance. I have always remarked that when a man gives himself up frankly to chance, he immediately assumes an air of force and liberty which it does one good to behold; such was the case with this wayfarer. As I wished to find amusement at any cost, and, as he did not appear very fierce, I went and walked at his side; he was a well-bred man, and was the first to speak.

"You are going to Paris, sir?" asked he, "if so, be kind enough to show me the way, for I have already lost myself twice in these quarries and woods."

"Willingly, my friend; come with me, we will go there together; but you do not seem in any great hurry to arrive."

"I am never in a hurry to arrive anywhere. Where I am well off I remain; where I am badly off I also remain, for fear of faring still worse. Such as you see me, a true highway hero, I have lead more the life of a quiet citizen than of a gentleman of the road. Patience is the virtue next to courage. There is in Italy more than one rock on which I have remained in ambuscade a fortnight together, with a listening ear, an open eye, and my carabine in my hand, waiting for prey that never came."

"What! are you one of those bold Sicilian brigands, about whom I have heard so many tales of assassination and robbery, and whose daring mode of life has so well inspired Salvator Rosa?"

"Yes," replied the brigand, "I was formerly one of those daring Sicilians, as you call them, a bold and merry bandit, able to carry off a man and his horse on the highroad with as much facility as a French pickpocket steals a miserable purse in a village fair." Here he let fall his head, and I heard him sigh deeply.

"I suppose you deeply regret this happy kind of life," said I to him, with an air of the greatest interest.

"Regret it, sir! to live in any other manner is not to live. Nothing under the sun can be compared with the bold inhabitant of the mountains; fancy, now, a mountaineer of twenty, with a green jacket and gold buttons; he has his hair elegantly tied behind and encircled with a fillet; his pistols hang at a rich silk girdle; his long sabre, sounding formidably, drags after him along the ground, and over his shoulder he carries a carabine as bright as silver; at his side is a poniard with a crooked handle — fancy, I say, a young bandit, thus armed, posted on the top of a rock, defying the abyss below, singing and fighting in turn, forming alliances with both the Pope and Emperor, settling ransoms on his captives as if they were slaves, indulging freely in *rosolio*, and forming the delight of every tavern and young girl for miles around, while he has the full certainty that he will either die on a gibbet or in a nobleman's bed; yet this is what I have lost!"

"Lost! It seems to me that it would have been no easy matter to hang you, and that, as you have left your profession, it must have been by your own choice."

"It is easy to talk," replied the bandit, "but if you had been hanged as I have —"

"You hanged?"

"Yes, hanged, and, what is worse, for my devoutness. I was riding in one of those impenetrable passes near Terracina, when one fine evening (the moon had just risen beautiful and pure), I recollected that for some time past I had not offered the tenth part of my booty to the Madonna. That day happened to be the *fête* of the Virgin; all Italy had been celebrating her praise; while I alone had offered up no prayer; I resolved to delay no longer; I descended rapidly into the valley; admiring the dazzling reflection of the stars in the lake, and I arrived at Terracina at the brightest part of the evening. I thought of nothing but the Madonna, and traversed the crowd of peasants who were enjoying the cool of the evening at their doors, without perceiving that every eye was fixed on me. I arrived at the doors of the chapel — one only was open; on the other a large placard was affixed; this was a description of me, with a price set upon my head. I entered the church, a church like those which are to be found but in our Catholic and Christian country, with carved vaults, bright tessellated pavements, a lofty dome, an altar of white marble, an agreeable perfume, and with the dying strains of the organ visiting in turn every place where the faintest echo lurks. The holy image of the Madonna was surrounded with flowers; I prostrated myself before her, and offered her a part of my plunder — a cross of diamonds which had belonged to a young English countess, a heretic, but the diamonds were of the first water; a small Spanish coffer of exquisite workmanship; a fine necklace of pearls, taken from a gallant French lady who laughed heartily, and who sent me a kiss into the bargain. The Virgin appeared satisfied with my homage; she seemed to smile kindly on me, and to say: — "A pleasant journey, Pedro! I will send you up some wealthy travellers into the mountains." I rose from off my knees, full of security and hope, and was returning home, when I felt myself violently seized from behind; I was dragged by the satellites of justice into a prison, whence it was impossible to escape, for there was no woman in it to pity me, and I had not a *paolo* to bribe the jailer with."

"And you were hanged?"

"I was hanged the next day; this was an honour paid to my courage and fame. A few hours sufficed to erect a gibbet and find a hangman; they came in the morning, and took me out of my cell, and outside the last gate I found, waiting to receive me, white penitents, black penitents, grey penitents, and penitents both barefooted and provided with shoes; each held in his hand a lighted torch; on their heads they wore the *san-benito*, which reflected a sinister light; they looked like a lot of phantoms; four priests, repeating the prayers for the dead, and carrying a coffin, walked before me; I marched bravely to the gibbet. The gibbet was a respectable one; it was a large oak struck with lightning, which stood on a slight eminence; at the foot of the tree there was a carpet of flowers formed by white daises; behind me were those happy mountains that still rang with the fame of my exploits. It was not without some grief that I saluted my fine domain for the last time; in front of the gibbet yawned a deep precipice down which heavily rolled a rapid torrent that sent its humid and refreshing vapours to where I stood; all the air around the fatal tree breathed light and fragrance. I advanced without faltering to the foot of the ladder, and was about to deliver myself up to the executioner, when a glance at my coffin made me draw back. "This coffin is not large enough to contain my body," exclaimed I, "I will not be hanged if you don't fetch another suited to my size;" and I assumed so resolute an air, that the captain of the *sbires*, approaching me, said: "My son, you would certainly have the right to complain, if this box were meant to contain the whole of your body; but, as you are well known about the country, we have decided that, when you are hanged, your head is to be cut off and exposed to public view on the most elevated part of our ramparts."

Such a reason wanted no reply; I ascended the ladder; in the twinkling of an eye I was on the top of the gibbet; the view was beautiful. The hangman was a novice, so that I had time to contemplate at my ease the crowd that was weeping for me. Some of the young men present were trembling with rage; the eyes of the young girls were filled with tears; the peasants regretted me as a gallant fellow who well know how to exact tithes from those travellers who came to visit the churches, sun, women, Pope and Princes of Italy without paying; the *sbires* were the only ones who openly rejoiced. Francesco, our worthy captain, stood, with his arms folded, in the middle of the crowd; his look seemed to say to me:—"Courage today, tomorrow vengeance!" While waiting for the executioner, I walked along the gibbet, over the precipice; a gentle wind slightly moved the fatal cord. "You will be killed!" cried the hangman, "wait for me." He arrived at last at the top of the ladder, but he was seized with giddiness, and his legs trembled beneath him; the cascade below, the burning sun above, and all those looks of pity for me and of hatred for him entirely deprived him of his self possession. At last, however, he placed the cord round my neck with a trembling hand, and launched me in the air; he tried to rest his ignoble foot upon my shoulders, but these shoulders are firm and strong; a man's foot can do no harm to them; that of my executioner slipped; the shock was great; at first, he caught hold of the gibbet with both his hands, but he gradually let go his hold, and, falling heavily into the chasm, was swept away by the rolling waters." Such was the brigand's story.

This cheerful gibbet, this scene of death, related with such gaiety, greatly interested me. I had never before imagined that the gibbet would become an agreeable subject of amusing recollections; never before had I seen death arrayed in such bright colours; on the contrary, all those who have entered this field so fertile in sensations, have vied with one another in darkening the picture, and making the scene appear bloody, as if, in our social life, the punishment of death were not a common occurrence, a sort of fine, the amount of which we always have with us on our shoulders, and nothing more. Now, such was the loyalty of the bandit in question, that he perfectly well understood that the gibbet was the counterbalance of his profession, and that Italian society had tacitly said to him,— "I allow you to pillage, to carry off, and even to kill Englishmen and Austrians, on condition that, if you force us to take you, you will be hanged." He had accepted these conditions, and he possessed too great a sense of justice to complain. I was desirous of knowing what became of him after he was hanged; on my expressing this wish, he thus continued:—

"I remember quite well," said he, "the slightest sensations I experienced, and I should not care a fig, if, an hour hence, I had to go through it all again. As soon as the cord was round my neck, and I was launched into space, I first of all felt a very disagreeable sensation in my throat, and then I felt nothing; the air came down to my lungs slowly, but the smallest quantity of that balsamical and refreshing element sufficed to keep me alive; besides this, I felt, when suspended in that aerial space, as if I were being rocked by an invisible hand. I fancied that the noise in my ears was a series of divine melodies from Heaven, and that the gentle breeze which caressed my burning lips was the kiss of my affianced. I saw everything as through a gauze veil; in the distance all appeared refulgent, as if Paradise were the closing object of my view. Evidently, the holy Virgin was come to my aid, for I was a martyr to her worship. Besides, had I not my scapulary, and the hair of my Maria on my heart? Suddenly, the air ceased to penetrate my lungs; from that moment I saw nothing more; I felt no more gentle rockings; I was dead!"

"Yet," said I, "you are still in the land of the living, and appear, at present, little disposed to leave it."

"This is a great miracle," replied the bandit gravely; "after I had been dead an hour, my worthy captain cut the cord of the gibbet; when I came to myself again, my eyes met the kind look of a woman, who was leaning over me and bringing back the breath of life, stronger and purer than it had ever been. This woman had an Italian voice, Italian gracefulness, a soft accent, a sparkling eye, and, in fact, all the perfections of an Italian. For an instant, I thought that I had just left my tomb, and that the Madonna of Raphael was receiving me in her arms. That, sir, is the history of my bandit life. I promised my gentle Maria that I would become an honest man, if I could; I hope to succeed out of love for her. In order to appear honest among you, I have already procured myself a decent coat and a new hat, which is a great thing."

"You would still require to know some trade, and I am afraid you have learnt none."

"That is what I am told everywhere, your Honour, yet I never knew that a trade led to anything among you."

"Do you think you are luckier in Italy?"

"The country round Naples, like a good mother, produces every morning enough champignons to feed a whole city; but, in your country, everything must be paid for, even your champignons, which are poisonous."

"Do you think, then, that the calling of a *lazzerone* is the calling of an honest man?"

"There is none more loyal; a *lazzarone* is neither master nor valet; he depends but on himself alone; he only works when there is absolute necessity for so doing, but, as long as the sun shines there never is any necessity; finally, he can go to Rome when he likes, and crawl round Saint Peter's on his knees, by doing which he will obtain two hundred indulgences. That is the life of a *lazzarone*."

"Why, then, I beg, did you not become a *lazzarone*?"

"I had thought of doing so," replied he; "Maria, even, begged me to do it; but I am too much afraid of the eruptions of Vesuvius."

[67]

The Dead Donkey

We here entered Paris.

The entrance to Paris by the *barrière du Bon Lapin* is perhaps the most agreeable, although the least pretending of all the entrances to the capital of France. You arrive across the fields, and traverse a large plain, where the cavalry exercise every morning; then you enter a narrow road, and, leaving to your left the *Grande Chaumière*, and all the public houses that surround it, you suddenly find yourself in presence of the Garden du Luxembourg, the tranquil and favourite promenade of this retired quarter. My Italian friend questioned me at every step; everything astonished him; the old woman who lived in the garden, and the young peers of France, who came, whip in hand, to make laws for their country; the Odeon, so large, and the Sorbonne, so paltry in appearance, and the large mansions of plain stone, without a single marble statue; besides this, he saw no one basking in the sun, but he perceived instead numbers of *lazzaroni* working like convicts, while other *lazzaroni* were singing out of tune in the middle of the street, and accompanying themselves on instruments still more out of tune than their own voices; wretchedly daubed engraving met his eye at the glaziers shops; earthen pitchers without the slightest pretensions to elegance and with nothing antique about them; dirty streets filled with infectious air; young girls, weighed down by misery, and who never smiled; and noisy fish-women also met his gaze, but not one Madonna! The bandit was thunderstruck. "How shall I be able to earn my living here?" said he to me, with visible uneasiness.

"In the first place, what can you do?" said I, somewhat embarrassed as to how I should get rid of him.

"Nothing," replied he; "but yet I would sing better than those do who are singing now, and paint better pictures than those, and make finer statues than the ones I have seen; I could guard a palace better than those that I have already seen are guarded; and, as to your vendors of poison, here is a poniard that is better than all the rubbish they sell," added he, with an energetic smile.

"If you have no other resources, I sincerely pity you; we already have fifteen thousand painters, thirty thousand musicians to take care of, and I don't know how many poets; as to your poniard, I advise you to let that alone, for it would assuredly get you hanged at a certain gibbet, the cord of which can never be cut."

"Still I can say without boasting, that I know how to sing a love-song. When I was at Venice, the gayest noblemen there used all to want me to conduct their serenades, which I did so well that I often finished for

[68]

myself the enterprise I had began for others."

"Serenading would be a dull trade with us, in France, there is but one sure means of obtaining a woman's smile, and that is to give her something; all the songs in the world would not be of the slightest use. Were you even a Metastasio, they would laught at the plaintive sounds of your guitar, and the melodious ditties of your summer's night love."

"In that case," said the young man, throwing back his head, "I will go and ask the king to let me serve in his army; I will show him how I can handle a carabine and keep a battalion in order; if he will let me serve under him, I'll promise to mount guard on the hottest day in summer, without an umbrella."

"Know in the first place, young hero, that it is not possible to speak to the King of France. Then, as to your skill in handling a carabine, you will find that we have two hundred thousand men, with five sous pay a day, who can use it quite as well as you; you must also know that there is in the whole world but one foreign nation that has the right to guard the King, and that, ever since the Ligne, the Italians have never been for an instant thought of."

"Ah!" exclaimed the bandit, knitting his brows; "what a miserable nation is that which is not rich enough to keep a good company of brigands, with a captain at their head! If you had the honour to possess one, I would, regardless of Maria, go this very evening and offer those brigands my services as cook, and I should be heartily welcomed."

"What do you say? You a cook? Pray, what do you cook?"

"Egad! cook what we do on the highway, to be sure, and I don't very much think that there is any one among you who is so nice but what he would joyfully partake of a joint roasted and seasoned by me. When I was at Terracina, I was the most renowned man in the place for jugged hare and stewed adders; so, at least, thought his eminence, Cardinal Fesh, whom, Heaven preserve! I was sent for one evening in my forest-home to prepare his supper, and when the repast was over, he swore by everything holy that he had never tasted anything more exquisite, not even in his own palace."

I here approached the bandit, and said to him with a solemn air:— "I congratulate you; you are saved! your talent as a cook will give you a better welcome among us than you would receive if you were merely a great musician, a poet, a painter, a sculptor, or a general. You have it in your hands to raise yourself to power, for we are in the golden age of equality; nay, at this very instant, the whole of France is occupied in

The Dead Donkey

combating the sum demanded for the expenses of a minister's table. Visit the whole of Paris; enter boldly the first house you think will suit you, and say to the master:— "I am a great cook," then prove it, and you will soon be the leader of a party."

The bandit thanked me with a friendly gesture, and, at last, relieved in mind with respect to his fate, I left him.

CHAPTER XV ◄§ ◄§ ◄§
Impalement

The bandit's story often filled my thoughts. In France, England, Germany, and everywhere else, a new school of publicists had just sprung up, who, in the first article of their code, condemned capital punishment. The question was debated for a long time, as every theory will always be among nations sufficiently learned and skilful to play at paradox. Carried away as I was, without knowing it, by this crowd of argument for and against capital punishment, I esteemed myself lucky at having spoken to a man who had been hanged; I was quite proud at being able to relate the history of a person of the other world, without being forced to content myself with the incomplete narration of a culprit only walking to the scaffold. In my eyes I had an irrefutable argument in favour of this penal law, so strongly attacked by our wise men; I was only waiting for an opportunity to develop it according to my fancy.

This opportunity soon arrived. One autumn day, when all the leaves were gone, and when winter and frost already began to be felt, we were assembled in the country in a large cold, damp room. The company was numerous, but those who composed it felt for one another very little of that active sympathy which connects men closer together, and prevents them from thinking the fleeting hours long. In the middle of the apartment sat the ladies, who, entirely isolated from the rest, were silently engaged in needlework. The men spoke to each other at long intervals, without having anything to say; in a word, the whole evening would have been lost, if this question of capital punishment had not stepped in and spread some animation over the gloom and irksome aspect that prevailed. The effect was electric; everyone had in reserve, an argument for or against, and everyone spoke with all the force his lungs permitted, without even waiting for his turn; as to me, like a skilful man, I waited until the first clamours had subsided, and then, as soon as I thought the moment favourable, I narrated the bandit's story.

It did not produce much effect; it only appeared true and probable when told by the Italian himself: related by me it merely seemed a most unlikely thing. This subject, however, caused the discussion to begin again, hotter than ever; my adversaries, that is, the adversaries of capital punishment, retrenched behind that grand *humanity*, as behind an inaccessible rampart, had already gained the advantage over me so far that nobody dared to side with me any longer, when, in the midst of the clamours raised against the truth of my story, I met with a most powerful supporter.

This was a venerable Mussulman. He raised his head, admirably well set off by a long white beard, from the corner of the sofa, which was economically covered with a casing of faded printed calico, in which he had buried himself, and gravely taking up the conversation where it had been broken off, said — "I am quite ready to believe that this Italian was hanged, for I myself have been impaled."

At these words the greatest silence suddenly prevailed; the men drew near the narrator; the ladies forgetting their work, lent an attentive ear. You have, perhaps, sometimes seen women formed into a group, while listening to the recital of something that interests them; if you have you must have admired their animated physiognomy, their eyes wide open, their suppressed bosoms, a pretty neck extended like the swan's, and two listless hands which fall carelessly at their possessor's side; it was in admiring all these that I occupied my time, until it pleased the Turk to begin.

"Mahomet be praised," said he, "but once I penetrated into the abode of the sacred wives of his highness."

Here the attention of all became greater; I remarked a young girl of fifteen, who, seated by her mother's side, was listening to the Turk; she pretended to take up her work again. When you work you cannot listen.

"My name is Hassan," continued the Mussulman: "my father was rich, and so am I. Like a true Turk, I have had but one passion in my life, a passion for beauty; but the more my passion increased the more difficulty did I find to satisfy it. It was in vain that I visited all the most celebrated markets, I could find no woman handsome enough for me. Every day I was shown fresh slaves: women as black as ebony, and others as white as ivory; this one came from Greece, the country of beauty, but she did nothing but weep; one came from France, but she laughed in my face, and plucked me by the beard. "Have you then, nothing finer?" said I to the slave merchant. "Recollect, Hassan, we must not tempt Heaven. Woman is certainly a fine creature, but we must not expect her to be finer than her maker deemed it fit she should be," answered the slave merchant. The worthy man was right, he did not cry up his merchandise, but sold it for what it was. I, however, required impossibilities, and, incited by my desires, I one evening scaled the ramparts of the imperial palace.

I never thought of concealing myself, but climbed over the walls, as if his Highness possessed neither janissaries nor mutes, and in consequence was perceived by no one. I luckily penetrated the three impenetrable halls, which protect the sacred seraglio; and when daylight appeared I rashly rushed to look into the inviolable sanctuary. Great was my surprise when, by the white pale glimmer afforded by the sun's first rays, I perceived that women of Mahomet resembled all those I had already seen. My undeceived imagination could hardly believe this sad reality, and I had already begun to repent of my undertaking, when I was suddenly seized by the guards of the palace.

It was not my life alone that was in danger, but the lives of all these unfortunate women I had surprised in their sleep were in equal peril. It was however determined that this act of pollution should be kept secret from his Highness, but I was dragged from the sacred place, and taken to receive the punishment I had merited.

"Perhaps, gentlemen, you don't know what impalement is. The instrument used for this punishment is a pointed rod placed on the top of our minarets, and which is not very dissimilar to the lightning conductors invented by your Europeans, as if to defy destiny even in the clouds. I was stuck on this sort of tapering arrow, and, in order to make me keep my equilibrium the better, they tied two cannon balls to each of my feet. At first the pain was agonising; the iron slowly entered my body, and the sun, whose burning rays now fell on the glittering domes of Stamboul, would not, perhaps, have found me alive at noon, if the cannon balls on each foot had not come untied; they fell with a loud noise; my torture then became more supportable, and I began to hope that I should not die. Nothing can equal in beauty the sight that spread itself beneath my eyes — an immense sea, covered with little islands clothed in verdure, and ploughed in every direction by European vessels. From the height where I was placed, Constantinople appeared to me the queen of capitals. I was right above the sacred city, and saw at my feet, her gorgeous mosques, her

Roman palaces, her gardens suspended in the air, and her large cemeteries, the refuge of hydromel drinkers. In my gratitude I invoked the God of true believers. Doubtless my prayer was heard, for a Christian priest delivered me at the peril of his life; he took me into his hut and saved me. I was hardly cured, when I returned to my palace, my slaves prostrated themselves before me. The next day I bought the first woman I could find, filled my long meerschaum, which I dipped in rose-water, and, giving myself up to my reflection, came to the conclusion, while thinking of his highness's mutes, and their mode of punishment, that we must be content to buy women as they are, and that if the Prophet has not made them handsomer it is because the Prophet did not deem it necessary. Allah is just."

Thus spoke the Turk: this long narration had fatigued him; he fell languishingly back on the cushions of the sofa, and reassumed the voluptuous attitude of a true believer smoking his pipe at the hour of noon. If I were a painter I would depict tranquillity of mind and happiness in this attitude. In my opinion nothing better expresses repose than a happy child of Mahomet reclining on a Turkey carpet, free from anxiety, ambition, and desires, and wrapped in the luxurious sleep of the East which does not even force you to close your eyes, as if to do so were too great an effort for a mortal.

I have often remarked that an interesting story, well told, exercises a remarkable influence, often changing the tone of conversation and turning tediousness into pleasure. When once you are in a room full of people, what else can you do but boast about yourself and cry down others? Thus, after the first narration, the evening assumed a new aspect; everyone drew nearer his neighbour, and the mistress of the house, stifling the voice of parsimonious economy which warned her against touching her woodstack before the almanack had positively announced the winter, talked of having a fire made. This announcement was received with a thousand unanimous bravos; in an instant the fireplace was cleared of its rampart of grey paper, the lighted wood made the brass dogs shine, while every face, rendered gay and smiling by the gentle heat, bespoke unexpected satisfaction. There is a whole descriptive poem contained in the first fire of the last day of autumn, which fire gives you unawares a foretaste of the enjoyment procured by the crackling hearths of winter.

The fire burnt brightly: at the moment when its white and blue flame, accompanied with a strong odour of fir tree, shone out in its greatest brilliancy, it suddenly fell on the face of a young man who had not spoken yet. He was seated in a corner of the room, and all the part he took in the conversation was to notice, from time to time, its witty sayings, by a smile of satisfaction or irony, so that the attention of all was soon directed towards him. He was, besides, young and handsome; his eye was black, and everything in him announced a man of taste and wit, who thinks himself neither superior not inferior to those around him. The curiosity contained in the looks of the company made him instantly judge that they expected a tale from him; consequently, without giving them the trouble to ask him more directly, he leant his arm on the chair of a lady behind whom he was seated, and then with his head nearly touching her young and lovely face, began his story in so sweet and pure a voice, that you would have thought it was his beautiful neighbour, who was speaking, if her half-opened lips had not remained perfectly motionless, and if she herself had not assumed an attitude of the greatest attention.

"I greatly fear, ladies," said he — This unexpected departure from that social custom established in France, which required you always to begin with gentlemen when speaking in public, appeared so piquant a novelty for which the ladies present were much obliged to the narrator. By this skilful manner of proceeding the young man really procured himself the honour of a female *tête-à-tête*, and separated himself from the rest of the company; in consequence, there arose a murmur of approbation, which forced him to begin again; like a man of sense he began in quite a different manner.

"As for me," said he, "I have only been drowned, but the circumstances attending my death are rather curious. Some of you are doubtless acquainted with that finest of all landscapes under the sun, just without the walls of Lyons."

"It was a summer's day, one of those days when the whole sky is blue, and the air warm and pure. I was softly reclining on the bank of the river, or rather on the bank of that common shore where the Saône abruptly unites with the waters of the Rhône, which, at first stoutly resisting, and then more gently, the advances of the former's yellow stream, at last owns itself vanquished, is entirely lost in the waters of the conquering river, and rolls along with it in the same bed. It was twelve o'clock, the heat was overwhelming, and the water limpid; I was dozing, in a reclining posture, on the grass at the side of the river, and was in the same state of beatitude as a man who has taken opium. By dint of contemplating this vast extent of water, which appeared so calm and peaceful, I fancied that I perceived at the bottom of the river, on a piece of rock, I don't know what young

[75]

and ideal beauty, stretching out her hands to me with an angelic smile. The charm was irresistible. The vision swang softly to and fro in the mirror of the waters; an old lime tree that grew on the banks of the river lent the white flowers which covered its branches to protect the young nymph's head, and with its green leaves formed for her a transparent robe. I remained at the side of the river, motionless, enchanted, and burning with indescribable love, which realised all the mad dreams of youth; I fancied that I was the hero of Tasso, the handsome Roland stepping in the garden of Armida, by the side of those marble basins in which sportive nymphs sang of love, while playing in the silvery water; these same lovely beings I fancied smilingly stretched forth their hands to me from the bottom of their limpid habitation — and I succumbed. I dashed into the river, and neither the coolness of the water, not the irresistible force of the current which carried me away, not the flight of my transparent goddess, could arouse me from my poetical dream. I was swimming in the middle of those two great rivers, the Rhône and the Saône, which fought for my body as a prey. Without thinking of the danger I was running, I abandoned myself complacently to their desires; one moment, I was gently borne along in the arms of the Saône, and the next moment the Rhône violently tore me from the former's soft embrace, and impetuously drove me forward; at other times I found myself on the confines of these two powerful rivals, and then being propelled by the one and stopped by the other, I remained nearly stationary, while the nymph reappeared as lovely, as smiling, and as youthful as ever; once she was so near me, that I rushed forward to seize her. After this I recollect neither what became of me, nor to what happiness I was admitted, nor with what delightful reward I was presented; but after a whole day of ecstacy, I awoke in the loft of a peasant. Night was slowly descending on the mountains, the oxen were returning to their stalls, and their melancholy lowing fell on my ear as I lay with my head supported by one of those fine and vigorous oarsmen of the Rhône, such as are still seen in my own native village of Condrieu; everywhere else these once bold, but now degenerate navigators, are become timid and crafty merchants; they have not preserved in their veins a single drop of the blood of their forefathers.

"Such was my death; it was, as you see, a delicious dream. I am of exactly the same opinion as the Italian and the Turk. You see, death by order of the penal law in Italy, death by command of despotism of the East, and voluntary death in the West, are not to be feared, the one more than the other. From that day I became of the opinion of the philosopher who thought that to live and to die was the same thing; only, as I had once fallen asleep, I am very sorry that I ever woke again."

Such was the young man's narrative; and when, on leaving off, he saw that he was the object of general attention, his face became purple, he quickly withdrew from the chair on which he was leaning, and his cheek touched by accident the cheek of the young girl who was sitting before him. I soon remarked that his blushes were contagious, and it was really a pleasure to see the countenances of these two young people simultaneously lighted up with the deep carnation of bashful youth.

When the company was a little recovered from the surprise caused by these strange stories, the discussion began again stronger than ever; the adversaries of capital punishment had nothing to advance against such arguments. While they were racking their brains, in order to find some plausible answers, the timorous partizans of punishment by death, who had for an instant appeared beaten, and who feared being accused of cruelty, came back to the charge with more force than they had displayed before, and found no limits to their demonstrations. Everyone did his utmost to remember that he had been dead at least once in his life. One had fallen pierced through with a sword, at the Bois de Boulogne, and he recollected perfectly well that the cold steel, as it traversed his body, had produced anything but a disagreeable sensation; another had received a ball full in the breast, without feeling the least hurt; while a third had fallen down and fractured his skull, without recollecting anything. I make no mention of the putrid fevers, malignant fevers, brain fevers, and all the other numberless fevers that were spoken of; in a word, such were the arguments brought forward, that it was unanimously voted that death was free from pain; that capital punishment was, on the part of society, rather a precaution for the safety of all, than satisfaction taken as an equivalent for the perpetration of a crime; that society paid too dearly for death on the battle-field, by rewarding it with that immortal recompense, glory; and, finally, that to fear death in one's bed was acting more like a fool than a coward.

In the midst of this dissertation on penal law, which even Beccaria would have been puzzled to cope with, a fat abbé, who till then had remained buried in a large arm-chair, in the posture of a man digesting a good dinner, having risen with an effort from his seat, took up his station in the very centre of the disputants, and right in front of the blazing fire-place; having taken his position, he settled himself firmly on both his feet, and as he was a man of sense and good counsel, one of those old priests, with a kind and indulgent conscience, whom the French revolution had driven abroad, and who on returning to their country, had attempted to reconstruct to the best of their ability, canonical life, so full of easy comfort for themselves, and of active charity for others, the worthy man was listened to with attention.

"By Saint Anthony," exclaimed he, "yours is a fine discussion on capital punishment. My opinion is, gentlemen, that you are talking very coolly; if, like me, you had but just escaped from dying of indigestion you would certainly speak of death with more respect."

CHAPTER XVI ⋅⤐ ⋅⤐ ⋅⤐
The Capucins

It was in vain that I tried to forget the double passion, the double study of my life — Henrietta and moral deformity. Nothing could turn me from this fatal passion — from this fatal study. Every day I was goaded on by I don't know what fresh and frightful desire to dive deeper into the horrible, and to learn whether I could proceed still further, or whether, in fact, I should be vanquished in my researches. In my eyes, however, the horrible existed but with Henrietta, that false and unfeeling woman, a very abyss of egotism and weakness, a human being devoid of moral nature, a magnificent envelope, to complete whose perfection nothing was wanting except a soul.

One morning I again met with this inanimate and heartless thing, to which I had attached myself, and which I was following, step by step, in every course of vice. Yet how shall I ever dare tell you where I found her? Still I must. My story would not be complete if we did not wade through all the loathsome degradation traversed by Henrietta. The dreadful place to which vice had brought this woman — with society as it is at present constituted, it is, however, as fatal, as necessary, I was about to say as unavoidable, a place as the Bourbe or the Morgue — was no other than an infectious, degrading hole, ringing with cries and misery, and filled with howling and gnashing of teeth. This place was a hospital, but a hospital that no one respects. The doctor himself despises his patients there, and looks upon them with more disgust than pity. This hospital is a prison, and the patient an ulcer. Illness in this place is designated under all sorts of horrible names, which are pronounced in a whisper. The public point, with a deriding smile, at the victims who are being carried there. It is the Prefect of Police, and not the Sister of Charity, who keeps open this fatal asylum. The police is the queen and sovereign mistress of this place. The hospitable Sister of Charity flees far from this abode of misery, while covering her face. The countenances seen there must indeed be hideous and distorted, for even you thus to turn away your eyes, gentle and holy women, chaste queens and guardian angels of the Pitié and Hôtel-Dieu! The unfortunate creature whom vice throws into these places generally enters at the end of a banquet, with her lips still stained with wine, her bosom uncovered, her head crowned with flowers. She leaves as she entered, with her bosom uncovered, her head crowned with flowers, and ready again to abandon herself to the madness of intoxication; yet the narrow space in which she is shut up, the air she breathes there, the fetid tortures that await her, the shame and ignoble misery of which she is about to become the vassal, everything, in fact, turns this dreadful place into damnation nearly as terrible as that which awaits crime after death.

At the top of the Rue Saint Jacques, between the Cochin Hospital and Val-de-Grâce, and just by the Bourbe, is seen an old monastery; it stands alone, and has a wretched appearance, bearing a strong likeness to the shabby buildings of the eleventh century. A dirty, infectious candle manufactory casts its greasy shadow across the left side of this building. At its right angle a poor apple-man has built a wooden hut; before the door of this hut stalks a large, thin, bony goat. You enter, and you see keepers without kindness or pity, doctors without compassion, and patients without confidence. The manners, fright, and egotism of a city ravaged by the pest reign there, and what is more dreadful than all is, that the shame of the patients does not allow them to own the poignant suffering that tortures them. Within these walls are horror, hunger, corroding passions, ever increasing uneasiness, disgust, loathsomeness, and illness, that assumes every form, that takes every name, and usurps every place. Such is life there, if to breathe so foul an air can be called to live. The atmosphere is mephitic, the water that runs about the place poisonous and slimy. I have seen there young men, pale, livid, green, stupid, deprived of their nascent reason, insipid victims of an insipid passion. I have also seen there fathers of families, still in mourning for their wives and children; horrible old men, whom the faculty take great care of as being curious phenomena, that they show to strangers, saying, "See, our pestiferous patients are more dreadful to view than yours." A worthy subject of pride, indeed! All these wretches, distorted, bent, crushed by their maladies, without memory or hope, were moving about with a slow and silent step. Out of this crowd of patients not one would have dared to complain, not even to his Maker, so afraid are they of being heard by their fellow-men. The same leprosy, the same shame, the same infectious filth, the same despair are depicted in every face, and harboured by every person there. "Ah!" whispered I to myself, "you wished for something horrible; you are seeking after every kind of ignominy. You leave your house in the morning solely for the object of contemplating all sorts of misery, putridity, and corruption. Well, now satisfy yourself — glut yourself with infection and vice — yet let me leave, let me leave as quickly as I can, this lazar-house." I was about to go out, when someone said to me, "There is another side to the hospital; this side is for the men, but the woman are over there. Do you not wish to see both sexes?" Women here? Women? Alas! I had hardly crossed the passage, when I met nurses infected by the feeble child they carried at their infected breast; yet their look was rather one of pity than of anger; poor young country girls, who, bathed in tears, but understanding nothing of their malady, and at a loss to account for the derisive smile that fell on them, hid their heads in their cotton aprons. At the door of this den, a young and innocent woman, the pitiable victim of the marriage bond, stood motionless, like a statue of Niobe, waiting for a place in some vacant wretched bed. What! the woman who suckles a child with her milk; the young girl who abandons herself to her love; nay, even the virtuous woman, they, also, are attacked with this horrible malady. Unfortunates! How much more are they to be pitied than those other patients whom you hear laughing aloud in the wards. The latter are at home; they look upon an hospital as a place of luxury — a bed of repose. I entered the ward; it was immense; the women were making the place ring with laughter, and playing at all sorts of games; some were adorning themselves with a veil, others with a dressing gown. The youngest, who were nearly naked, were disputing as to who was the youngest; others were swearing frightfully, or else singing some ribald song with a hoarse voice. Most of the women here were as florid, clean, and happy as the men were haggard, pale, and wretched. Unfortunate women! handsome enough to appear handsome even there; thoughtless enough to be able to sing in such a place; and strong enough to be able to laugh at the tortures they endured. Merciful Heaven! what treasures of beauty hast thou not given them in thy anger. Poor, accursed creatures! they might have been an honour to youth, the pride of the conjugal roof, the force of enterprise, and the consolation of old age; yet they have blasted everything before the age of twenty — youth, virtue, beauty, family, love and marriage, infancy and old age; they have lavished, sold for a mere nothing, exchanged for ulcers, all those precious gifts they had received from Heaven — grace, youth, smiles, health, and happiness. Oh! it is indeed horrible — most horrible! Suddenly, at a certain signal their games stopped, silence succeeds the uproar they were making, they take their places in order, and drag themselves, one after another to where the doctor is awaiting them.

This was at the bed of misery. This bed of misery is in a small, low room, lighted by a single window, which looks out on a drain; its walls are of a dirty grey colour, and grotesquely embellished with a few obscene drawings, traced by the idle hands of the patients. On this bed is a thin straw mattress, over which is thrown a black cloth. By the side of this wretched couch are scattered here and there all sorts of sharp operating instruments. A chafing-dish, full of charcoal, is presently brought in — the irons are heated — around the bed stand the old incurable inmates of the place, who, by their services, have merited to be present at the spectacle about to be exhibited. On the only seat in the room is the elegant operator, who is talking with his pupils about actresses and newspapers. I was in the midst of these young followers of Esculapius, who were more learned than the god of medicine himself, as he was lucky enough to be entirely ignorant of so many maladies; and I alone was moved and attentive. Through the half-open door I contemplated all those women who, hardly clothed, were awaiting their turn with as much impatience as if they had been waiting for the rise of the curtain at the theatre. Among them were the most charming faces; children's faces, delicate and modest, with a half-open mouth encircled by a faint smile; handsome faces with well arched eye-brows, an expressive look, and black hair; it was, in fact, a confused and varied assemblage of all kinds of beauty — a veritable seraglio — which, when awoken at night by the Sultan's order, rushes, with naked feet, to the door of his harem, and awaits, with amorous respect, his orders and his handkerchief.

A voice was heard, and then a name — "Henrietta!" "Henrietta!" and from the midst of the crowd, which made way for her, I saw her emerge, with a haughty step, an arrogant look, and still beautiful. She threw herself on the bed of misery with as much unconcern as on the grass at Vanves, and awaited the pleasure of the operator. The greatest silence prevailed; the surgeon took up his curved scissors, and cut into the living

[81]

flesh; nothing was heard but the sonorous clashing of the instrument; and when, overcome with pain, the young woman flinched, or uttered a cry, she was answered with words of rage and contempt. For myself, divided between horror and pity, between love and disgust, I silently contemplated this unfortunate, and admired her courage, her pale figure, her pure form, her soft delicate hand, her slender, graceful neck, her whole beauty so mercilessly annihilated. She who might, said I to myself, have formed the happiness of a king, was fallen to the lowest rank of degraded humanity. When the operator laid aside his intruments of iron, he had recourse to fire; he unrelentingly burnt all those bleeding wounds, looking every now and then at his dreadful work with the satisfaction of a young painter, finishing a landscape. At length he said, in a harsh voice, "Make room for the next, trollop! and don't let me see you here again." she got up, pale and suffering, and hardly able to walk, but still unabashed and insolent: another patient had already taken her place before I perceived that she had left.

CHAPTER XVII ◄§ ◄§ ◄§
The Return

I hardly know how I found my way out of this fatal place. When beyond the gate, I got into the vehicle that was waiting for me, a rough-looking country cabriolet, but large and commodious. I remained there buried in stupid astonishment, that somewhat partook of despair, when, after waiting about an hour in the middle of the Rue de la Santé (*la Santé!* what a bitter derision! a witticism by some municipal councilman), at the edge of the heaps of eternal dirt that stagnate there, I perceived something white and shivering, that appeared to be waiting for the means of getting out of so disagreeable a position. My determination was soon taken. "Give me your coat and hat, and get up behind," said I to Gauthier, the driver. I then threw the braided coat over me, and drawing the glazed hat across my eyes, I advanced, like a veritable hackney coachman, towards the two women.

It was Henrietta and that young and honest married woman, whose decent appearance and grief had so much struck me: cured at the same time, they had both been turned out of doors together, half naked and dying with cold, the one having no home to go to, and the other afraid to return to hers.

I alighted. "Will you get into my cab?" said I to them. I had scarcely spoken, before Henrietta had taken her place in the spacious vehicle, without waiting for further entreaty. "I dare not, sir," replied the other women; "my husband lives a long way off, and I am afraid that your fare would not be paid," and she hid her face in her old black shawl, the only one of her things which she had not given to her companions in misfortune, or which the latter had not stolen from her; she leant against the wall for support, while her feet were only protected by a pair of slippers, that let water in at every step she took.

"Never mind, ma'am," I replied, "get in all the same." I placed myself between them in the cab. At this moment all the women who were discharged that day as cured left the hospital. One would never have imagined, on seeing them so cheerful, through what horrid ordeals the unfortunates had passed. They laughed, jumped, and sang. "Huzza for wine! huzza for love!" They returned at the same time to the world and to debauchery. What is the lesson taught them by this dreadful malady? The greater part of these liberated women were received with rapture by men with suspicious-looking features; the neighbouring public-house resounded with exclamations of joy, and all the hackney-coaches around were quickly filled; in the midst of the crowd a few old women of ignoble appearance came to seize their captives, poor young girls whom they had bought in and round about Caux, in all the virginal brilliancy of their twentieth year, whom illness had momentarily taken away from their degrading druggery, and who were not yet out of their time.

"Where shall I drive to ma'am?" asked I, addressing the young and unfortunate women who was trembling at my side.

She was so troubled, that she hardly heard me. At length she told me that her husband lived a long way off. Yet the unfortunate had implored him so earnestly to come and see her, and withdraw her from the misery in which he himself had placed her, but he came not. "Were it not for you, sir," said she, "I should have died of cold and shame in the streets." Those were her words, spoken in so sweet a voice, and accompanied with a look so full of thankfulness! Poor woman! So chaste and so defiled! So modest and so degraded, especially made for the creation of sweet, domestic bliss, and yet passing her honeymoon at a hospital! At every new street we entered she become more sad. On remarking this, I slackened my horse's pace. "What troubles you so much?" said I. "Alas! sir," answered she, "how will my husband receive me? — how will he ever forgive the harm he has done me?" I turned to look at her. She was pale and livid; her fine face bore indelible traces of every sort of suffering of the soul and heart, of the mind and body. "Take courage, ma'am," said I. At this moment we passed under the arcade of the Hotel de Ville.

"Courage! Good Heavens! I have had great want of it for the last year! Unfortunate that I am! A year of torture and of prison for a month of marriage!" We thus arrived at the door of her house. I stopped my horse — the young woman was speechless; I gave her time to recover. As for Henrietta, numbed with cold, she had buried her head beneath the lowest cape of my coat, and had fallen asleep, with her two hands resting on my knees.

At length I said to the young woman, — "Shall I accompany you to your husband, ma'am?" She cast on me a timid look, but full of gratitude. I then cautiously raised Henrietta's head, and opened the flap of the cab; the air passed across the face of the sleeping girl, the cold air seized her, and she uttered a vague complaint. The young virtuous woman was already on the threshold of her door, when, without saying a word, she took off the black shawl that covered her shoulders, and getting on the step of the cab, enveloped with this sympathetic rag the shoulders of Henrietta, who was still struggling with sleep. Gauthier descended, and held the horse's head.

When this last act of charity was done, the unfortunate woman seemed to take fresh courage: she ascended the staircase, leaning on my arm, for though she no longer trembled, her limbs were very weak. The house was quiet, clean, cold, as well conducted as a usurer's; we stopped at the second story, I knocked, and a voice said, "Come in!" I opened the door; my companion was as pale as death; her fine bosom, no longer concealed, heaved convulsively; I entered first. A man, surrounded with green pasteboard boxes and papers, received us; he welcomed his wife, as if he had parted with her but the evening before; he had for her no word of consolation, no smile, no expression of regret, no look of pity. The wretch! he still dared give this woman a kiss, which made me tremble, for his eyes were streaked with red, his dull hair fell down his face in matted knots, and large pustules were scattered over all his face! "Wretched woman!" exclaimed I approaching her, "what madness has made you return to this place? What destiny has brought you back here to your ruin? Here! why it would have been better for you to remain in the place you have just left!" The man smiled with an air of derision, and continued the examination of his papers.

His weak and innocent young wife began to weep; then she cast a look on me, and that look seemed to say, "I know my lot; in a year, come, and you will again find me at the same place."

Oh poor unfortunate! that is what your duty then brings you to! What worse thing, I ask, could debauchery accomplish? Can the wretched Henrietta be right? You at least, who are all virtue and honour, are yet more to pity than the street-walker. Poor woman, poor woman! I descended the staircase, trembling convulsively, and my head ran against the head of my horse.

Henrietta still slept.

CHAPTER XVIII ⋰§ ⋰§ ⋰§
Lupanar

"Where do you want to go?" asked I of my other companion, as soon as I was somewhat recovered from my emotion.

Henrietta replied nothing; she looked at me with an air of astonishment, as if she had never thought that she ought to go anywhere; the unfortunate! she had, in fact, no place to go to; formerly, before she entered the hospital, she still had a charming little house, of so coquettish and inviting an appearance, and the abode of such elegant vice, that the vice practised there might almost be tolerated. Everything the house contained was hers, and she herself the queen of it; she had velvets and lace, silks and gold, to embellish and increase her beauty; her foot hardly lighted on the carpets, so strewed were they with flowers. She smiled on herself in brilliant glasses, and everywhere her listless eye fell on *chefs d' oeuvres* of the past century. There were flying cupids, sighing shepherds, and shepherdesses stretching their well-formed tapering legs along the mossy grass. The most expensive furniture adorned this sumptous dwelling; old bronzes, marble polished by age, clocks which struck alarums, and announced with certainty the hour when it was time to love; a thousand invisible perfumes floated between those profane walls, as blood circulates through the body; a discreet and laughing echo repeated in a whisper tender words, and in the cornices was heard, on listening attentively, the sound of kisses given and returned. The entire world had sent its *spolia opima* to this house. China had contributed her old grotesque and licentious lacquered porcelain; England her richly chased and highly polished plate; Sevres its noble vases, more precious than gold; and our old royal mansions their thousand nameless yet graceful knick-knacks. Servants, few in number, but knowing well their duties, surrounded the idol of the place. She had to guard her door an old woman, who, as occasion required, was both a severe duenna and an engaging matron. The footman who rode behind her carriage was a fine young peasant from Vanves, who, like her, was corrupted, and wore the same livery. To flatter her night and morning, and from whom she might borrow gaiety, knowledge, and piquant effrontery, she had a pretty girl of sixteen, a *soubrette* with the finest prospects, and who was soon about to begin to trade in vice on her own account. Her kitchen was always burning hot, her drawing-room ever quiet and cool; and her bed-chamber was surrounded by jasmine and roses, while its alcove was dumb, its door discreet, and its window inquisitive. There her beauty reigned in all its brilliancy and power; she possessed everything necessary for its support; it would have been impossible for her to desire to be more elegantly dressed, or more often fêted, to be treated with greater care, to receive more flattery, or be more gently lulled to sleep; she could not wish to have a more refreshing bath, nor a softer bed, not more generous wine, nor a table better served, nor more skilfully conducted obscurity. Thus surrounded, thus entertained, thus seen to advantage, the most mediocre beauty would have appeared superlatively handsome; judge, then, what was Henrietta's beauty! Every one of her hours brought with it a *fête*, an act of treachery or pleasure; every morning, when she awoke, Rose, her *soubrette*, brought her numberless newly printed calumnies on all that was beautiful, witty, youthful and virtuous. While reading these calumnies and words of vile abuse, Henrietta consoled herself with the thought that she was separated from that petty world whose contempt she so well returned with her own disdain. Then followed the journal of fashions, the theatrical gazette and her *billets doux*, and she hastily chose a bonnet, a theatre, and a lover for the day. As twelve o'clock struck the horses were put to her carriage, which was adorned with lying emblazonry; it is at this hour that the Rue Vivienne is visited, and at which are taken those strolls so dear to a pretty woman, when, stopping at every shop, and listening to the flattering whispers of the young girls who fill it, she hesitates between a thousand *nouveautés*, looks at one stuff and then at another, adds a flower to her bonnet, or takes one away, chooses for her dress a plain gauze or the

there were any place she could go to. I waited patiently till she had taken
a resolution. This new kind of struggle interested me. I was desirous of
knowing where an unfortunate woman, who had but just left the degrading hospital of the Capucins would be welcome.

Reduced to the last extremity, and overcome by so much misery, the
wretched woman tried in vain to remember the men who formerly
surrounded her with their protestations, their homage, and their love.
What was become of the old men who called her their child, and of the
young men who wished to die for her? She herself had forgotten even
their names; they certainly must have forgotten her face. If she had then
possessed but the money she had spent in perfumery alone, she might
have bought twenty acres of land at Vanves. No hope, however, was left
her. During the year she had been separated from the world another
generation of old men and young gallants had arisen to love and lose their
female fellow-creatures; as also had arisen another generation of young
women to seek celebrity, and ruin themselves as Henrietta had done.
Thus she was no longer on a level with gilded vice, but was only now
fitted to revel in the depths of low debauchery. Turned out of her
drawing-room, henceforth her sole refuge was the street. She soon understood, confusedly and in trembling, on what still more horrible course of
life she would shortly have to enter. Prostitution was nothing now with
her but a question of poverty and hunger. She then recollected certain
advice, certain mysterious information that her companions had given
her while she was at the hospital. It is principally in the hospitals for the
leprous that the agents of corruption at present recruit their wretched
victims; an infectious ward, how fit an anti-chamber to such a boudoir!
By dint of thinking, Henrietta recollected the name of an unknown
protectress, to whom she had been strongly recommended to apply, as a
person able to offer her an asylum. After many efforts, all she could think
of was the name of this woman, but she had entirely forgotten the address.
Such was still her thoughtlessness, and such her confidence in her
fortune. So, after much reflection, she said to me — "Do you know where
Madame de St. Phar lives? They told me that she would treat me like her
own child, and would always be happy to place at my disposal a bed, a
dress, and a place at her table. Take me to Madame de St. Phar's."

I have already told you, and you must have long since perceived that I
am no libertine, I did not even know there was such a person; yet the
name is very popular among students, military men, and commercial
travellers. Still less, then, did I know the address of this lady. Neverthe-

less, I naturally directed my horse's head towards the richest and most corrupt quarter of the town, when, in the course of my way, I luckily met with some soldiers in merry mood, fine handsome fellows of the Royal Guard, on whose arms were hanging women about three feet high, and horribly ugly; yet these men appeared as proud as if they had conquered Italian princesses. "Gentlemen," cried I to the soldiers, "would you be good enough to tell me where Madame St Phar lives?" The question flattered their vanity, but, at the same time, embarrassed them; happier than I, they were extremely well acquainted with the name and deceptive calling of the lady mentioned; more than once, while passing the night in the guard-room, had they heard their officers talk of such abodes as the true believers talk of the paradise of Mahomet; but it was out of their power to tell me exactly where the house was situated. Their amiable companions were no better informed, and quite mortified at their ignorance, silently remained hanging on the arms of their gallants. At length, a corporal, twisting his moustache round his fingers, said, — "If Agatha can't give you the address of Madame de St. Phar, you must go and ask for it of my lieutenant, who could find his way there blindfold."

Agatha, who was a little behind, came up slowly, and in great majesty, like a woman who possesses gloves, and condescends, in her own idea, to keep low company. I bowed to her respectfully. "Would you have the kindness," said I, "to direct me to the house of Madame de St. Phar, if as the corporal says, it is in your power to do so." "If it is in my power to do so!" exclaimed Mademoiselle Agatha; "as if I didn't know St. Phar! Thank heaven, I might know more of her, if I liked; I should think I am entitled to that!" And while pronouncing these words in a tone of disdain, she proudly threw back her head, drew up her person and her dress, the bottom of which was beginning to appear rather dirty. "Then, Mademoiselle, you will, I am sure, be kind enough to tell me the way." "For what do you take me?" said Agatha, her eyes darting fire. "Come on, Agatha, be obliging now," interrupted the corporal, "and don't want so much asking to oblige a polite, gentlemanly man; devil take it! can't you show others that we keep good company, and that we don't limit our acquaintance to little thoughtless girls who have never quitted the Faubourg Antoine." The poor girls bit their lips; Mademoiselle Agatha smiled gracefully, and, pointing with her forefinger, whose long black nail had worked its way through a cotton glove, said:— "Go straight on; at the end of the street turn to the right, and keep on until you come to the Palais Royal; on reaching the third street on the left you will find yourself at St. Phar's door." While listening to these amiable directions, the corporal was proud of his companion, the soldiers were proud of their corporal, and I, myself, was proud at having so quickly found an address which was certainly not to be met with in the "Court Guide." See how each interprets pride according to his own idea.

As I drove on towards the spot designated, I examined Henrietta, and tried to account for her immobility and assurance.

What! could she take so terrible a resolution in so short a space of time! And this, too, without a moment's hesitation, or a shadow of remorse! It was, however, evident that she was about to undertake a dreadful task, and that she had her foot raised to descend still another step in the deep abyss of vice. In my eyes such a resource was horrible. On seeing her so calm and tranquil, one would have thought that she was merely accomplishing an agreeable duty. But I, who by the irresistible force of circumstances was conducting her along this fatal road; I, who was the blind instrument which she made use of to accomplish her destiny; I, who had seen her so innocent, so free, so happy — alas! I shuddered to think that I was about to be a witness of the last transaction a woman can make — a witness of the incredible sale, through which she abandons herself to the first comer for a flimsy dress, or a crust of bread. When we arrived in the street inhabited by St. Phar, I immediately recognised the house by the calm and silence which surrounded it. It was the calm of opprobrium — the silence of shame. One would have thought that the neighbouring houses had fled back and hidden themselves, in order not to be polluted by the contact of the one in question. What a frightful thing it is to think that there is not in the world one single city free from this impost of crime and vice! This house was also easily known by its door, mysteriously half open; the inquisitive side-glances of the passers-by; its broken windows; its walls covered with pawn-brokers' addresses; and the names of quacks professing to cure diseases that we dare not name; as if ruin and affliction were worthy prospectuses for these poisonous abodes! I boldy stopped my cab at the door — at the door where no vehicle is ever seen, not even a hearse. Henrietta alighted leaning on my shoulder; she was already become more gay; she felt at home. We entered the house; I naturally gave her precedence. The staircase was dark and dirty; an old woman, who was in mourning, I know not for what, received us on the landing. Without uttering a word, she led us into a room, well, though modestly, furnished. Although it was in the middle of the day, this room was lighted by a lamp, the doubtful glimmer of which was engaged in a faint and melancholy combat with a stray sunbeam, pale and watery, which made its way through a hole pierced at the top of the closed shutters. This was in accordance with the orders of the Prefect of Police. By this regulation everyone could enter the house in safety; the executioner, the convict, the assassin, the spy himself; all, in fact, except the sun. This was the only contrivance the magistrate had been able to find for the support and protection of morality.

Seated round a table in this room were three woman of respectable appearance. They were discussing their affairs over a book kept by double entry, and carefully balancing their profits and losses. They were no less than the three partners of this commercial enterprise. Two, who were mothers of families, were dividing the dividends of the concern with the greatest conscientiousness and probity. The woman who sat at the top of the table, and who appeared to be presiding over this settling of accounts, had brought into this joint-stock company the popularity of her name and good reputation of her house, and her old experience in these kinds of transactions. It was she who first addressed Henrietta. Retired into a corner, I did not lose a word of the conversation.

"So you wish to enter our house?" said the woman, in a very natural tone of voice, and like an honest housewife engaging a new servant, while her acolytes were examining the neophyte with the most scrupulous attention.

"Yes, ma'am," answered Henrietta, in a voice full of respect; after which she was silent. Here they all three examined together her figure, hands, arms, legs, throat, hair — in a word, her whole person — with her thin and suffering face.

"She is handsome enough," said the youngest of the woman. "Something may be done with her; but we shall have to take great care of her. In the first place she is too thin and too pale; besides which, she has not clothes to cover her. Her hair, also, is in great disorder; and her fingers are horridly emaciated. She has evidently just left a hospital, and were it necessary, I could say which hospital."

"Never mind," remarked the woman on the right; "you know, my good friend, that even virtuous girls go there; and let us hope that she will profit from the lesson." Then turning to the postulant — "I do not think, my dear, that I have ever seen you anywhere?"

"Nowhere, ma'am."

"So much the worse," remarked the woman who presided; "for you have, no doubt, contracted expensive and independent habits, which will not at all suit the tranquillity of our house. If you wish to remain any length of time with us, Mademoiselle, your submission must be profound; your obedience unlimited. You must be neither noisy, nor greedy, nor ill. You will have to go yourself to the Commissary of Police to ask for permission to pursue your profession respectably; and you will have to submit without a murmur to all the exceptional rules of the affair. You will be allowed wine or beer but once a week, and will never go to the theatre more than once a month. On these occasions we shall be happy to give you all the encouragement in our power. But yet, ladies, even if we take her, what is it in your opinion that we ought to make of her?"

"My opinion is," said the first, "that she ought to be made a *grisette*; in the first place, there is a great want of *grisettes*, and then, nothing attracts a gentleman, or a man who is used up, like a white stocking drawn tightly over a well-formed leg, with a black apron; and consider also, that this dress is not very expensive for the house."

"As for me," replied the other, "I think that we have already too many *grisettes*; they are to be met with everywhere, — in the shops, on the stage, and in all the novels on morality; most men are either not courageous or old enough to openly attack a round cap and a black apron. Now, a lady of the middle-class could be seen with anyone. She would compromise no man. She can be followed, and a gentleman can offer her his arm without blushing. Besides, a lady is quickly improvised; a silk dress, a kid shoe, a Leghorn bonnet, a Baragé shawl, coloured gloves, a strong smell of musk and amber, with a modest air, are sufficient to turn the head of any Stock-Exchange man, or Government Office Clerk."

"Excellent!" replied the other; "but this young girl is not old enough for that sort of lady; she will be competent to the fact in five or six months; but, for the present, I should prefer dressing her with a bare neck, a dazzling robe of yellow satin, open-worked stockings, her ears loaded with mock pearls, Indian feathers in her hair, and Old Felicity at her side, to serve as her mother, in the evening."

"I am tired," replied St. Phar, who had been listening quietly, "I am tired, I say, of all these princesses; they ruin us with their gauzes, finery, and jujubes; nothing pains me more than to see their fine satin dresses come home covered with mud; I will have nothing more to do with them; and if I were you, Mademoiselle, I should prefer a peasant's pretty gown, bare arms, a gold cross hanging from an original velvet ribbon, a white flower in my hand, my hair twisted behind in a knot, and a straw-bonnet tastily placed on one side of my head; certainly, such rustic *nonchalance* would well become her!"

At these words, which brought to my mind (oh, dear and chaste recollections, what right had you in such a place?) the plain at Vanves, I rushed from my seat, and resolved to make a last attempt to rescue the wretched Henrietta from this dreadful haunt. "Yes," exclaimed I, "yes, poor girl, there is yet time; resume your cotton gown; again cover your neck with a plain muslin kerchief, and place on your head the modest faded straw-bonnet that you once wore; come, be again the young, pretty, laughing peasant, whom I formerly knew revelling in the freshest colours of health; come, let us return to Vanves; come, hasten, and let us flee this place! I love you, and will save you, if you like!"

The three women, on hearing me speak thus, looked at each other with uneasiness. This prey was too fine to be allowed to escape. "We do not wish to force the young lady," said St. Phar, "if she wants velvet dresses, a gold chain, and embroidered handkerchief, and open-worked stockings, she shall have them this very evening ——"

All was said!

CHAPTER XIX ✺ ✺ ✺
Sylvio

I am bound by the tenderest friendship to a young man, not so old as I am, named Sylvio, a frank, fine, good-natured fellow; strong, well-made, and slim, with enough affection and passion in his heart to supply a whole dramatic company. The dream of Sylvio's whole life — imprudent and inexperienced man! — was a woman's love all to himself; he looked upon women as being far superior to the human kind, and hardly dared breathe in their presence; but his admiration was dumb, and his silent homage was not of much good to him. Young and handsome, rich and brave, bearing an illustrious name, which he himself graced still more, he had hardly obtained from the beautiful creatures he adored a few indifferent and disdainful looks. But this was his own fault; for why was one so handsome so extremely modest? Entirely taken up in contemplating themselves, women are incapable of penetrating a man's character; at the most, they are only able to appreciate him when he openly parades his qualities. This is what Sylvio dared not do. I had tried, but in vain, to turn him from so dangerous a state of exaltation; he received with a smile my best advice. I don't know how he had discovered that I was tormented by a melancholy passion, but he knew it, and often bantered me about my mysterious sentiments; he counted all my sighs, found an explanation for my half-uttered words, and feverish absences of mind, and more than once he cast on me such a look of pity that made me tremble; for I imagined that he knew my secret, which is to say that he knew all my wretchedness! It was the day after my fatal adventure; I was extremely melancholy; I was reflecting that I myself, my love and youth, had been sacrificed to a velvet dress! to a tarnished, prostituted velvet dress! Wretched woman! Yes, thrice-wretched woman! Here Sylvio entered my room; he was accompanied by his good humour, which never abandoned him, not even in the midst of his strongest attacks of passion. He had imagined that, at a ball, the evening before, a woman of forty, a thick heavy gossip, who was old enough to be his mother, had pressed his hand. He was proud of this; and, in his pride, he came to tell me of his good fortune.

"The devil! so she pressed your hand! That has advanced you much, certainly," said I sighing.

"Advanced me much!" replied he. "The heart is touched through the hand as well as through the lips; yet I think, Mr Disdainful, that you would esteem yourself happy if you were only advanced as much as I."

"I assure you, Sylvio, that, with respect to my affections, I am much more advanced than I wish, and that you would jump for joy, if you knew how much you also are advanced, without even being aware of it."

Sylvio stared at me; his young and ardent imagination was already constructing a whole complicated romance of love, built upon a word that chance let fall.

At the same time I began to play with my purse, and mechanically spread its contents on the table, separating the gold from the silver, and the silver from the small change. Sylvio was still dreaming.

I suddenly drew him from his reverie. "Can you, Sylvio, who so much adore women, guess what is the usual price of the woman I love, and for whom I am dying?" exclaimed I, scattering my money out on the table.

Sylvio gave me no answer.

"Do you know," continued I, "what a woman is worth? I mean a charming and ideal creature, such a one as you have never even thought of in your dreams; a young girl as beautiful and fresh-coloured as a rose, of scarcely twenty, with the experience of an angel beneath her fine and streaming hair; a woman whom I saw, not a year ago, running about the plain at Vanves, and caring for nothing but the ass on which she rode, and the straw hat that sheltered her face from the sun? Do you know at what they esteem this happy peasant, who would have done honour to a Spanish grandee — at what they esteem this beautiful girl whom I loved as soon as I saw her? Do you know for how much money you, I, and everyone else, could possess her — do you know?"

The young man listened to me in trembling. "She whom you love! She of whom you ever think! She whom you pursue night and day! She for whom you neglect your flowers, friends, and poets! Well, what is her worth?"

I took a piece of gold. "To you, Sylvio, who are young, handsome, and timid, she would, doubtless, value herself at this, and laugh at your simplicity."

I then took the half of the same sum in silver. "To the vulgar man, to the first-comer, this would be her price; but to a drunken soldier, or an avaricious, obstinate old man, she would not cost more than this;" and I pushed to him a five-franc piece, on which was the effigy of his Majesty Louis XVIII; then I was ashamed of myself, and fell back in my despair.

A moment of silence ensued. Was this a reproach or a complaint from Sylvio?

At length he rose, approached me, and took up a piece of gold. "I wish to be satisfied," said he; "where is she? I will go and buy her."

"You, Sylvio?"

"Yes, I! What does it matter to you who buys her, since everyone has the right to be your rival? Madman! Just now you railed at my wandering passion, and you are now crushed beneath the shame in which you have had no hand! All the earth can possess your mistress, except yourself, who will die of rage on the threshold of her door. It would be better if you had no money in your purse. But you have the wherewithal to pay twenty times over for the worth of the thing you love! You hold this venal creature on your table. You can buy, if you like, three months of this woman's life, and when the lease is out, renew it for three months more, or a single hour, and yet, like a coward, you lament, without speaking or acting! We might now well say with Iago — 'Put money in thy purse!' Yet I, Sylvio the innocent, Sylvio the young lady, will go and see your mistress, and in order that you may behave generously to the last, I will take these pieces of gold, for it is only by borrowing your purse that I can commit an adultery. Poor man! poor lover! come, arouse yourself; I don't wish to outrage your feelings, I only wish to have this beauty for my money! I wish to see," continued he in a milder voice, "to what sort of love you have abandoned yourself; I wish to to tell you what happiness and repose are to be found in the arms of this woman. If you have not the courage to buy her, I will buy her for you; after which I will come back and tell you whether she is worth your regret, whether she is worth a single one of your tears, or merely this piece of money. So I will go alone and purchase her, unless," added he, "you would like to be present at the sale."

"Certainly, I should, Sylvio; we will go there together; come" And I took my money, all my money, and went out in a state of consternation, like an incendiary or an assassin whom crime calls away from his home.

We turned our steps towards the abode of Henrietta; but as I advanced — "Sylvio," I exclaimed, "it is impossible for me to allow her to remain any longer in this vile haunt; I cannot, Sylvio, allow her any longer to remain exposed for sale to all buyers; I should die or go mad, Sylvio! Let us then buy her wholesale, so that she may no longer be sold bit by bit."

"Spoilt goods," answered Sylvio, stopping at every woman he met.

We were at the beginning of the street, and already had our eyes upon the house, when we perceived at the fatal door a noisy crowd, which continually kept increasing. A detachment of soldiers surrounded the place, and the Commissary of Police, encircled with his scarf, had just arrived. Sylvio knew the honest magistrate, who allowed us to enter the fatal house with him. Everything was in disorder; the inmates, pale and with their hair dishevelled, were seated on their beds, and were looking at one another with a stupid air; their wretched companions in debauchery, ashamed at being surprised by the crowd, in so sad a plight, hid their faces — hypocrites, who looked to their good character, and who wished to unite the impurities of vice and the honours of virtue! In the street there was an immense multitude, eager to know the crime, and to see the criminal. A murder had been committed in the night; the details of it were already spread about, and made everyone shudder; I alone felt a sort of infernal joy of learning the name of the culprit. Yes, it was Henrietta; she herself who had just washed away her fault in blood! Heaven be praised for having saved her by a crime! At length, then, she had escaped the public, and henceforth belonged but to the executioner; at length, then this world, to which she had prostituted herself, had no longer over her any other but legitimate rights; it could now only ask for her head, but not her body! She will no longer be made a show of in the street; at present the only place on which she will be exposed to view is the scaffold! Now, the justice alone of men can reach her; she is sheltered at last from their vile passions. Thus I finally triumphed over this woman.

I went up into her room with the Commissary of Police. Before we reached the grey alcove in which the loathsome bed was placed, we were nearly stifled by infectious smells. Disorder reigned triumphant: dirty dresses, torn kerchiefs, old shoes, ragged petticoats, filthy grease and wine stains, and all sorts of tarnished vestiges of very equivocal opulence, formed a pell-mell frightful to look on. Lastly, behind the curtains was the corpse of a man, weltering in blood, still warm. She had killed this man, after having allured him to the house, and had thrown him out of her mercenary bed, without well knowing why, just as she had made him enter it.

When we entered her room the creature of vice was again become an ordinary woman — thanks to her crime. She was modestly enveloped in a dressing-gown, and her fine hair was scattered over her white shoulders; one would never have imagined that she was a courtesan who had just committed a murder. Moreover, she perfectly well understood that she belonged, body and soul, to the Commissary of Police, and that he was her living law, against which there was no appeal. Consequently, she was quite prepared to follow those who came to apprehend her. She had already packed up her wardrobe; a few embroidered rags, a broken comb, piece of soap, some pomatum, a pot of rouge, and a few other articles of a toilet-table of the lowest order. Meanwhile, a police officer arrived. Henrietta stretched forth her two little hands to receive the handcuffs, which were much too large. One would have thought, from her infantine grace, that she was trying on some new bracelets. The rough iron made her arm red, but her hand appeared all the whiter. When everything was ready, she traversed the crowd, got into a hackney coach, and was slowly driven away, in the midst of the cries and execration of the crowd.

"Rejoice," said I to Sylvio; "we have lost her!"

"Could you tell me now," asked Sylvio, "how much she is worth?"

"At present, all the gold in the world could not buy her; and I thank heaven for it! By means of this crime she is become more inaccessible than the most rigorous virtue."

"Extremes touch, my friend," said Sylvio.

"Bars or virtue, it matters to me not which. She is saved; she has returned to the right path; at present I can love her as much as I like; I can be proud of my love, and owe it to both judge and executioner. She has no longer the power to sell her body; she has escaped prostitution, her sovereign mistress. Laugh, Sylvio, and mock me! At present I can love

her with more security than you could your young wife, four and twenty hours after your marriage, Sylvio."

And I abandoned myself to my infernal joy, as far as it was in my power so to do.

CHAPTER XX ⊷§ ⊷§ ⊷§
The Court of the Assizes

This murder, the only just and courageous action of this woman's life, was committed under the following circumstances:— When she had taken up her abode in this haunt of vice, she was taught in a few words her new profession. She was to be ready at every hour of the night and day; was to wait patiently with a smile on her face; be pleased with everyone; refuse but him who had no money; walk every evening from one pavement to another, in the rain and in the mud; be exposed to every insult and every desire. See her beauty the constant object of vile, degrading, biddings. Oh, agony! Be covered with rags, and wear them as proudly as a queen would her imperial robes; have no longer to herself her heart, nor her body, nor her corpse, for presently, perhaps, the hospitals will claim it for dissection; have for horizon in this world nothing but the limits of her prescribed beat, and never go beyond.

Thus to wade through all this misery, without knowing whither she is going, or rather, alas! while whispering to herself — "You are walking to your grave!" And then to be attacked by melancholy even in her debasement, by this same melancholy that follows the rich and powerful; melancholy, and yet so vile! melancholy, and yet be trampled in the dust! melancholy among all those howling passions! What remorse can be more dreadful than this?

It was the unfortunate woman's first evening; she wished to make herself welcome to the honourable firm who turned her beauty into a mercantile speculation. She wished, since she had let herself out on lease, that the proprietors should have no cause of complaint. She said to herself, before going into the street, that she should not have to wait long for her first customer. It was not very long ago that both old and young ran after her as she passed merely to touch her dress, or to obtain a single look. What a sensation she used to create when she appeared in the grand walk at the Tuileries. The air immediately became milder, the old trees amorously shook their branches, and saluted her with their hoary heads; the orange shrubs scattered their flowers beneath her feet, and the eyes of all were directed towards her, while every heart thrilled with love. She heard whispered around her all sorts of praise and admiration, but yet she hardly deigned to give in return a look. "What," said she to herself, "will be my triumphs now that I am here on purpose to obey everyone's desire, receive everyone's embrace, and encircle with my arms the entire public to whom I at present belong? What will they not do, now that I am their slave, and they my masters — now that they have merely to stoop in order to pick me out of the dirt?" It was thus the poor girl reasoned with herself, or rather with her wasted ruined beauty. But she had scarcely entered the domain of degradation, when heaven! what a change appeared. She, formerly so admired, so loved, so venerated, when she still was mistress of herself, was now avoided by all honest people; those whose cloak accidentally touched her dress, shook their cloak with horror; then laughter, nicknames, imprecations, blasphemies were showered on her as she went along. "She is ugly!" was uttered more than once, so horrible does even beauty seem when fallen to that depth of vice. Loaded with all these insults, she hardly believed her eyes and ears; she asked herself whether she was not the play-thing of a dream. How did this happen? She offered herself to everyone, but nobody would notice her. At this very instant, when she was perhaps near going mad, a drunken man ordered her to follow him. She obeyed this man without looking at him, according to her orders. But, O, surprise! O, grief! O, vengeance! this man, who was the first to profit by her prostitution, was the same who had been the first to profit by her innocence. Virgin and courtesan, she had met with this vile libertine at the two extremities of her life. Then, indeed, a light crossed her mind, a passion in her heart, a pang of remorse her soul.

When the primitive cause of all her crimes, the man who had snatched her from her home, he who had sent her tainted to linger in a hospital, came like a vile, thoughtless *roué*, again to seek the ignoble pleasures of an easy love; she had not been able to contain herself — she had killed him — she had killed him, because she recollected all at once the many affronts and unbounded misery she had endured; because, I don't know what horrible light broke in upon her, and made her see at once her destiny laid bare; because with this man were connected the last and bitter remembrances of her innocence. She had killed him in the midst of his sleep, killed him by one single blow, as if by inspiration; after which, she had cleared her bed of his vile corpse, and had gone tranquilly to sleep again; for anger came but at intervals, and her passions were but transient glimmers; everything was dead within her, heart, soul, intelligence, mind, virtue, passion. Consequently, when she owned her crime before her judges, her cause was immediately despaired of. The defence of this unfortunate creature had been entrusted to a young beardless advocate, the nephew of the Attorney-General. The young orator had a head of twenty summers abandoned him to begin his apprenticeship with. What could a child in a gown and wig understand of this poor creature's life? I think that she even frightened him, and that he was not at his ease, when alone with her in her cell. This young advocate, whom, to begin his career his uncle had gratified with a murder, defended his client according to all the rules of rhetoric. He had written his exordium after the *quousque tandem*; he evoked in his peroration all that was lamentable, and was pathetic in the manner of the great orators of former times; his good old uncle rendered justice, in his address, to the *young orator*; but in this tilt of words between the uncle and nephew the life of the young culprit went for nothing; it was, at most, a question of politeness, or, at least, a question of vanity. Moreover the uncle, who was a kind man, would not have been sorry to make his nephew a present of this young girl's head, and to let her live in order to encourage the youthful eloquence of the rising Cicero; but the facts were proved, and the prisoner herself, in the softest voice possible said:—

"It was I who killed this man!"

Oh! woe to me! Now that I recollect all these frightful circumstances, I can rightly say — "It was I who killed this woman!" I alone could defend her; I alone was acquainted with her life; I alone could tell by what fatal and miserable path, the unfortunate creature had arrived at the degrading dock of the Criminal Court; I alone knew what had ruined her; the neighbourhood of Paris, which daily distributes among the surrounding villages its sweepings and its vices; Paris, the corruptor of all virtue, which withers every rose, and tarnishes all that is lovely. Insatiable debauchee! how formidable are you to whatever is pure and spotless! If I then had told the Court, as I could have done, the life of this woman, her cruel vicissitudes of misery and opulence, of flattery and neglect; If I had shown her today covered with flowers, and tomorrow writhing under opprobrium; if I had said to her judges — "This is the work of your young sons and old fathers — this is what Parisian corruption has made of this young girl!" Yes, and if I had added — "Though she is lost and sullied still I love her; in my eyes this blood purifies her; by killing this man, she hardly did justice to herself, for she has only made a corpse of him, while he had made a prostitute of her," she might, perhaps, have been saved. For that is what I could have said; that is what I ought to have said; but I let her die. I was too selfish to let her again escape me. She henceforth belonged to me, until the day when she would become the property of the executioner. I alone felt indignant, and remained faithful to her; not one of those who had pursued her with such admiration and outrage even gave her a thought at present. She, however, was calm, so certain was she now of death. I had never before seen her look so lovely. The pale light of the Court, the bleeding crucifix above the Judges' heads, all those courtesans who came, by their unanimous depositions, to enlighten justice; those speeches both for and against, which never contain a word of the question; nothing, in fact, could trouble her; nothing could disconcert her. The strength of mind which had impelled her to commit this murder never abandoned her for a single instant. She leant her head on her hands as if she already felt it waver on her shoulders. She answered her judges with the most exquisite politeness; her voice was soft, her whole demeanour proper; and yet, close behind her was death, the scaffold, the sound of the falling hatchet — all which things protected her from I don't know what eloquent influence that might have saved her, had it not been for her infamous calling. But how would anyone have dared take an interest in this abandoned creature! save a courtesan from death! What would the wives and daughters of the jurors and judges have said? Public morality and the Attorney-General demanded an example. The most humane thing that it seemed possible to do for the unfortunate Henrietta was, to debate during six hours her condemnation to death.

CHAPTER XXI ◄§ ◄§ ◄§
The Condemned Cell

When the judge pronounced the wretched woman's sentence, I though in myself that I had at last found the solution of the philosophical and literary problem so long sought after; still a little more courage, and my work would be accomplished, — the horrible could go no further. I resolved to bear up till the end of the drama, and not to miss a single scene, but be present at the entire expiation of a life so badly employed. The victim now interested but me in the whole world; I loved her; I wanted to see her again, and never more to quit her. Sylvio, who had taken pity on me for some time past, did not abandon me in this last extremity; thanks to his acquaintance with some high personages, he got me admitted into that vast prison, the happiest inmates of which are those condemned to the galleys, a bastard punishment, as horrible, though less apparent, than the tortures suffered at the *bagues* of Brest and Toulon. In this dreadful place, which might be called Hell, if we were not afraid of passing for calumniators, I only heard moans and cries of joy, blasphemies, and prayers; I saw rage and tears; but these general circumstances interested me very little then. Among all those lost females the place contained, I only had to do with one, — with her who was about to die. The head that was soon to fall had been thrown alive into that common grave of the guillotine, or *bague*, called the Salpêtrière. In what cell had the condemned woman been placed? It required all my perseverance and love to discover it. The cell she occupied was secured by a triple lock, and situated low under ground, at the angle of a deserted yard; by the side of the vent-hole communicating with this cell was a rotten bench, covered with a thick layer of moss, having the appearance of a fine green carpet; I sat down here and surveyed, with greedy eyes, the darkness that dwelt within. I am as well acquainted with this bench as I am with the hospitable seat of the paternal roof; were I to live a thousand years I could still describe it hidden under that peculiar kind of slimy moss that grows on prison walls. Time and the weather had hallowed out this bench; it might have been taken for a trough or coffin; between one end of it and the wall there was sufficient space for me to sit by the side of the vent-hole, without casting my shadow in the cell, and, consequently, without fear of being seen. From this place I could constantly watch the palpitating corpse within, which still enjoyed the power of thought in its dismal tomb. I remained there whole days together; that yard surrounded by thick walls, was become my domain; through the interest I commanded I was almost looked upon as a supernumerary turnkey. In this manner, I was enabled daily to study the least movements of the captive.

This study was painful. How was it possible for me to restrain my anger, while viewing the mournful picture presented by those damp walls, that pale light, that ragged straw, and, on that straw, a woman whom the scaffold was already waiting, without any other chance of escape (faint hope!) but that afforded by the Court of Appeal? This woman was my daily study, thought, and sorrow in her prison, as she had been already in the world. In the morning I was at my post as soon as it was light; the first sunbeam that fell upon her bed of straw made her start out of her sleep; affrighted she hastily opened her eyes, and sitting up, remained melancholy and pensive. By and by she arose altogether, and, faithful to certain habits of elegance and refinement, arranged her dress, and put her prison in order. First of all she made her bed, that is, she picked up every bit of straw that lay scattered about the cell; she raised her earthen pitcher to her head; the cold water fell down her pale face, and animated it for an instant; she washed her hands, already so white, arranged the long black hair of her pretty head, examining in turn her foot, hand, and elegant figure; she gently stroked her lovely slender neck, and, while doing so, shuddered from time to time, as if her hands were made of polished steel: she prolonged this important occupation as much as possible, for her whole soul was in it, and when everything was finished, when she had no more pins to use, no more ribbons to tie, she sat with her legs bent under her, and let her arms slowly fall at her side; you would, alas! have said that she thought of nothing.

About twelve the jailor brought her the ordinary prison allowance; black bread and some warm soup in a thick wooden bowl, with a pewter spoon in it. The jailor put the bowl on the ground and retired. Then the convict taking it in her lap, and bending her head over the smoking liquid, inhaled its genial vapour; her two hands held the bowl, and became slightly coloured by its penetrating heat; when she had thus seized her soup by all her senses, she devoured it in an instant to indemnify herself for having wanted so long. As evening came, at the hour when she used formerly to receive at table all her lovers eager to obtain a look, the jailor silently threw her in a piece of bread at the grating of her prison door; she slowly ate her black bread, raising her eyes toward the vent-hole through which darkness gradually began to penetrate, and thinking of the length of the night that was about to follow, she remained in an attitude of painful meditation, with her eyes filled with tears, her mouth half full, and letting the rest of her hard bread fall on the damp ground. What slow agony was hers! what profound solitude! what chaos! and what mournful episodes might I not add to this melancholy story!

One hot day, when the large cobweb hanging from the sinister roof shone with violet-coloured streaks of light, and while the joyous insect was visiting its work in every direction, and multiplying without end its fine-spun threads, the young captive began to sing. At first she hummed an air in a low voice; then she sang louder, and finally exerted all her strength; her voice was fine and sonorous. The air she sang was insignificant, one in the bravura style a happy hit for a street ballad-singer, accompanied by the ambiguous sounds of a guitar; yet she imparted to it an undefinable expression, while I, motionless on my seat, listened to its funereal accents with trembling emotion. It was like the last sigh of a young man, who falls as if he would rise in an instant, and be revenged. Another time she was gay, and laughed immoderately; then she rubbed I know not what on a piece of cloth, or her ragged blanket; but she rubbed with great activity and perseverance. Sometimes she remained a whole quarter of an hour without examining her work; at others she looked at her piece of metal every instant. Was she trying to render it bright and shining, and to clean it of the rust that covered it? The task was difficult. The captive grew impatient, became tired, seemed discouraged, and then again resumed her labour; suddenly she uttered a cry of joy; her work was accomplished; she had stolen from her jailor a brass button, and had polished it enough to use it as a mirror.

At first she appeared happy. A mirror! it was so long since she had seen herself. But when she looked on this perfidious metal, she sought in vain for all that beauty, the object of her worship, passion, religion, relief and love. She became sad; the face she saw was no longer her face; she discovered neither her brilliant eyes, nor her skin so soft and white, nor the carnation of her lips, nor the pearly teeth that her smile unveiled, nor the grace of her whole person. She saw nothing but a phantom, the pale

and melancholy reflection of a shadow. Indignant, she dashed to the ground the lying mirror. A moment afterwards she picked it up and looked at herself again; she began to think that this mirror was deceitful; that it was its form that made her face appear so long; that it was the reflection of its yellow colour that cast its shade across her, and that it was her dungeon's dismal light which lessened the whiteness of her skin; and then, thanks to her recollections, she fancied herself such as she once had been; she discovered one by one her roses and her lilies; she returned slowly by the most flowery paths, to the finest days of her limpid beauty; her recollections still embellish them, and a smile achieved the rest. At the moment when, happy and proud, and forgetful of everything, she was thus smiling on herself, the jailor entered her cell.

CHAPTER XXII ◆§ ◆§ ◆§
The Jailor

This man — but can he be called a man? — had, like myself, been subjugated by such unrivalled beauty. A harsh outside enveloped the heart of this strange lover. He had not been much more happy in life than the unfortunate of whom he was the keeper. He was born in the prison, and his father had been jailor there before him. A woman of the galleys had engendered him under dread of the lash, and yet this abortion was born soon enough, and with sufficient intelligence to become jailor in his turn. He was hideous, above all, when he laughed; I saw him make his declaration of love. He first prudently placed himself against the half open door, and, thus supported while fixing his two uneven eyes on his unfortunate prisoner, and opening his immense mouth, the thick lips of which hardly allowed his sharp fox-like teeth to be seen, he began to speak to her in an unintelligible language; he signed to her that her head was to fall within a fortnight; his signs were horrible expressive; he raised himself on his two feet, carried his heavy hand to the back of his head, bent his enormous neck, and pretended to strike himself; from his breast issued a dull sound, similar enough to that of the guillotine's falling knife; then he raised his head, showing together his long beard, thick lips, pointed teeth, and hideous grin, which he carefully preserved, in order, no doubt, to avoid the trouble of beginning this pantomime.

The prisoner viewed this man with a wild look. He, notwithstanding, approached her; he took her hand less brutally than could have been believed: and explained to her, with that eloquence which belongs but to passion, that she might be saved. I know not what were his words, they did not reach me, but she appeared to consent to everything; she did not withdraw her hand from his. They appointed, in a low voice, a more comfortable time; then he wished to embrace her, but she drew back with horror; at length he left, still grinning with that horrible grin which he had stereotyped on his horrible face.

At this sight I was forced to call my courage to my aid. Heavens! in her cell! on her death bed! her jailor! — and then what jailor! I was mad; mad with misfortune, despair, astonishment, rage. I thought I had exhausted every view of grief, and a new mind of corruption opened to my view. I thought her long debaucheries at an end, and they were about to begin more recklessly than ever. I was satisfied with moral deformity — which more than sufficed me — and I had it now in my power to be, if I liked, a witness of the coupling of physical with moral deformity, of an executioner with a murderess, of a heartless woman with an abortive man. But when? on what day? at what hour? This very evening, in a few minutes, immediately, perhaps! And I remained nailed to my seat, trembling with emotion, with my pulse stopped, breathless, bewildered, lost. I would have given my soul, — yes, Satan, my soul to enable my troubled eyes to penetrate the dark shades of that dreadful dungeon. What, then, is about to take place in that abode of gloom, Oh! malediction on me for having allowed this woman thus to perish. Malediction on me for not having snatched this pea from the bed of filth on which her life was passed. But, Heaven be thanked, day breaks. Silence! some one comes. The door opens, not violently, but so gently that it announced the lover's approach. Yet this was the same man who was there the evening before. Henrietta, on seeing him, crouched to the end of her cell; besides her customary food, the man carried under his arm a truss of clean straw, which he strewed gravely over the old; then he left, impassive, and without even casting a glance at his prisoner. I heard a distant sound of bolts pushed into their fastenings; I breathed more at my ease; Heavens be thanked, it was not for that day.

But, after this instant of calm, uneasiness soon returned. Suppose the jailor had seen me! suppose it was put off but till the next day or that evening! It was night — one of those nights which are too dark for lovers, too dark even for murder. I could not sleep, an insurmountable presentiment haunted me; I groped my way into the yard; the air was bitter cold;

the fog, imprisoned between those long high walls, fell to the ground in a heavy glacial rain; the cell was dark, similar to some deep and sombre tomb, with no sign of life, and where you cannot even perceive the white skeleton lying at its damp, unwholesome bottom. All was silence; the only things that clasped each other then throughout the prison, and that were locked in close embrace, were the night and silence, remorse and crime. Had Henrietta been laid, all bleeding, on her last bed of straw, she would, perhaps, have made more noise. I felt tranquilized; the man was, no doubt, afraid of such a noise; perhaps, the woman also. I was about to return to my room, and had already left the vent-hole, when I fancied I perceived, through the large key-hole, at the bottom of the cell, a faint ray of light, a small glimmer, a sort of will-o- the-wisp, like that which misleads the traveller at night, the small lamp of a glow-worm, hidden under a rose leaf. It was he — the other monster — the male — the jailor! The door opened slowly; slowly, too, did the ray of light penetrate the dungeon, and slowly did the jailor enter, holding in one hand a fetid lamp, and with the other clasping his keys to keep them noiseless; presently I perceived, by the lamp's flickering light, the bed, the fresh straw, and Henrietta stretched on it, but not asleep. She was waiting — she was waiting for him! After all, this man was her last slave, her last love, her supreme triumph, the triumph of a woman nearly dead! The lamp, a torch worthy of such a hymen, was placed on the ground, the jailor advanced with an air of assurance, his hand already passed her elegant figure, his horrible visage already touched her lovely face; I wished to speak, but could not, I wished to flee, but my limbs were numbed; I wished to turn away my head, but my head was fastened, chained, riveted to the spot, and I unavoidably forced to witness everything! My brain was turning, when, luckily, the lamp went out: everything disappeared; I saw nothing more, heard nothing more, imagined nothing more. Oh, Heaven! the greatest of all thy boons to man is madness or phrenzy; the knowledge of such great misfortunes as he sometimes meets with would often kill him!

I was delirious for a fortnight. It was not till a fortnight afterwards that I was able to account for this mystery. Sylvio, in order to bring me to my senses, was forced to talk to me of her and to affirm that she was the handsomest and most charming of women.

"Tell me again, good Sylvio," I used to say, "that you have never seen a more enchanting being." "I really have not," replied Sylvio, "she is the most lovely creature in the world, and I think that she has excited pity, and will not have to die." On hearing this my fever returned. "Not die!" exclaimed I; "Oh! if I thought so, Sylvio, I would go and kill her with my own hands! Oh, let her die! let her ascend the scaffold! let her guilty hand fall! let her tender look close in death beneath the hatchet! Go, go, and bespeak me a good place at a window at the Grève. Oh, if you but knew her crimes! 'tis dreadful!" Thus whether she was accused or pitied, I relapsed into the same state of mental agitation. Meanwhile, there was talk of a long delay in favour of the condemned woman. I had perceived her when, tranquil and pensive, she had abandoned herself to the jailor, pressing every instant her body with her hand, and examining it with the most mournful curiosity. When the principal turnkey came to tell her it was time to die, adding that someone wished to speak to her, she listened to him calmly, for she had a reply even for death. An instant afterwards I saw two men dressed in black enter; two physicians; one was severe looking, already old, with an anxious, thoughtful air; the other one was young, smiling, heedless, who took the prisoner's hand with grace and politeness, while his colleague appeared scarcely to touch it, and envinced much more horror than he really felt. The old doctor immediately said to the officer of the prison,— "This woman is not enceinte; let justice be done;" and he went out. The soldiers were already dragging Henrietta away, when the young doctor, calling back the other, exclaimed;— "This woman is enceinte; she is a mother; the law, humanity, everything forbids her being put to death;" and he spoke with such conviction, and gave such decisive proofs, that a respite was granted to the prisoner; she had given an hour of her love for nine months more of her melancholy life; of all the bargains she had ever concluded this was perhaps the most horrible.

CHAPTER XXIII ✒ ✒ ✒
The Salpêtrière

I let alone for a while the mother, father, and child, and went and took a walk on the newly-formed boulevard. "Young doctor," said I to myself, "you have certainly done a fine thing; you have rendered a great service to the embryo of this woman and of crime; but you have not snatched this child from the executioner for any length of time; let him only grow up, and reach the age when he will have the right to inherit! His head, too, will fall. He has but little chance with respect to future inheritances, but then, to make up for this, he already possesses every chance that has attended both his father and mother. In truth, young doctor, you have rendered a great service to all; and why? Besides, what right had this woman, already cut off from the world to become a mother? And by what right does this child come into the world, or what does he come to do in it? His birth will be a second death-warrant for his mother; but this time the Court of Appeal will be deaf to all entreaties. At all events, the mother might be allowed time to suckle her infant, but she had hardly nine months granted her to give him birth. The milk which ought to nourish this child will flow, in the place of blood, under the scalp of the operator, and will become an object for mirth in our anatomical schools. Young doctor, what a skilful man you are!" Thus reflecting, and going from prison to prison, I arrived at the place of the Salpêtrière, the asylum of all those old female outcasts whom society has rejected, and refused even for fish-fags or bone-gatherers. The Salpêtrière forms an entire village, as populous as a town; but, good heavens! what are its inhabitants? Women without husbands, mothers without children, grandmothers without grand-children, and all sorts of abandoned decrepitude are heaped together between its walls. This hospitable house only opens its doors to those women who are neither old or mad. It is, in fact, a perfect catacomb of living bones, where the women with one foot in the grave are separated from man with more care than the most chaste and youthful daughters of Flora are protected. The building rises grandly, like all such receptacles for the poor, beggarly and lying palaces. They are dignified with a gilt dome and marble facade, but beneath this dome the poor are isolated, and behind these splendid blocks of stone daily practise the art of dying at the smallest possible expense. The old people huddled together in this frightful loneliness are horrid to look at. In spite of yourself, you think of all the blighted hopes that such an hospital represents. It is here, then, that vice and virtue, idleness and labour, mercenary and legitimate love, meet and live together. I was trying to find out by what fatality so many old people of such different character arrived at the same point, when at a turn of the path, opposite a pretty house, I perceived a poor woman and her two children. This woman was twisting hemp to make ropes; a child of six or seven years old, with a curly head and bare-footed, was turning the wheel; his poor mother was walking backwards and pulling out, from time to time, with an avaricious hand, the hemp contained in her apron. She had been at work ever since the morning, yet, she had not done much, for she was obliged to consider the weakness of her young workman still more than her own. By the side of the wheel, and on the dried-up grass, a little female child was sleeping; her infantine head rested on her right arm, her long silky hair, which had been blown up by the wind, fell over her cheeks, which were then coloured with a slight rose tint; her little brother looked at her now and then, and perhaps envied her repose and sleep; the poor mother looked at them both in turn, but she suddenly broke off her maternal contemplation, reproaching herself for having devoted an instant to repose and hope.

"Poor little child!" said I to myself, on seeing the little girl asleep, while her brother and young mother were earning her a drop of milk; "misery watches over your cradle, your support will be misery — your counsellor misery! There is not the slightest chance of your escaping from a life of poverty, neglect, and vice — no hope! no happiness! Your mother, too, who loves you now so dearly, while she has still a drop of milk to give you, will hate you as soon as she has no more bread for both herself and you. She will not even have the time to talk to you of God and another world, so entirely will she, yourself, and brother, be soon wrapped up in all the necessities of this life. Poor, pretty, delicate child! how quietly you now sleep in the midst of the noise made by this wheel, which turns like the wheel of fortune, but yet you will never to able to hope for ought else but a hempen rope. Poor little being, who after twenty-four years' hunger, neglect, and work, will be too happy to have a bed at the Salpêtrière, and a tattered sack for a winding sheet!"

CHAPTER XXIV ◄§ ◄§ ◄§
The Kiss

My victim had escaped me. They took her out of her dungeon, and shut her up in a chamber suited to the living. When I could no longer see her I left my voluntary prison, and returned to my former adventurous mode of life. I was well aware that the last day of her miserable existence would soon arrive; but, in order to keep from me, as much as possible, the dreadful thought, I plunged more than ever into my favourite study of everyday life, noticing the smallest incidents, examining the most vulgar natures, and learning daily a thousand innocent secrets too simple to be called study, and yet so fertile in emotions. It was thus I diverted my thought, and forgot for a while all I knew. I fancied it was a dream; I surrounded myself with smiling faces. Spring was returned, and with it those lovely walks in which one's admiration every instant excited, wanders, without ever being fatigued, from one discovery to another. In the midst of these raptures, always new, an invisible companion is constantly speaking to your heart, a mysterious voice softly warbling in your ear; you are not alone, or rather you are more than alone. I was one day passing through a pretty little village in the neighbourhood of Paris; I here observed a small house with a large yard full of timber-work; numberless planks were placed in order against the wall. At the bottom of the yard a skilful tasty hand had laid out a little garden, whose fine, half-blown lilies filled the air with odoriferous perfume; above the house was seen a pretty dove-cot, roofed over with red tiles, and constantly sending forth repeated sounds of love; on the edge of the projecting board a handsome pigeon, with a gold plumage that took a different hue every time it turned its neck was walking proudly in the sun, and coquettishly flapping its white amorous wings. This pretty house had such a pleasant look of comfort, cleanliness, and elegance, that I could not resist the desire of taking a closer survey of it. I entered the yard, and after having more copiously inhaled the fragrance of its perfumed lilies, I was about to continue my walk, when I perceived, on the ground floor in the middle of a roomy work-shop, a large, half-finished machine. This strange machine consisted of a long oak platform; a slight railing ran round each side; at the back was a staircase; in the front rose two large threatening posts; each of these posts was grooved out down the middle; on the platform at the bottom of the machine, between the posts, was a plank with a round hole cut out in the middle near the top, where it was divided, there was also another plank that was movable behind the other, the work appeared nearly finished. A young man, cheerful, strong, and well-made, was gaily hammering away with all his might at the half-joined boards, and giving the finishing stroke to his work, on the lowest step of the staircase was seen a bottle, nearly empty, with a glass half full; from time to time the young man took a sip, after which he resumed his work, singing.

The aspect of this strange machine troubled me, in spite of myself. What was the meaning of this platform, and what was its use? I might have remained fixed a whole day to the spot, without finding any satisfactory explanation. I was thus standing silent, motionless, and anxious,

listening with an involuntary shudder to each blow of the hammer, when
the young workman was interrupted by a pretty little boy, who came to
offer him some cord for sale; this child was the same I had seen at the
Salpêtrière; he brought with him the labour of a fortnight, and it was easy
to see by his timidity that he was afraid of being refused. The carpenter
spoke kindly to him, and took his cord, without examining it very closely,
paid the child handsomely, and sent him away with a kiss and a glass of
the good wine that was at the bottom of the staircase. When left alone
again the young carpenter did not resume his work; he walked about, with
an anxious air, and his eye fixed on the door; he was evidently waiting for
someone — that one who always comes too late, and goes away too soon;
for whom you are thankful to lose your time, and with whom the hours
pass quicker than thought. At length a young, handsome girl, both *naive*
and inquisitive, arrived; after having wished her lover good day, she
turned her attention, like me, to the machine. I did not hear a word of
their conversation, but it must have been lively and interesting. After
some time the young man, unable, no doubt, to give any further explana-

tions, made a sign to the young girl, as if to induce her to take a personal part on the platform; at first she refused; then she seemed to hesitate, and at last entirely consented; here her lover, assuming a grave and serious air, tied her hands behind her back with the cord brought by the child; he assisted her to ascend the platform; when there he tied her to the movable upright plank, in such a manner that one end of the fatal wood touched her breast, while her feet were fastened to the other; I began to unfathom this horrid piece of mechanism. I was fearing I understood it, when suddenly the plank fell slowly between the two posts, the upper part of the hollowed boards descended, and when her head was thus lodged in the circular hole, the carpenter suddenly jumped to the ground and clasped in his hands the neck of his imprisoned mistress, and, a jovial executioner of the sentence he had himself pronounced, applied his burning lips to those of the lovely head thus placed at his mercy. The fair and laughing victim tried in vain to defend herself; not a single movement was permitted her. It was only at the second kiss the young man gave his sweetheart, that I thoroughly understood for what this machine might serve.

CHAPTER XXV ☙ ☙ ☙
The Last Day of the Condemned Prisoner

A slight tap on the shoulder drew me from my horrible contemplation; I turned round affrighted, expecting to find behind me the man for whom the carpenter was working, but all I saw was the mild, melancholy, compassionate face of Sylvio. "Come, my friend," said I to Sylvio, with the smile of a madman, "come, and see this machine on which these two lovers are as amorously sporting as those pigeons on yonder branch. Would you think that on this even platform, between these two posts of such white and sweet-smelling fir, on this innocent theatre of such pure love, a horrible scene of murder could ever take place? — nay, the most horrible of crimes, a cold-blooded murder, committed in the face of God and men? Would you believe that through this hollow circle, where now the lovely, smiling head of that beautiful girl so amorously hangs, a head, newly severed from its body, could fall for ever? Yet it is too certain that such a thing will happen. Tomorrow, perhaps, the executioner will come to see if the machine is ready. He will climb the ladder to see if it is solid; he will examine all these well-joined boards, to assure himself that they will be able to bear the dying struggles of the culprit; he will try the spring, for the spring must act well and quickly, and act as promptly as the knife descends. When he is certain of the goodness of this work, on which depends the peace, honour, fortune, and tranquillity of our fellow citizens — a terrible pile-work on which the whole of society is built — he will smile with an air of satisfaction on the master-carpenter, and will tell him to send the machine early the next morning, or perhaps that very night; then this theatre of smiling love will become a scene of murder, and this boudoir be turned into a blood-stained scaffold; never again will be heard there the sound of kisses, unless you so designate that last act of charity which the priest throws from the end of his trembling lips on to the pale and livid cheeks of him who is about to die. And yet, Sylvio, now that I think of it, I recollect that once, in times comparatively happy, when I entirely belonged to paradoxy, I have heard persons ridicule capital punishment. But what is more, these same persons boasted, the one of having been hanged, and having swung for a long time at the end of a cord over one of the finest landscapes in Italy; the other, of having been impaled at the top of one of the towers of Constantinople, whence he could admire at his ease the Thracian Bosphorus; and a third, of having amorously drowned in the transparent waters of the Saône, while pursuing some young and lovely naiad with a neck of alabaster. I own that on hearing them thus embellish death I had become accustomed to trifle with it; I looked upon the executioner as a complaisant minister, as a person more skilled than others in closing the eyes of men; but at present the sight of this machine, still so innocent, the aspect alone of this wood which has till now been stained but with virgin wax, shakes all my sanguinary convictions. I have, you recollect, told you the story of the man who was impaled, and the story of the man who was drowned; what do you think of them all, Sylvio?"

"I think," replied Sylvio, "that you were running after paradoxy, while paradoxy met you itself halfway. Truth is less apparent, or less acceptable, and hardly admits of approach even when we advance towards it with a resolute step. Unfortunate man! now that you have accustomed yourself to the dazzling light of paradoxy, I am afraid that you will not rest satisfied with the more calm and steady one of truth. I have been following you all the morning, to relate to you the story of a dying man, written by himself. You will hear the words of a man who did not certainly trifle with death. You can put implicit faith in what he says, for he has really had his head in the hands of the executioner, felt the fatal cord round his neck, and

died upon the scaffold." Here Sylvio hurried me from the carpenter's
house. We passed through several green hedges, whose tops were white
with blossom, and sat down in the shade — or rather in the sun —
beneath an old elm, whose leaves were still wrapped up within its bright
red hands; my friend slowly unfolded one of those immense American
newspapers, whose number and size are still an object of surprise in
France, and when he saw me somewhat calm, and ready to listen to him,
he read the following melancholy and true account of the last sensations
of a man condemned to death. I have since learned that, in order not to
afflict me too much, Sylvio suppressed that last interview of the prisoner
with Elizabeth Clare, a young girl whom the latter passionately loved:—

"It was four o'clock in the afternoon when Elizabeth Clare left me; as
soon as she had left everything appeared finished between this world and
myself. I should have wished to die then on that very spot, and at that
very hour, as the last action of my life — the bitterest of all — was done.
As evening descended, my prison became more cold and damp; the
evening was dark and foggy; I had neither fire or candle, although it was
in the middle of January, nor sufficient clothes on my bed to warm me. My
mind, too, was becoming weaker by degrees, and my heart contracted
beneath the misery and desolation that surrounded me, and little by little
(for what I write now must be the entire truth) the thought of what would
become of Elizabeth banished the feelings attendant on my own unhappy
situation. This was the first time, though I cannot tell why, that I fully
understood the sentence under which I was soon about to suffer; and
while reflecting on it, a horrible terror seized me, as if I had but just heard
my sentence pronounced, and as if I had really not understood before that
I ought to die.

I had eaten nothing for four and twenty hours. Near me, however, was
plenty of food that a good man, who had visited me, had sent me from his
own table; but I could not touch it, and, while I viewed it, the strangest
ideas entered my head. It consisted of the choicest viands, and not such as
is given to prisoners; it had been sent me because I was to die next day. I
then thought of the beasts in the field and the birds in the air, that are
fatted in order to be killed. I felt that my ideas were not such as they ought
to have been in such a moment; I believe that my thoughts were wandering. A sort of low buzzing, similar to the hum of bees, incessantly filled my
ears; though it was night, bright, luminous flashes passed to and fro before
my eyes, and my mind became waste; I recollected nothing. I tried to pray,
but I could remember but a single prayer, which was entirely unconnected

with any others; it seemed to me that the words I thus confusedly addressed to Heaven were nothing else but so many blasphemies, and cannot now remember what this prayer was, nor even in what form its words were couched. Suddenly, I thought that all my terror was vain and useless, and that it was madness thus calmly to await death. Hope — but was it really hope? — arose in my breast! I sprang with one bound to the bars of my window, and seized them with such force, that they bent beneath my grasp, for my strength was like the lion's. Then I carefully examined every part of the lock on the door; tried to raise the door itself with my shoulder, though it was heavier than the massive gates of a fortified town; felt along the walls, and in every corner of my prison, although I might have known, had I been in my right senses, that its walls were formed of massive stone, three feet thick, and that even could I have passed through a crack not bigger than the eye of a needle, I should not have had the slightest chance of escape. In the midst of my endeavours I was suddenly taken with a fit of fainting, as if I had swallowed poison; I had scarcely strength enough to reach my bed-side. I fell on the bed; and I think I fainted. But this did not last long, for my head swam, and the room appeared to turn; and, half-awake and half-asleep, I dreamed that it was midnight, — that Elizabeth had returned as she had promised, but that they would not let her enter. It seemed to me that a heavy snow was falling, that the streets were covered as with a white sheet, and that I saw Elizabeth lying dead on the snow, in the middle of the night, before the prison-door. When I came to my senses I was struggling for breath. In a minute or two I heard the clock of Saint Sepulchre strike ten, and then I knew that I had been dreaming.

"The chaplain of the prison came to me without being sent for. He solemnly exhorted me to think no more of the troubles of this world, but to turn my attention towards a future existence, and to try to reconcile my soul with Heaven, in the hope that my sins, though great, would be forgiven if I repented. When he was gone I felt for a moment a little more collected. I sat down on my bed and seriously began to examine myself and prepare to meet my fate. I reflected that, under all circumstances, I had now but a few hours to live, that there was no further hope for me, and that I ought, at least, to meet death bravely and like a man. I then tried to recollect everything I had heard said about death by hanging: 'It was but the struggle of a moment; it caused little or no pain at all, and produced instantaneous death.' Then I passed on to twenty other strange reflections. Little by little, my mind again began to wander. I carried my hands to my neck, which I clasped tightly, as if to see what strangulation was. Then I stroked my arms at the places where the cord would bind them; I felt it pass round and round until it was strongly fastened; I felt my hands tied behind me one after the other; but what horrified me more than anything else was the idea of feeling the white cap slowly drawn over my eyes and face. If I could have been spared this white cap — this wretched anticipation of eternal night — the rest would not have appeared so horrible to me. In the midst of these mournful ideas the whole of my limbs were slowly seized with a general numbness.

"The giddiness I had felt was followed by a state of heavy stupor, which diminished the suffering attendant on my thoughts, and yet, even while I lay nearly unconscious, I still continued to think. The church clock then struck twelve. I heard the sound, but it fell on my ears indistinctly, as if it had first penetrated through several walls, or come from a great distance. Then I gradually saw each object that filled my memory turn round and round, become less distinct, wander here and there, and, at length, entirely disappear one after another. And then I fell asleep.

"I slept till within an hour of my execution. At seven o'clock in the morning I was awoken by a knock on the door of my cell. I heard the sound, as in a dream, before I was thoroughly awake, and the feeling I at first experienced was that of a man put out of humour by being suddenly aroused, when tired, out of a pleasant sleep. I was fatigued, and wished again to close my eyes. A minute afterwards, the bolts outside my prison door were drawn back; a turnkey entered carrying a lamp; he was followed by the governor of the prison and a chaplain. I looked up; a chilling shudder ran, like an electric shock, through my whole body; I felt as if I had just been dipped in a bath of ice. One glance had sufficed. Sleep soon fled as if I had never known, nor ever would again know, what sleep was. I cruelly felt my situation. 'Roger,' said the turnkey in a low but firm voice, 'it is time to get up!' The chaplain asked me how I had passed the night, and asked me to join in prayer with him. I huddled myself together on the side of the bed. My teeth chattered, and my knees shook, in spite of myself. It was not yet very light, but I could see into the little paved court through the half-open door of my cell; the air was thick and dark, and it rained slowly but without ceasing. 'It is more than half-past seven, Roger!' again said the turnkey. I gathered all my strength to beg them to leave me alone till my last moment. I had thirty minutes to live!

"I tried to make a second observation when the turnkey was about to leave the cell, but this time I could not articulate a single sound. My breath failed me, my tongue stuck to the roof of my mouth; I had lost, not my speech, but the power of speaking; I made two violent attempts to open my mouth, but it was all in vain, I could not pronounce a syllable. When they were gone I remained in the same place on my bed. I was drowsy and numbed with cold, probably on account of the sharp air that had penetrated through the open door, and to which I was unaccustomed. In order to keep myself warm I remained huddled together, with my arms crossed on my breast, my head hanging down, and trembling in every limb. My body appeared to me an insupportable weight, which it was in my power neither to raise nor move in any way. The day became lighter and lighter, though dull and dingy, and gradually entered my cell, exposing to my view its damp walls and black flag-stones. Strange as it may seem, I could not help remarking all these puerile things, though death was awaiting me an instant afterwards. I observed that the lamp which the turnkey had placed on the ground burnt dimly, with a long wick that seemed oppressed and suffocated by the cold and foul air; and I then thought that this lamp had not been trimmed since the evening previous. I looked at the cold, naked bars of the bed on which I was seated, and at the enormous nails in the door of my cell, and at the words traced on the walls by former prisoners. I felt my pulse; it was so weak that I could hardly count it. In spite of all my efforts, I was unable to bring myself to think, understand, say, or own to myself that I was really about to die. In the midst of my anxiety I heard the chapel clock begin to strike, and I inwardly said — 'Oh Lord, have mercy on me a miserable sinner!' But no, no, it could not yet be three-quarters past seven; or, at most, it could not be more! The clock continued to strike; I heard the third quarter, and then the fourth, and then the clock strike eight — the fatal hour!

"They were again in my prison before I was aware of their presence. They found me in the same place, in the same posture in which they had left me.

"What I have now to say will not take up much more time. My recollections are very precise till that time, but they are far from being distinct on what followed. I remember very well, however, in what manner I left my cell to go into the large outer room. Two little wrinkled men, dressed in black, supported me. I know that I tried to rise when I saw the turnkey and his two men enter; but it was impossible for me to do so."

"In the large room I found two other wretched men who were about to undergo the same sentence as myself. Their arms and hands were pinioned behind their backs, and they were lying on a form waiting till I was ready.

"Another thin, old man, with scanty white hair, was reading something to them in a loud voice. He came to me and said — but I cannot exactly remember what he said — I think, though, that I recollect the words — 'We ought to embrace one another' — but I did not hear him distinctly.

"The most difficult thing for me was, to keep myself from falling. I had thought that my last moments would be full of rage and horror, and yet I felt neither one nor the other; but in their place I experienced a nauseating faintness, as if my heart was failing me, and as if the floor on which I stood was giving way beneath my feet. I nearly fell. All I could do was to sign to the old man to leave me: someone interfered, and sent him away. They finished pinioning my arms and hands. I heard an officer of the prison say in a low voice to the chaplain — 'Everything is ready.' As we were leaving, one of the men in black put a glass of water to my lips, but I could not drink.

"We began to travel the long, vaulted passages that led from the large chamber to the scaffold. I saw the lamps still burning, for the light of day never penetrates those gloomy passages; I heard the measured tolling of the bell, and the deep voice of the chaplain, saying, as he walked before us. 'I am the resurrection and the life, saith the Lord; he that believeth in me, though he were dead, yet shall he live; and though after my skin, worms destroy this body, yet in my flesh shall I see God.'

"It was the funeral service; prayers composed for those who are stretched lifeless in their coffins, that they were reading over us who were still alive! Till this moment I could still feel and see, but soon all power of perception left me. Yet I felt the sudden transition from these subterraneous, warm, silent passages, with their lighted lamps, to the cold, open platform with its creaking steps leading to the scaffold. Then I discovered an immense dark, silent crowd, that filled the whole street beneath me; the windows of the shops and houses were occupied by spectators as high up as the fourth story. I saw the church of Saint Sepulchre through the yellow fog in the distance, and heard the tolling of its bell. I recollect the cloudy sky, the murky morning, the humidity that covered the scaffold, the enormous mass of all those black edifices, and the prison which rose at our side and seemed still to cast on us its withering shadow; I still feel the cold, fresh breeze that blew against my face. I still see the whole sight which pierces my heart like an arrow; the horrid perspective is stretched out before my eyes; the scaffold, the rain, the multitude, the roofs of the houses covered with people, the smoke which beat down heavily among the chimney-pots, and the carts filled with woman come to take their part of the general emotion from the yard of the inn in front; I hear the low, hoarse murmur which ran through the crowd when we appeared. I never saw so many objects at the same time so clearly and distinctly as in that one look; but it was soon over.

"From this moment I became unconscious of all that followed. I recollect neither the prayers of the chaplain, nor the adjusting of the fatal noose, nor the cap which inspired me with so much horror, nor my execution, nor my death; were I not quite certain that all these things really took place I should not have the slightest knowledge of them. I have since read in the papers the details of my behaviour on the scaffold. It was there said that I had conducted myself properly and courageously; that I had died without any great suffering, and that I had not struggled much. In spite of all my endeavours I have not been able to call to mind even one of these circumstances. All my recollections cease at the sight of the scaffold and street. What seemed to me immediately to follow this moment of agony was a feeling of being awoke out of a deep sleep. I found myself in a room, lying on a bed, near which was seated a man who was watching me attentively. I had recovered all my senses, although I could not speak for any length of time consecutively. I thought that a pardon had been brought me; that I had been carried from the scaffold, and that I had fainted. When I knew the truth, I had a slight recollection, like a dream, of having been stretched naked in a strange place, with a number of faces turning round me; but this idea only rose in my mind after I had been told what had taken place."

Such was this dismal story. It was full of sadness, gravity, and resignation, and was well suited to the melancholy that enveloped me. I listened to it with a sort of terror; and even this terror itself reconciled me to death. The least that can be done is to leave the wretch about to die the dignity of his punishment. I felt all the agony of this man, but felt it to congratulate him in the bottom of my heart. Let us not trifle with this immortal soul that is violently driven from the body it inhabits.

Good Sylvio! he had just given me the only consolation that was suited to my grief. He had just proved that I could respect Henrietta, who was about to die.

The history of this man was so great a source of relief to me, that I returned for a while to literary pursuits, which I had neglected for so long a time.

"But do you know," said I to Sylvio, "that with such a hero, a condemned criminal relating, himself, the details of his own execution, a fine book might be written?"

"My dear friend," answered Sylvio, "let us not meddle with this story, and do not let us make a book of it, for it is already one."

A little later I saw that Sylvio was right.

CHAPTER XXVI ◄§ ◄§ ◄§
The Bourbe

Time flies quickly both for the fortunate and unfortunate of this world. Death hastens towards all with an equal step, and when near at hand, we ask with affright, "What hour is it?" The wise man alone knows how to count the hours, nor thinks them too long nor too short. The wise man listens, the clock strikes, and he blesses Heaven for having granted him another hour.

Thus, hours, days, months had passed by without my recollecting, unless confusedly, the fate of Henrietta. Henrietta! Was she not that woman who ought to have died long since? At length, one evening, by I know not what fatal foresight, and as if awoke from a long sleep, I suddenly counted the months, the days — I counted them twice over — and then I hastily rushed towards the Bourbe. No one was admitted in the evening. I returned very early the following morning, and waited at the door. If I had calculated right, Henrietta's child must have already come into the world! The fatal sentence was pronounced without appeal; the melancholy respite was expired; the prisoner had become a mother, and now it only remained for her to die. By what an appropriate name is that impotent and cheerless house designated, which cannot save from the executioner the nurse whom the scaffold claims — "La Bourbe."

The Bourbe is the last refuge of those poor girls who have become mothers, of those young wives whose husbands are gamblers, and of these woman who are condemned to death, and whom the executioners wait for at the door. At the Bourbe misery engenders misery, prostitution engenders prostitution, crime engenders crime. The children brought into the world on its wretched beds have no other inheritance to expect but the hulks or the scaffold. These are their entailed domains — their only right. When a woman has given birth to a child at the Bourbe, the

Bourbe grant her three days rest, after which she is turned out of doors with her infant; but then, by a philanthropic precaution, the turning cradle of the Founding Hospital is placed as a branch establishment next to the Bourbe. In this manner the poor child the Bourbe vomits out of one door, is nearly always received by the other. I asked for the prisoner; I saw her; over her mild and resigned face was spread that extraordinary whiteness which is often a great compensation to a young mother for all the suffering she has borne. Henrietta was seated in a large arm-chair, suckling her child, with her head bent over it. The infant clung with charming tenacity to its nurse's inexhaustible breast. This breast was white tinged with blue, and it was easy to see that it belonged to a healthy nurse, to a young and strong woman, formed to be a mother. The word *mother* commands everywhere something of respect, including even the Bourbe. A mother offering to her child her swelling breast, the uncertain life of the feeble little creature which depends on the life of its mother, that attentive and tender care which a mother alone can give, that little heart which begins to beat against its mother's, that nascent soul gorged with milk and covered with kisses, which the mother gently presses to her bosom, while holding it with both her hands, suffice to make us forget all a woman's crimes, her infidelity, her coquetry, her weakness, her phrenzy, and that fatal blindness which goads them everyone on to ruin; poor creatures predestined to perdition! Yes, a mother's love should be esteemed sufficient to expiate all these amounts; a single drop of milk should be able to wipe out all these perjuries. More than all this, if this woman has killed a man, has she not just given another man to the world? a man who will be younger, and stronger, and handsomer? Thus I entered the Bourbe the morning of the very day that Henrietta was to die. Her calmness, her attitude, her weakness, her beauty, and all that I knew of her first moments of life and of her misfortunes — shall I confess it? I could hardly restrain my sobs. I begged the Sister of Charity to leave us alone: I told her I was the victim's brother, that I wished to speak to her without witnesses. The kind sister said to herself as she left us, "Let us go, perhaps he is not her brother." Henrietta's child had fallen off to sleep without quitting hold of its mother's breast.

I approached her. "Do you recognise me?" said I. She raised her eyes slowly on me; she made a slight movement with her head to say she recognised me. It was evident the confusion cost her a pang. "Henrietta," I said, "you see before you a man who has loved you, who loves you still; he is the only man for whom you never had a glance or a smile; at present he is the only friend you have left; if you have any last wish, tell it me — it shall be fulfilled." She replied nothing; but yet her look was tender, and her blood again mounted into her cheek; the beautiful oval of her face became animated for the last time with the fire of her glance — with the ineffaceable charm of her smile. Poor, poor young girl! Poor head, doomed to fall! Poor neck so delicate and so white that might be severed as easily as the stem of a lily, and on which a hundred weight of lead, armed with an immense knife, will soon descend! Oh! if thou hadst but looked at me thus, once, only once, you would have been mine, mine for life; thou would'st have been the queen of my world for a certainty, thou was the most beautiful of all women. "Henrietta," I said, "it is true then you must die, die, so young and beautiful; you might have been my wife, have brought up with me our young family, led a long, happy life, and been for ever honoured; and when you were become a grandmother, with white, silver hair, have died calmly, some fine autumn evening, in the midst of all your grandchildren. A few hours more, and I must say adieu! adieu for ever!"

Henrietta still remained silent; she pressed her child against her breast, without answering me, and wept. These were the first tears that I had seen her shed; I watched them trickle slowly down her face, and they nearly all fell upon her child; thus bathed in these tears, which redeemed its mother, I looked upon the child as mine.

"This child, at least," said I to her, "shall be my son."

At these words, the poor woman hastily embraced the little creature, and had already stretched it towards me with a convulsive movement, when the door opened before I had finished speaking, and a man who entered, exclaimed in a hoarse voice, — "This child is mine." I turned round, and recognised the jailor of the prison; he was still as ugly as ever, but less hideous. "I am come for my child." said he; "no one else shall have him; though I cannot leave him my place as jailor, as my father left me his, I yet can give him a *chiffonnier's* basket to carry. Come along with me, Henry," and he drew out of his basket some child's linen as white as snow. He advanced towards Henrietta, without, however, looking at her, and seized the child with tender anxiety. The poor little creature was sleeping at its mother's breast; it was necessary to use force, in order to tear it from its nurse, so tightly did it cling. The old *chiffonnier* wrapped the child up, placed it in his basket, and exclaimed with an air of triumph, — "Come, Henry, misery does not dishonour one; you shall never be touched by Charlot!"

[126]

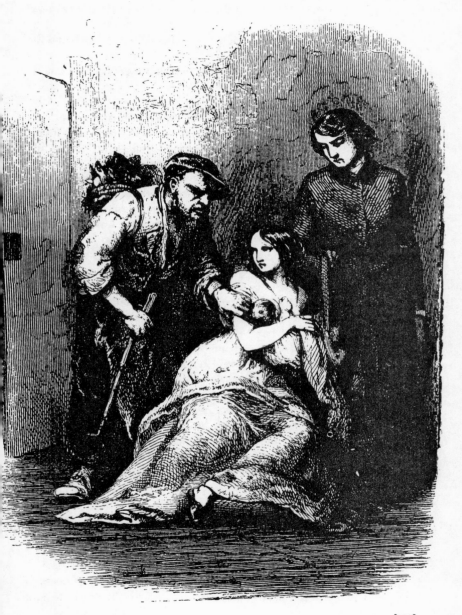

He left; it was time. Charlot! At the name of Charlot Henrietta raised her eyes.

"Charlot!" said she, in a trembling voice, "what does he mean?" and she shuddered convulsively.

"Alas! Charlot is the name by which the executioner is known among the people, and in the prisons."

"Oh, yes, I recollect," said she.

Then with an indescribable expression of anguish and regret, she repeated:— "Charlot! Charlot! why that was your watchword, was it not? That was my remorse. Oh, unfortunate woman that I am! How guilty, too! What severe warnings you gave me; what a frightful name you continually pronounced before me, without knowing it! Charlot! That word means my infancy, my childhood, and my girlish innocence! Charlot! It also means the probity of my father, the benediction of my mother, work and poverty without remorse. Unhappy girl that I am! It was my vanity that ruined me! When you met me while yet so innocent on Charlot's back, I was frightened of you, and avoided you from pride. My vanity led me into all the vice you have seen me in, and through which you have pursued me, with the name of Charlot ever on your lips. You gave me good advice, but I took your advice for so much derision. In order to give the lie to my recollections of Charlot, I determined to be rich, honoured, powerful, fêted; but the recollection of Charlot always came to embitter all my joy, and spoil my triumphs. The presence, the voice, the look of you who had seen and loved Charlot, terrified me; and yet how often have I not been ready to throw myself into your arms, and say — 'I love you! oh, return my love!' Oh, forgive me, forgive me!" added she; "in the name of Charlot forgive me! Pity, pity for me, a sullied, lost, guilty, criminal woman! Oh sir, for the love of Christian charity, do embrace me!" She stretched forth her arms to me, and I felt her burning cheek touch mine — it was for the first and last time!

Here they came to tell me that I had already remained too long.

CHAPTER XXVII ✑ ✑ ✑
The Executioner

I ran, I flew through the crowd, which as yet was thinking of nothing extraordinary, but was simply wending its way to the *Halls*, until the hour of the execution had arrived. After having wound my way through a long labyrinth of turnings, I reached a house without a number, in a street without a name. Everyone knows the house. A strong gate, lined with planking, defends the entrance of the court-yard. This gate is only opened on grand occasions. A low door, garnished with thick-headed nails, leads into the house. In the midst of the door gapes a brazen mouth more redoubtable than the Brazen Mouth at Venice; for be certain that when anything is cast into this opening it is a sentence of death; above this gaping mouth is a knocker, eaten up with rust, for few hands have ever knocked it. The house is surrounded by silence and by terror. I knocked; a servant came and opened the door. I was surprised at his respectable appearance and civil demeanour. He ushered me into a handsome drawing-room, and went to see whether his master was visible. While left to myself, I had an opportunity of examining two or three elegant rooms, furnished with great care and taste. The paper on the walls was of the freshest tints, the engravings were remarkably well selected, and the furniture most comfortable. On the chimney-piece were flowers newly gathered; the clock represented a mythological subject, "Cupid and Psyche," and was a quarter of an hour too fast. On the piano, which was open, lay a romance by some genius of the day, with its cadences and fugitive sighs, composed for the benefit of Parisian feelings; a pretty little woman's glove had been dropped on the carpet. In a small room at the end, some clever artist had painted the portraits of the couple to whom this charming retreat belonged, smiling at each other. I thought for a moment that I had mistaken the house.

A little further on, through a glass door, I discovered a venerable old man, whose head was covered with white hair. Near the old man, standing in an attitude of the most profound respect, was a fair-haired child, with eyes of azure; it was the grandfather giving his grandson a lesson in history. It must have been a curious thing to hear a lesson in history given by that old man, who was descended, by a genealogical tree of blood, from a long line of executioners, and who himself had been the executioner of an entire generation! He, indeed, had seen the nothingness of royalty and glory, if any one ever did. He had seen Lally-Tallendal and Louis XVI bend before his knife; he had laid his grasp upon the Queen of France and Madame Elizabeth — on majesty and on virtue! He had seen crouching in silence at his feet the crowd of good men whom the Reign of Terror sacrificed without pity, all the great names, all the great minds, all the great heroes of the eighteenth century; all that Marat,

Robespierre, and Danton combined had but dreamed, that old man alone had accomplished. He had been the only divinity and the only king of that epoch without authority and without belief, a terrible divinity, and inviolable king. He may be said to have had at his fingers' ends all the tints of the most noble blood, from that of the young maiden who arranges her dress in order to die to that which runs half-frozen in the veins of age. He had been the confidant of every kind of resignation, and of every description of courage; and how often has this red philosopher been confounded at seeing the villain die as courageously as the good man, and the disciple of Voltaire offer his neck with as much firmness as the Christian! he had seen virtue treated like vice; he had beheld the courtezan tremble with affright on the same scaffold that the Queen of France had mounted with a steady step. He had seen at the block every virtue and every crime: one day it was Charlotte Corday, and the next Robespierre. What *could* he understand about history, and how did he understand it? This is a difficult question to answer.

At last the person I was expecting entered the room. He was dressed in a dress coat, and had his gloves already on his hands; he was ready to go out; I knew whither.

"Sir," said the individual, casting an anxious look toward the clock, "my time today is not my own: may I have the pleasure of knowing what has procured me the honour of this visit?"

"I came to ask a favour of you, sir, which you will not refuse me."

"A favour, sir! I should be happy to have it in my power to show you one; many ask favours of me, but always in vain; 'tis like begging for mercy from the falling rock."

"If that is the case, you must often have felt yourself very unhappy."

"As unhappy as the rock. It is true that I fulfil a cruel duty; but I have right on my side, the only right which has not been disputed, even for a single instant, in the age in which we live."

"What you say is quite correct; you are a legitimate authority, an authority that is inviolable, sir; and, if we would be good historians, we must trace legitimate authority up to you as its source."

"Yes," replied the man, "there is no case in which my right was ever disputed. Neither revolution, anarchy, the empire or the Restoration has ever attacked it; my right has always maintained its position, without making one step forwards or backwards. Under my axe royalty, the people, and the empire have bowed their heads; all have passed under my yoke; I alone have acknowledged no yoke; I have always been stronger than the law itself, of which I was the supreme sanction: the law has changed a thousand times, I alone have changed once; I have been as immovable as fate, and as powerful as duty; and I have issued from this long series of ordeals with a pure heart, hands steeped in blood, and a conscience without a stain. Show me the judges who could say as much as I, the executioner, can! But, I repeat, I am pressed for time; may I ask what you wish?"

"I have always heard," I replied, "that the condemned prisoner who was placed in your hands was your sole and entire property; I come to beg of you to give up one I particularly wish to have."

"You are aware, sir, on what terms the law gives them to me?"

"I am; but when the law is once satisfied, there yet remains something, a trunk and a head; that is what I would purchase at any price."

"If that is all, sir, the bargain may be soon made;" and then, again looking at the clock, he continued, "but first of all, allow me to give some orders that are indispensably necessary."

He rang hurriedly, and two men came in obedience to his directions. "Be ready at half-past two," he said. "Dress yourselves decently, for we have to do with a woman, and we cannot show her too much attention." When he had spoken, the two men withdrew; at the same moment his wife and daughter came to bid him adieu. His daughter was a young person about sixteen, who, as she viewed him, said with a smile, *"au revoir!"* "We shall expect you by dinner-time," continued his wife. Then drawing nearer to him, she added in a low voice — "If she has fine black hair, do not forget to put it on one side to make me a front!"

The man turned towards me. "Do you bargain for the hair?" he asked. "For everything," I replied, "trunk, head, hair, everything, even the brain imbued with her blood!"

He kissed his wife as he said to her, "You must wait till another time."

CHAPTER XXVIII ◄§ ◄§ ◄§
The Shroud

The hour was nearly arrived, the audience were waiting for the sanguinary drama to begin; everyone had made his various little arrangements to see the victim die. Such is Paris: vice or virtue, innocence or crime, it matters not who is the victim, so long as there is death. Of all the sights that are to be seen gratis at Paris, the last moments of a fellow-creature on the Place de Grève is the most agreeable. Yet how much blood has that horrible Grève already drunk up! While the whole of this pitiless city was rushing to meet the fatal cart, I returned to the top of the Rue d' Enfer; for the last time I dived into this remote quarter, which almost seems to be the general depôt fixed on by Parisian humanity for every infamy and for every misery. I passed once more before the Capucins, where she had once been; before the Bourbe, where she was no more; before the smiling house of the young carpenter; neither he nor his betrothed were at home, they had both gone to see the effect of the machine. In the court-yard was still a vase which had contained the red paint that had served to give the scaffold its first light tint of blood. I passed the Salpêtrière; the child and his mother were employed in twisting another rope, as if they knew that the one the executioner was about to sever must be replaced. At the barrière I again met the beggar who performed the hero; the little boy, too, again defied me. Horrible fact! two old persons, leaning upon each other, were slowly pursuing their halting course, in order that they might see at least something of the execution — it was Henrietta's mother and father. Unconscious and curious, they, too, were proceeding to this *fête*, where their own blood was about to flow. At the same moment an important-looking major-domo arrived in a lumbering carriage. I recognised the Italian. Thus did I meet almost all the heroes of my book: their life had not advanced a step; they were two years older, and that was all; while I had drained my life, and lost for ever the lost illusions of my youth. For my last walk I was going to wait at the Cemetery of Clamart for the bargain I made that morning.

It was two o'clock; the sun moved but slowly, and I was walking under the shade of the dusty poplars at the side of the high road, when, in the midst of a green meadow, I perceived a large quantity of clean clothes hung up in the open air, on a number of lines that were fixed to the trees; a few women kneeling by the side of the neighbouring brook made the place echo again with their frequent blows, as they beat the linen. I recollected for the first time that I had no shroud; I resolved to obtain one whatever it might cost. I entered the meadow — it happened to belong to my little Jenny; Jenny herself was seated on a truss of hay destined for her horse, and was superintending at the same time the hanging out of the clothes, and those still under the process of washing; she was cheerful and kind, as usual, and her figure had acquired a certain degree of *em bon point*.

"You are very melancholy," she said, after she had wished me good-day.

"Do you think so, Jenny? It is because I must have without delay a large piece of linen to wrap up a poor young girl who is dying."

"Dying!" replied Jenny; "there may yet be hope, perhaps. I know many young girls who were very ill — so ill that they were believed to be dead — recover, and enjoy at present as good health as you or I."

"For her alone, Jenny, there is no hope; she will surely be dead at four o'clock. Make haste, then, and give me something in which I may wrap her up, for there is no time to lose."

Jenny conducted me into the midst of her lines, and showed me the clothes. "That is not what I want," I said; "I must have something finer, a woman's chemise, for instance. You can say that you have lost it — that it has been stolen. Jenny, you can say what you please, I will buy you another, but I must have it."

The kind-hearted girl did not wait to be asked twice; she guided me past all the clothes, but I could find nothing of Henrietta's size; sometimes the garment was too wide, sometimes the defect was on the other side; on other occasions I was stopped short by the owner's name. I desired that as she could not be in consecrated earth, the unhappy girl should at least have a chaste shroud. Jenny followed me closely, without in the least understanding my caprice.

At last, hung on the branches of one of the almond trees in the meadow, and covered with its smiling flowers, I discovered the most beautiful shroud that could possibly be imagined; it was a fine piece of cambric, as white and soft as satin, ornamented at the top and bottom with a slight edging of embroidery, and so swelled with the breeze of spring that at times you would almost have said the fine tissue enveloped a youthful figure. "That is what I have been looking for Jenny, that is what I want, give it me, and I am satisfied."

Jenny hesitated. The garment belonged to a beautiful young creature, as innocent as a child, and who was to be married in a week. I looked so pleased, however, at what I had found, that the good-hearted Jenny resisted my wishes no longer. I wrapped up carefully my rich and chaste shroud, and was about to depart, when I again turned back.

"This is not all," I said to Jenny; "I must have something else — a smaller shroud — a kind of bag — "

"Is it for a woman in childbed, then?" asked Jenny.

I started back in horror, as if she had penetrated my secret. "A woman in childbed! who told you, Jenny?"

"Yes," she replied, "I understand; a shroud for the mother, a shroud for the child," and then casting a glance upon her own rounded figure, she added — " 'Tis a sad death!"

"Alas, yes, dear Jenny, it is a sad death; they should not kill a woman who has not long been a mother!"

"Or, at least," replied Jenny, "she ought only to die when she has no longer a child to love!"

I added, then, to my first shroud, one of my own pillow-cases, on which my head had so often and so deliciously reposed.

As I was going, Jenny made the sign of the cross, and murmured the prayer for those in the pangs of death.

"So be it! — Amen!"

CHAPTER XXIX ◦§ ◦§ ◦§
Clamart

Clamart can scarcely be termed a cemetery; it is a piece of ground in which a corpse is now and then interred, but no priest has ever conse-crated it. The only monument at Clamart is a theatre of anatomy. By mere chance a few crosses have been erected there, but they have fallen to ruin. The service for the dead is never heard within its limits, no flower is ever strewed upon its graves, and if any one kneels down to pray, he hears invisible voices groaning in his ears. Clamart is the resting place of those that have been executed, but they hardly remain there two hours, or, to speak more correctly, they make but one step from the scaffold to the dissecting table. In this inhospitable place the rite of burial is but a mere form, the bier of the departed but a loan; the corpse is buried at five o'clock, to be deprived of its coffin two hours later for the instruction of future Hunters. We are curious creatures; out of human crime we have composed the book of the Sybil! But among all the different crimes of man the science of modern times will scarcely have aught to do with any but those of the most horrible kind. Hardly has the executioner placed his blood-red hand upon a human head ere the surgeon arrives to complete his work. Whoever has been a parricide, a poisoner, an assassin, or a traitor to his country, can claim his place in the Phrenological Museum. We are not content unless we know the weight of his heart and the conformation of his head; and we preserve his remains as if they were holy relics. On the other hand, however, we close the tomb, without so much ceremony, over him who has merely lived like a honest man, and, having done this, abandon him to the worms and to oblivion.

Our solitary grave-digger was employed in the cemetery of Clamart, digging a grave.

"You seem to take your time, my good man, and it appears to me that your grave is not a very deep one."

"I can't say I hurry," he replied. "As for the grave, I warrant it will be deep enough for the purpose it was made. Besides, if the body were to be there till the end of the world, it would not breed a fever; as a general rule, those we have here are not diseased — the rascals are as healthy as you or I."

"I see that you are pleased with your place, my good man, and that you envy no one."

"Envy no one! Ah! how I wish I were but a supernumerary at Père La Chase! A place there is both lucrative and amusing. Everyday there are lots of presents, and processions as fine as the evolutions of a regiment of the line; with no end of afflicted mothers, inconsolable sons, and weeping widows! Besides which, there are superb monuments, flowers to be strewn over the graves, weeping willows to clip, and little gardens to keep in order. At every instant of the day these rich people think it necessary to pay some one or other to give a favourable idea of their own grief. That is a place worth having, if you like;" and so saying, he drove his spade in the ground, and then continued. "Here, on the contrary, in this cursed place, there is nothing to be done. You never see the smallest procession — never behold a relation in tears, or have an opportunity of selling a single flower. The only persons you meet are the executioner's assistants, who will hardly give you something for a drop of drink. It is a wretched occupation! I would as soon be a gendarme or a custom-house officer;" and speaking thus, he leaned upon his spade, in the attitude of some honest country-men, when a long summer's day is drawing to its close.

"In this case, however, the grave must be deep," I replied impetuously, "It must be six feet; dig on, and when you have finished you shall be well rewarded for your pains."

"Six feet for one who has been executed — the thing is impossible! It would take an hour this evening to dig it up again."

"Six feet, at the very least; the corpse belongs to me."

"If it does, that's another argument in favour of what I say, sir," replied the grave-digger. Then, turning his head, he continued, — "It is late, they will not be long now."

He was right, for at that moment I saw a lumbersome cart approaching in the distance. At the horse's head walked the driver, while two men, who might have been mistaken for a couple of butchers coming from the *abattoir*, sat on the front seat with their arms crossed over their breasts. Inside the cart could be distinguished the vague form of something which resembled the rough outline of a coffin; it was the basket provided to receive the corpse of the victim, after justice had been allowed to take its course.

On reaching the gate of the cemetery, one of them jumped down; the grave-digger went up, cap in hand, to assist him, and, while the man who had remained in the cart held one end of the basket, the other two took it in their arms. The burden was not so heavy as it was cumbersome, and they managed so awkwardly as to let it fall at my feet, sprinkling the earth, as they did so, with a few drops of blood. As for me, I was half seated against the door-post, and beheld all that was passing as if in a confused dream. One of the assistants came up to me.

"It was you was it not, whom I saw this morning at the executioner's?" he asked.

"It was: what is your wish?"

"As you claimed the body of the deceased, my master supposed that you were perhaps a relation, and would not wish her to die in debt; he therefore told me to give you this little bill."

I took the little bill; it was like all other little bills — like a grocer's bill or a milliner's bill, written on fine white paper in an excellent hand. I read it slowly, like a man who had no objection to pay, but who did not wish to be imposed upon. The following is a literal copy of the bill:—

	fr.	c.
To placing and removing the guillotine — Prosper the carpenter	50.	00
To driving from the Palaise-de-Justice to the Grève	6.	00
To having had the knife newly ground and other friendly offices	2.	00
To a candle for greasing the groove	0.	30
To the bran in the sack	0.	20
To *Monsieur*, for his fee	200.	00
To the head Assistant	20.	00
To three glasses of brandy which we are about to drink in honour of the deceased	0.	30
To the body, entire	60.	00
Total	338.	80

Received the above.

"Is that all?" said I to the head assistant.

"It is the exact price," he replied, "you do not pay one sou more than the

City of Paris itself. You will, at least, have the consolation of knowing that the defunct did not die at the expense of government."

I went over the bill again. "There are three francs too much charged," said I, casting up the items, but I paid as if there had been no errors.

I then took an inventory of the basket, which the assistant opened. The first object that emerged from it was a head without the least drop of blood, and with the hair cut as close as if with a razor. The mouth was horribly contracted, and the eye was dimmed, although it seemed to look at one still. The convulsions of death had been so strong that the jaws were no longer parallel, so that the same mouth which had once been the seat of a thousand smiles and charms was closed on one side and gaping hideously on the other.

"Unhappy creature! how she must have suffered."

"Well — no," replied the second assistant, who was holding the upper end of the basket. "We showed her a thousand little attentions from the moment she was delivered into our hands. We let her sit down a little; we cut off her long black hair with new scissors, and then, without keeping her in suspense, we carried her to the cart. She was not a heavy burden I can assure you."

"You carried her! She trembled then? Poor girl! to be killed thus, so young and so beautiful!"

"Yes sir, you are right; she was indeed beautiful. She was said to have been a courtezan; but she did not look like one, at all events, she was so timid, reserved, and bashful. She had got on a black stuff gown reaching to her shoulders; a little crape handkerchief covered her neck. Her shoulders were delicately formed, her breast was beautiful, and her neck was very white."

"And you may also add," continued the other assistant, that her hands were lovely. I tied them; how soft, delicate, and white they were! And then her feet, I tied them also, but merely for the look of the thing; I was afraid of hurting them. All in all, she was a most perfect and beautiful creature."

"And yet, beautiful creature as she was, you killed her without pity."

"We did for her," replied the head assistant, "all we could do. We supported her, and hid the scaffold from her, and the consequence is that she died nobly."

"Before dying did she ask for no one?"

"For no one — only on leaving the prison, and all along the road, which is a good distance, she often looked around with an anxious air, as if she expected to see some acquaintance or other in the crowd."

"Yes," added the other; "and on seeing no one, she repeated in quite a low voice, — 'Charlot! Charlot!' and gave a deep sigh. I could not help laughing on seeing my master turn round on hearing the name Charlot; he thought some one was calling him."

I ended this conversation by saying to the two executioners, "Leave me, leave me! Give me the body, and begone."

Half the body had fallen out of the basket of its own accord; and the other half was drawn out — naked!

The grave-digger placed the coffin near the corpse. "Sir," said he, "I will just go and drink a glass with these gentlemen, and be back in an instant."

I then spread out the two winding sheets. I took the severed head in my two hands, and entwining it with its beautiful black tresses, placed both head and tresses in the pillow case, and deposited them at the end of the coffin.

The body now remained; but how could I think of burying it unaided? Sylvio was at my side — kind Sylvio! With his courageous hands he raised the upper part of the poor, decapitated trunk. As for me, I raised the two feet, as white and as cold as snow. Alas! blood and milk flowed simultaneously from the lovely body. We placed the corpse in its transparent winding sheet, the white chemise, which hardly covered the two finely tapering hands. The shoulders, however, were completely covered, and there was even sufficient of the neck left for us to fasten the funeral garment round it.

Old women and young women — all the women of the neighbourhood — had entered the cemetery, and stood looking at Sylvio and myself.

"Holy virgin!" cried one of them; "is it not a crying shame for such beautiful linen to be thrown on the ground like a mere corpse?"

"And the ground is not even consecrated!" said another.

"I'll wager that a wretch who has been guillotined has got better chemises than many a Christian!" continued a third.

Among these women there was a fat, red-faced man, with a soft, fluted voice — a philosopher — an orator, who stood at the edge of the grave as anxious to see as to hear all that was going on. He was so calm, so tranquil, so curious, and so comfortable in the position he had chosen! One of his observations was atrocious, and I recollect it now. I had just fixed the winding-sheet with a trembling hand, and was murmuring a last adieu to the object of my unhappy passion; he was explaining to the women why their chemises were more adapted for executions than ours.

"The last preparations are much sooner made," said he. "The executioner is not obliged to cut the chemise of the victim; and you can imagine how horrible it must be to feel the cold scissors grating against the back of the neck that the axe will soon divide."

Seeing the heavy tears swimming in my eyes, he continued, shrugging his shoulders, —"Lovers' sorrow! How foolish men are! For ten years I was in the musical chapel of St. Peter's, at Rome; I was conductor at Florence; I was first singer of the Theatre of La Scala, at Milan; I have been the object of the most ardent passions that ever inflamed a fair Italian's breast; I have traversed Venice in the rose-coloured domino and black mask of the Carnival; have seen women die for love, and I never once felt the stupid passion that is called love."

After pronouncing these words, the man sheltered himself behind the flowery hedge of his own egotism.

The women looked at him with horror; and, by my faith, you will easily believe it; this man, so happy and so rosy, was a Neapolitan soprano.

So, in the whole course of my story, not one pang was spared me — not even the consolation of a soprano!

When all was properly arranged, and the head placed at the top of the body, as if it had never been separated from it, Sylvio shut the coffin; and having done this, we both crossed our arms and kept guard at the graveside, for the grave-digger had not returned. Meantime, night was slowly drawing in, and the sky was gradually assuming those calm bright tints which end a fine day. At my feet, Paris, that same town which had just pitilessly immolated the young girl stretched before me, was preparing, without remorse, for its nightly *fêtes*, its pleasures, its concerts, its dances, and its intrigues. Where art thou, my poor Henrietta? Whither has fled, not thy soul, but thy beauty? Where does thy last smile now appear? Poor girl! at the moment I speak the place of thy beauty and thy vice is already filled up. Other maidens and other vices of twenty years old have supplied the void left by thee in the love and the admiration of men. Already, no one — not even those old bald-headed men to whom you gave your love as an alms — no one remembers more thy youth, which dazzled like the lightning, and which passed as quickly! Not one even recollects thy name! They do not even say, when speaking of thee, "She is dead! — she was killed!" for they do not even know that thou art dead; they are not aware that it was a woman who was immolated today. But they, the happy ones of this world, ungrateful as they are, will deliver themselves up to fresh victims, whom they will, crush with the same pitiless unconcern.

Oh! that thou should'st die thus! — die, for them and by them! — die, because thou wast beautiful, poor, and weak, and because thou revengedst thy wrongs! — die, assassinated by the town which corrupted thee! — die, when thou hadst naught but thy blood to offer the infamous city which had robbed thee of thy innocence and of thy beauty! — die! For whom, by whom? Gracious Heaven!

Yes, I suffered cruelly while I was thus waiting at the side of the grave. As I stood near the corpse all my melancholy recollections crowded on my mind. All the deceitful or terrible apparitions of my life passed before me with a smile or a malediction. I was the victim of a horrible nightmare. At one glance I cast my eyes over the whole of this sad story, half vice, half virtue, in which truth is more powerful than fiction, and where the piece of kingly purple is hideously joined to the most revolting rags. My dream was endless, and, oh! how horrible!

Night had completely closed in, when the grave-digger returned. He was half tipsey, and was singing some drunken song. He was greatly astonished at finding us still on the spot, but, however, set about work. The coffin was lowered into the grave; the earth fell upon the sonorous wood, which returned a plaintive sound; by degrees the reverberation become fainter. "Courage," said I to the grave-digger; "there must be a great deal of earth in this grave." In order to obey me better, the worthy man began to dance over the grave, resuming at the same time his song, *J'aime mieux boire*.

We were now alone, Sylvio and I; the inquisitive crowd, finding there was nothing else to be seen, had departed. I plucked up courage enough to fall upon my knees. I searched my heart, but in vain, for some holy prayer. It was with difficulty that I could recollect a few of the words consecrated to those that are no more: *De profundis clamavi ad te*, and the grave-digger replied in *faux bourdon*; *J'aime mieux boire*.

Sylvio tore me forcibly from this terrible scene. Adieu, Henrietta; adieu, courtezan, who was the object of my tender and innocent love! I will return to-morrow.

The next day I returned alone, my thoughts filled with prayers, my heart filled with pity, my eyes filled with tears, and my hands filled with flowers; but on reaching the spot where a few drops of blood were still visible, there was no longer a tomb. The grave, which had been ransacked and half filled up again, had already delivered up its prey; the School of Medicine had stolen the body; the hungry grave-digger had once more taken possession of the miserable shell, to dispose of it to another victim;

the women of the neighbourhood had battled with each other, as to who should have the shroud, in order to dress their living bodies in the garment of death; the pillow-case had fallen to the share of the Neapolitan soprano; another courtesan had already bought the beautiful black hair in order to adorn her own bald head. Nothing was left.

This last outrage, or rather this last execution after the last execution, struck me as horrible. This fatal instance of the poor girl's eluding my pity was the most horrible of all. Now, indeed, it was impossible for me to find even the smallest vestige of her; I felt that I was hopelessly conquered; by dint of calmness, perseverance, and an amount of melancholy courage, I had followed her to the end of her sad path of candour and of vice, of roses and of thorns; but there I lost her track for ever; I had been enabled to dispute the possession of her with corruption, with disease, with misery, with prostitution, with the executioner, with the grave-digger . . . I might have done so with the worms of the tomb, but how could I hope to snatch her from the surgeon's knife? Unhappy wretch that I was, had I not also wished to snatch her from the new poetic school of my native land?

I reserved my useless prayers for myself; I drove my grief down again into my heart; the morning breeze dried the last tears in my eye; I scattered from me the flowers I had brought to the tenantless tomb. And this, unhappy wretch that thou art, I exclaimed, in my despair, is all that thou hast gained by thy pursuit of the horrible; no hope in thy soul, no tears in thy eyes, no flowers in thy hands; not even in this tomb.

"Mort de Charlot à la Barrière du Combat."
Vignette by Dévéria for the first edition (1829)

The Paper-Knife

Chapter XXX of *The Dead Donkey and the Guillotined Woman*

by Honoré de Balzac

"I am extremely satisfied with myself at having found the means by which to exhaust the entire range of human emotions," I remarked to Sylvio, "from the coldest degree below freezing point to the hottest temperature that is known. From talk of the friendship that one can feel for a donkey to the joy one expects to obtain in the presence of the most beautiful woman on the face of the earth, between Charlot (the donkey) and Henrietta (the guillotined woman), I have squeezed life so thoroughly, I have witnessed the accomplishment of so much unhappiness, that my heart has become completely hardened. I can now walk without fear through the midst of civilisation. Horror can go no further, I have dipped myself in the Styx. What a tremendous advantage it gives a man to be armed with such precious insensitivity. If I were stupid enough to become a statesman, I would have no fear of an aneurysm; if a politician, no concern that anyone would ever call out a remark that would leave me at a loss for words. I am like the man who in order to avoid being sickened by the base conduct at Versailles said that he swallowed a toad every morning."

Instead of replying to these observations, Sylvio, haunted by some memory, asked sadly:

"Did you really manage to get any sleep last night?"

"Why not?"

"But it was only yesterday that — Henrietta was buried!"

"And legally executed," I added. "But, yes, I managed to go to sleep, and I slept as soundly as if she were only a character in a novel or a play, an Amy Robsart.[1] Is she not at peace now? And should one not feel happiness at the thought that the innocent have been spared any further part of human misery?"

"And not only buried, but also stolen from her final resting place . . . " continued Sylvio, as he threw a last glance at the empty grave. "Where can the poor creature be now?"

[143]

Chapter XXX

"In the hands of a group of studious young men who will have paid for her for the last time. Only this time, she will not receive the money for prostituting herself."

On these words, we left the cemetery of Clamart and started to make our way back towards Paris.

"You no longer consider Henrietta a criminal?" Sylvio enquired, thinking over one of the words I had used to describe her.

"Criminal! Whatever makes you say that? She is in the first rank of those meticulous individuals who fill in the list of bills for discount and who would cut a centime in half in order to pay you no more than your due. She killed a man who a long time ago had himself killed all the happiness, obscurity of birth, and innocence within her. The law cannot concern itself with such things, it knows only facts. I applaud the judgement that was delivered. Henrietta was still virtuous enough to seek revenge; her crime was that her repentance was badly thought out; if she had been a man, she would have given the cad a box about the ears, called on me to act as her second, and lodged a bullet in his heart. That way she would probably be dancing on the most brilliantly polished parquet in Paris instead of being six feet in the ground . . . Poor woman! She's virtuous enough now. One can shed a tear at her memory, though if the wretch had propositioned her two years later, she would no doubt have said nothing and merely stolen his watch . . . God has probably pardoned her already, while in two years' time she would have been so odiously vile that she would have been damned for all eternity."

"You turn everything upside down."

"No, I just give voice to my thoughts on cause and effect. God preserve me that I should upset things. Everything works so well!"

Suddenly, we heard some joyful laughter and we met some former school friends who were likewise returning to Paris by way of the barrière d'Enfer; they were on their way back from a botanical expedition. We renewed our acquaintance.

"You look as if you are in a hurry?"

"Well, yes, we are," said one of them. "A first rate specimen has turned up and we're on our way to the dissecting room, then we're having a bachelor party to welcome a new student. Have you ever seen an autopsy performed?"

"Never."

"Well, come along, then . . . You'll find it amusing. It's tremendously interesting."

[144]

by *Honoré de Balzac*

Chatting about our school days as we went, we soon arrived at a house situated near the School of Medicine. We went up to the attic, Sylvio and I going in first. The walls of the dissecting room were painted a greeny-brown colour. Daylight came in through windows in the roof and fell upon a table around which a number of young men were standing wearing green aprons and, on their arms, those green canvas sleeves to which nurses are so partial. So preoccupied were they that none of them heard the door open.

"They've started without us, the rotters!" exclaimed my friend from school, whose name was Michel.

"That was very unfair of you, gentlemen! . . . " remarked the three others to the company at large.

The four who were operating on the body turned their heads; but they were in such a hurry to cut into the livid flesh, open veins, study I don't know what mysteries of the life in this cadaver, that they started back to work amidst a torrent of exclamations.

"There! Do you see them?" "See what?" "The lungs." "The heart." "The plexus." "The . . . " I remember little of the words they employed, but I shall forever recall the spectacle which greeted my eyes. The corpse of a woman, as white as driven snow for the most part, turning livid in places, cut into quarters and slit open like that of a hare; pieces of flesh piled up beside her ready for dissection, and a woman, an old woman, sitting on a stool, calmly eating a slice of ham on a hunk of bread in front of all this. The complexion of this old woman was itself not unlike that of a corpse. She got up from time to time and picked up the human debris with her hook-like fingers and slung it into a basket.

"Good God! What a beautiful woman!" muttered Sylvio involuntarily.

"She would have been a good man's pride and joy," grumbled the old woman, "if only she had behaved herself." Her words went straight to my heart.

"And so, gentlemen," said the oldest student, "I think I can make a pronouncement of the greatest importance. This is the third time that I have encountered such a phenomenon in the organs of the head . . . "

I turned my gaze upon the speaker whose voice had given rise to such a religious silence, and I saw in his hand . . . the head of Henrietta. I uttered a cry so terrible that everyone stopped what they were doing.

"Horror has beaten me!" I exclaimed, as I slumped into a chair. "These entrails, now cold and scored by your scalpels, these pieces of flesh in this basket, this skin which hangs loose . . . only yesterday at half-past three

[145]

all this was Henrietta. She was alive, she could think, she was capable of suffering."

The students looked at me as if I were a madman.

"Yes, she was alive, she could think, she was capable of suffering at five minutes past four," replied the tall young man, "despite the fact that she had been decapitated. I am absolutely convinced of this matter. It will be a simple enough fact to establish once autopsies are performed on executed criminals in the presence of men of learning and an open mind. Personally, I believe that death by decapitation is caused, as with asphyxia, by black blood invading the vascular system. Now, as you can see for yourself, the state of the organs of the brain would seem to suggest that this girl was still able to think for two, three, four or five minutes — who can tell? — after the head was severed from the rest of the body. I would even go so far as to claim that the body itself did not die there and then but . . . "[2]

"So did she suffer badly?" I asked him.

"Yes," he replied coldly in order to be rid of me, "for we found signs of an aneurysm which must have started to form yesterday. Such that," he continued, "there are two deaths: the violent death which is contrary to nature and for which the organism is not prepared; and the slow death which nature causes to operate throughout all the organs. It would be a marvellous undertaking, gentlemen, to be able to prove it! For I have an inkling that the manifestations of these two kinds of death would be so different, and the factors surrounding them so diverse, that it would be impossible not to conclude in favour of the hypothesis I suggested a moment ago — namely, that violent death does not cause the immediate annihilation of all our moral faculties."

I was looking around for Sylvio when Michel, guessing my intention, said:

"Sylvio has gone out. He couldn't bear the smell, so I showed him into the room where the altar has been dressed."

I went to rejoin Sylvio. He was sitting in front of a table covered with the most appetising of dishes: the number of bottles of champagne suggested that a good time would be had by all. There was Bordeaux, Bourgogne, Rivesaltes, Roussillon, Hermitage — a deputation, in fact, from every wine-growing region in France. A generous block of foie gras stood out between a salmon-trout and a ham. The seven students soon joined us, and we ate, and we drank, and we joked about the autopsy, the foie gras, the salmon-trout and Henrietta.

Michel had broken off the poor girl's tibia and wanted to demonstrate something with it.

"Ha! ha!" I said, after having drunk a few glasses of champagne. "What's in store for Henrietta next. Where's she off to now?"

"Next," replied Michel, "as the bones are nice and white, Old Mother Virginie will . . . "

"What! The old crone over there?"

"That's right. Old Mother Virginie will sell them on to the domino-makers. Afterwards, all that remains is the flesh. The oedema will be extracted and used to make those beautiful, diaphanous candles."

"Thus, there is always the possibility that I may lose part of my fortune across the green baize of a gaming table which is illuminated by everything I found most charming in Henrietta! How horrible! Civilisation! Society is nothing more than a herd of swine, everything has its uses! Horror!"

"To the new doctor!" everyone cried in unison, clinking their glasses together. This toast concluded the meal.

"What would the ancient Greeks, who had such respect for the dead, have said about all this?"

"They would never have discovered the steam-engine, the circulation of the blood, the nervous system, and so on."

As I left, Old Mother Virginie pulled at my sleeve and presented me with a bone which had been carefully washed and scrubbed.

"The tibia was as white as driven snow. The gentleman may have it for only thirty sous. It would make an excellent paper-knife. They tell me she was a special friend of yours, dearie, wouldn't you like a souvenir to remember her by . . . "

"Thank you," I said gravely as I took possession of Henrietta's tibia.

A famous artist was employed to engrave a dead donkey on one side of the handle and a young girl on the other. I am now sure that I am the equal of that excellent pasha who, in Victor Hugo's poem, weeps over the loss of his Nubian tiger.[3]

1. *The tragedy of Amy Robsart — secretly married to Dudley, the Earl of Leicester, the favourite of Queen Elizabeth 1 — dominates Scott's* Kenilworth *(1821). Victor Hugo had collaborated on a stage version, the fourth to appear in almost as many years, performed in 1828.*
2. *There was a widespread debate in the 1790s and throughout the entire nineteenth century as to whether the victim's head retained life and therefore consciousness for a moment or more after the act of decapitation*
3. *Hugo's* La Douleur du Pasha *(1829), concerning an Eastern despot's indifference to the suffering around him.*

"Henriette dans son cachot."
Vignette by Dévéria for the 1829 edition

Afterword

Le Voyeur Sentimental: *Death and Desire in Jules Janin's 'L'Ane Mort'*

Tell me, though, I beg you, have you never thought of the consequences of all this revolution? Have you never thought of the executioner who dispatches, even as he adores her, the victim who has been thrown to him? What an abominable crime! What exquisite torture! —— Jules Janin, *Barnave*

L'Ane Mort et la femme guillotinée was certainly written at least in part with the intention of satirising what Janin considered both before and afterwards were the aesthetic and intellectual deficiencies of the *roman frénétique* — or the "new school of poetry" as he calls it. "Give me [...] something terrible, dark and bloody; this can be depicted — this easily excites the passions!" exclaims the narrator in the opening paragraph. "Courage, then! Wine no longer has the power to make your head swim, so swallow this tumbler of brandy. We have even gone beyond brandy; we have taken to spirits of wine; it only remains for us to turn drinkers of ether; but let us take care lest, by going from excess to excess, we may be enticed to imbibe opium."

Maxime du Camp provides us with further valuable first-hand testimony as to the author's intentions: "I have heard him say that when he started *L'Ane Mort*, he had no other intention than to ridicule the lugubrious inventions of Romanticism, but then, little by little, the subject seized hold of him and he finished by taking seriously a book which had begun as nothing more than a parody."[1] Arsène Houssaye likewise captures the paradoxical nature of Janin's achievement in his description of *L'Ane Mort* as a "strange masterpiece which is at one and the same time the soul and the raillery of Romantic literature."[2]

More recent critics, however, while recognising the existence of an underlying satirical intent, have preferred to treat the novel at something closer to face value. Thus, for Mario Praz, writing in 1930, Janin is little more than the ambiguous disciple of the Marquis de Sade.[3] Since then, Joseph-Marc Bailbé and Jacques Landrin have claimed that the work is mainly concerned with expressing the narrator's confused state of mind. "It seems [...]", writes Bailbé, "that *L'Ane Mort* exemplifies an internal conflict in the author's personality between the seductive nature of appearance and the desire to observe reality in all its cruelty."[4] Landrin makes a broadly similar point: "What is far more important than these scenes, half-horrific and half-burlesque, is the shock that the discovery of

Henrietta's infamy causes the narrator. [...] The real subject of the novel is the painful conflict between the idealism of a young man who is still full of illusions and the sad realities of existence."[5]

Such an approach, it seems to me, falls into the deceptive trap of taking the narrator at his own estimation of himself as being reasonable, sane and reliable. Nothing could be further from the truth. His fascination with Henrietta, with whom — let us not forget — he initially has no more than the most fleeting and superficial contact, is both obsessive and unhealthy. He is, moreover, at his own admission drawn to sadistic and bloody spectacles. Indeed, his voyeuristic tendencies are clearly emphasised by Dévéria in the two vignettes he designed for the 1829 Baudouin edition of the novel: in the first, he is shown surveying a pack of dogs tearing into the donkey; in the second he detachedly observes Henrietta languishing in prison.

What instead we shall argue here is that in *L'Ane Mort* Janin uses his narrator to mock the search for moral purity — a moral purity based at least in part on notions of revolutionary *vertu* deriving from 1789 — that characterised his generation.

A key element in this new ethos was the perceived collapse of the existing moral order (and the consequent undermining of the élites which controlled it) in the months leading up to the Revolution of July 1830 and its immediate aftermath. Thus, French Romanticism, at least in its *frénétique* aspect, should be seen in terms of a conflict between generations. This finds its clearest manifestation in the extreme youth of a large proportion of the central protagonists of such fictions. Indeed, many are mere students, and if not students, in early manhood: Frédéric de Wulfenbuttel (in *Barnave*), Anatole (in *La Confession*), and the anonymous narrator of *L'Ane Mort* (to mention the three novels by Janin briefly examined here). The works of other "minor Romantics" such as Pétrus Borel, Roger de Beauvoir, Alphonse Royer, and so on, furnish innumerable other such examples — as, indeed, do the writings of Hugo and Balzac.

In his seminal study of such student-initiated revolts, Lewis Feuer claims that students are fired by a conviction "that their generation has a special historical mission to fulfil where the older generation, other elites, and other classes have failed."[6] With respect to the *roman frénétique* in the years leading up to and immediately following on 1830 that special mission was mainly, though not exclusively, linked to the Republican ideology:[7]

"The Paris students," writes John Plamenatz, "were the first organized republicans in nineteenth-century France, and they were also revolutionaries. Students in Paris had, in September 1818, formed the first republican association, "The Friends of Truth," under the protective cover of Freemasonry. Less than two years later, they were plotting an insurrection of six hundred armed students, but the police got wind of it and it came to naught. The student leader, Bazard, shortly evolved into an ardent Saint-Simonian, proselytizing especially among the engineering students at the Ecole Polytechnique [...]. Meanwhile, another student plot to seize power, the so-called Charbonnerie, had failed in 1821, and students began to look for allies and physical power among the workers. The revolution of 1830 indeed took place under student initiative. A student organization, formed in January 1830, took to the barricades on July 27, 1830; the workers followed. [...] An American observer reported that when the barricades were going up in July 1830, the commanding officers were students [...].

It was that republican ideology, embodying as it did numerous themes and ideas deriving from 1789, that Janin mainly sought to attack in *L'Ane Mort*. What Bailbé mistakes for evidence of an "internal conflict" is — according to this reading of the novel — the exposure of the absurdities to which the narrator's moral zeal gives rise. The self-satisfaction, for example, with which he observes the gradual destruction of Henrietta was intended to remind readers of the cold logic which informed the Terror, a logic symbolised by that "most abstract of executions", the guillotine itself, which eventually dispatches her.[8] Ultimately, as we shall see, we should perhaps even view Henrietta's death as representing in some way the apotheosis of Marie-Antoinette.

Janin's narrator first encounters Henrietta on the road to Vanves, not far from a tavern called the Bon-Lapin. This was an area much in fashion with certain Romantic writers. Victor Hugo and his friends, for example, were regular patrons of another nearby *cabaret*: "The pantry of Mother Saguet was not well-stocked. She would go out to the poultry-yard and wring the necks of a few chickens, slice them in half, cook them over the grill, and garnish the dish with a piquant sauce. [...] We would take our places at the table at six o'clock, we would not stand up again until ten. The time rapidly sped by as we chattered away agreeably over more bottles of wine and more omelettes."[9]

Nothing could appear more charming. For a member of the bourgeoisie, however, such places could no doubt seem quite intimidating. On the way there one would have to cross the populous district of Montparnasse with its street performers and travelling shows, taverns full of carousing working men or groups of drunken artists, skirt the edge of a cemetery and penetrate the countryside.[10] More to the point, Janin's Bon-Lapin is also an erotically charged environment: "The garden lends its shade to less carnivorous gastronomists. There, you see young girls and young men, young girls and old men, young girls and soldiers, young girls and lawyers." It was also a place of chance encounters. Adèle Hugo recounts that returning from Mother Saguet's one evening with her husband, David d'Angers took down the name and address of a fifteen year old girl who was dressed in rags. A few days later Hugo called on the sculptor and was surprised to find the same girl stretched out naked on a table: "The poor little thing, thin, sickly and beautiful, was serving as a model for the artist

[151]

for a statue destined for the tomb of Botzaris which, in the mind of the great sculptor represented modern Greece."[11]

Not all such encounters served such lofty aspirations. On entering the Bon-Lapin, after his briefly and purely accidental exchange with Henrietta, Janin's narrator remarks: "I went and sat down in a corner of the garden, *quite alone, without a young girl, but, in reality, absolute master of all those who were present* [...]." (My emphasis.) This somewhat sinister reflection clearly stresses the narrator's isolation, his awareness of his lack of sexual companionship, as well as suggesting his feelings of inferiority. Indeed, this passage introduces the central ambiguity of *L'Ane Mort*: namely, the manner in which the narrator projects his sexual anxieties back on to women in such a way that they seem wholly reasonable.[12]

This theme of sexual inadequacy is highlighted in Janin's next novel, *La Confession* (1830). Anatole, still single at forty, marries a girl chosen for him by his mother. On his wedding night, such is his terror at approaching his bride he cannot remember her name.[13] Enraged by his own impotency, he strangles her. As she dies, he suddenly recalls her name which he screams at her. This noise is misinterpreted by the wedding guests as her cry of *jouissance* and the celebrations downstairs are renewed. Significantly, even as he kills her, Anatole is presented to the outside world as having changed sexual roles with his wife.[14]

René Girard has suggested that intense crisis within a community entails a fear of the loss of sexual differentiation.[15] The France of the late 1820s and 1830s was in such a state of crisis as the political instability of the period would indicate. Sexual identity remained a significant issue in Romantic literature throughout the 1820s and '30s, as works such as Latouche's *Fragoletta, ou Naples et Paris en 1799* (1829) and Gautier's *Mademoiselle de Maupin* eloquently testify.

The narrator of *L'Ane Mort* is likewise a member of a large class of social and sexual misfits — such as Balzac's Raphaël de Valentin (in *La Peau de chagrin*) and Lassailly's Trialph (in *Les Roueries de Trialph*, 1833) — who populate *frénétique* writing towards this period. Outside the cycle of productive labour, they are the archetypal *flâneurs* who strolled about Paris, their dandyish appearance symbolising their economic and political emasculation.

His notion of being *maître absolu* takes on added ironic significance if one considers the vast social distance which separate the hero and heroine of *L'Ane Mort*. Indeed, the greater the social distance between them grows as Henrietta sinks down the social scale, the more obsessive the narrator's passion would seem to become. He can find no rational justification for his desire. This is how he describes his love-object: "In my eyes, however, the horrible existed but with Henrietta, that false and unfeeling woman, a very abyss of egotism and weakness, a human being devoid of moral nature, a magnificent envelope, to complete whose perfection nothing was wanting except a soul." Yet it is only in opposition to Henrietta's lack of status that the narrator can define himself as a gentleman. Himself lacking status in the eyes of his peers, he imagines he

[152]

Le Voyeur Sentimental

may at least become the *maître absolu* of someone even lower down the social scale than himself.

The bourgeois youth's desire for women of low social status is a major theme in nineteenth-century literature.[16] Not surprisingly, there is also much psychological evidence for such a condition. During analysis, Freud's 'Wolf Man' recounts how "he saw a peasant girl kneeling by the pond and employed in washing clothes in it. He fell in love with the girl instantly and with irresistible violence, although he had not yet been able to get even a glimpse of her face. By her posture and occupation she had taken the place of Grusha [his nursery maid] for him."[17] It is not necessary to accept Freud's interpretation of this to acknowledge that it was the girl's posture of physical debasement (which his client lays great emphasis on) which was the principal eroticising factor.[18]

Another aspect of this same hierarchical organisation of the world concerns the topography of the city. Just as Henrietta is essential to the narrator for the maintenance of his own individual identity, so the Barrière du Combat, the Bon Lapin, the Morgue, the Grande Chaumière, the Bourbe, the *lupanar* (a low-class brothel) followed by all the institutions connected with Henrietta's trial and execution, are essential to the bourgeoisie for the construction of their collective identity. In all these places, once again, Janin's narrator could survey his own antithesis together with the operation of the state apparatus which holds the entire mechanism in place: "Many treatises have been written on the sublime and the beautiful, but they prove nothing; their authors have been satisfied with superficial appearances, whereas they ought to have dug to the root. What do I care about the drawing-room manners of that society which could not exist a day without spies, gaolers, hangmen, lotteries and dens of debauchery, pot-houses, and cut-throat theatres!"

It is, of course, relatively easy to take such passages at face value. Janin's narrator should certainly not be considered as making such remarks lightly. Behind them, however, there lies the main satirical mechanism of *L'Ane Mort*: the political (in the widest sense of the word, including sexual ideology) differences in attitude of author, narrator and reader.

Writing of the Republican ideal of virtue at the time of the French Revolution, Lynn Hunt claims that it was "profoundly homosocial; it was based on a notion of fraternity between men in which women were relegated to the realm of domesticity. Public virtue required virility, which required in turn the violent rejection of aristocratic degeneracy and any intrusion of the feminine into the public."[19] This homosocial aspect of the Revolution found its most chilling manifestation in the wave of executions of women who played a public role — Marie-Antoinette, Mme du Barry, Mme Roland, Olympe de Gouges, — and in the suppression of the women's political clubs. "In the general need to read crimes as bodily," remarks Peter Brooks, "where women were on trial there seemed to be a specific need to place criminality squarely on their sexuality."[20] Revolutionary rhetoric was indifferent to whether such women were monsters of depravity (as Marie-Antoinette was portrayed) or chaste.

[153]

After her death, an autopsy was conducted on Charlotte Corday which revealed her to be a virgin. "She was a woman who had simply cast off her sex," commented an official newsheet, "experiencing only disgust and annoyance when nature recalled it to her. [...] Decent men do not like such women, and they in turn affect to despise the sex that despises them."[21]

The guillotine is one of the key images by which the French Revolution has been represented, "no other stereotype of the Revolution is so widely recognized."[22] It is, therefore, perhaps not unreasonable to juxtapose Henrietta's death on the guillotine with that of her more illustrious sisters who perished during the Revolution.

As a courtesan, Henrietta is the living embodiment of social degeneration: the direct antithesis of the modesty and fidelity characteristic of good petit bourgeois wives whether of 1790 or 1830. Like Marie-Antoinette, she may be seen as driven by an ungoverned ambition, one which is ultimately attributable to an ungovernable sexuality, a carrier of corruption and debauchery infecting all those who come into contact with her.[23] Just as Revolutionary rhetoric insisted on the eradication of such enemies of Republican *vertu*, the "juvenocratic" ethos of much *frénétique* writing was likewise directed against such symbols of corruption. The need to protect society from such an invasion is stressed by the author in Chapter III:

After this, I perambulated the magnificent boulevards from one end to the other: they begin at a ruin, the Bastille, and terminate at another ruin, an unfinished church. I surveyed Parisian immortality in all its phases. At the Bastille it seems as if it were trying its strength; it is still timid there, and on a small scale, beginning with some young girl, who sings an obscene song to divert the men from the wharfs and warehouses. On advancing, you will perceive the venal woman changes her appearance. She now wears a black apron, white stockings, and a cap without ribbons; her look is modest, her step slow and steady, and she keeps so close to the wall, that you would think she was avoiding a person infected with the plague. Further on, the lady is gaudily attired; she is half naked, following the fashion you tolerate in your ballrooms; but reprobate elsewhere, and wears no cap; she sings snatches of songs out of tune, and with a hoarse voice, and leaves behind her a strong smell of musk and amber: this is vice, as patronised by the most refined amateur. [...].

In the 1829 version, the text then continues as follows:

Next there is the prostitution aimed at young men, a cashmere shawl, thirty-six years old, a brougham, a box at the theatre and a student ruined for a whole term; finally, there is the prostitution aimed at the nobleman: she is young and handsome, seductive and extravagant, with beautiful hair [...] By this time, the tableau of prostitution is complete: at the corner of a street an old woman sells

[154]

her own daughter, at the doorways of the places where you buy your lottery tickets, old women prostitute even chance. [...]

Janin's interest in the social problems posed by prostitution thus anticipates the pioneering work of social reformers by some years.[24] His discourse on the subject, however, is punctuated with elements indicative of revolutionary ideology. As in the scandalous tales that make up *Les Fastes de Louis* XV (1782), he is describing a female sexuality "run amok" which had taken over the centre of the kingdom.[25] The narrator's complaint about Henrietta's skills at dissimulation — "cette nature si vide et si fausse" (the English translation, "that false and unfeeling woman", is weaker than the original) — takes on a sharper focus when one recalls that the Republicans valued transparency — "the unmediated expression of the heart"[26] — above all other qualities. As an enemy of society, Henrietta is marked as a victim of Saint-Just's implacable logic: "What constitutes a Republic is the total destruction of everything opposed to it."[27]

At this point, the question should be posed as to how far Janin's own beliefs coincided with such an ideology. The answer is largely in the negative. In *Honestus*, a *conte fantastique* published in 1832, Janin explored the ramifications of a young philosopher's wish that vice would disappear from the face of the earth. He quickly seeks to rescind his wish. As his father explains to him at the conclusion of the story: "By eradicating vice and crime [...], you have killed the world, you have deprived it of its principal condition of existence, you have taken away its ethics, in short, by making it more common than sand on the river-bed, you have robbed virtue of its self-esteem . [...] Remember this, my son! this sad experiment was necessary to teach you that this is nothing more dangerous for men than a universal morality . . ."[28]

Balzac, it will be recalled, presents us with the image of the heroine in the dissection-room. This dissection-room was not to be found in a hospital, as one might expect, but in a private house — though those present are mainly students. To understand the significance of this scene, it is necessary to explore briefly the history of the French medical profession.

Until the eighteenth-century, development in the field of medicine had been restricted by the custom of physicians practising individually. As the century progressed, a number of reforms were undertaken to improve standards of care. One such measure, which occurred in the mid-1770s, led to the introduction of a standard system of instruction for physicians and surgeons based on practical experience in the dissection laboratory and hospital wards. This system was by no means abandoned with the advent of the Revolution. Indeed, progress in the field of pathological anatomy, especially in the emerging domain of histopathology (or tissue pathology), resulted in an increased reliance on postmortem dissection.

By the beginning of the nineteenth-century, postmortem dissections had become part of normal hospital training, and the Faculté de Médecine de Paris attracted students not only from all over France but also from England since such training was not so readily available in Britain. Indeed, between 1816 (the close of Anglo-French hostilities) and 1832 (after which time courses in morbid anatomy became increasing central to the process of certification in Britain), the number of English students enrolled at the Faculté de Médecine increased from less to a handful to over eighty.[29] Writing just prior to the passage of the 1832 Anatomy Act, one British commentator complained bitterly in the pages of the *Quarterly Review* about the dearth of cadavers:[30]

The medical and surgical students who come annually to London for this kind of education, are in number about eight hundred or one thousand. To instruct them in the knowledge of anatomy and the art of dissection, the only legal means are the bodies of executed murderers, which scarcely amount to twelve annually throughout England. In London, a year sometimes passes without the anatomical schools receiving a single body from this source, and they have rarely received more than one in a year.

Since the same writer estimated that each student needed to dissect three bodies to gain any degree of competence, it is clear that the Resurrectionists — who secured corpses for their clients by other, illegal, methods — had their work cut out for them. The shortage of subjects, moreover, had the result of raising the price from a couple of guineas to as much as sixteen — thereby making murder another option to grave-robbing. The writer urges, therefore, that the French system is adopted whereby any unclaimed body (which in practice meant those of the poor) could, after twenty-four hours, be passed on for dissection.

This tradition of postmortem dissection in French medical colleges goes some way to account for the fact that ghoulish stories relating to such practices were common in *frénétique* writing throughout the 1830s. Many of these writers were fresh from university, and not a few of the anecdotes they recount no doubt first circulated amongst the student fraternity. In an 1832 story by Louis Couilhac, the daughter of a surgeon at the Hospital Saint-Louis, who has been seduced and abandoned by a medical student, sinks into prostitution and is eventually dissected by her own father; the following year, Arago and Kermel went one better by publishing a story in which a worker asphyxiates one of his own children, the body later being sold on for dissection. The list could be extended almost at will. Not all such stories were quite so morbid however. The same writers also included in the same collection an amusing tale of a man hawking the body of a close friend round the craniologists and anatomists in order to recover a small debt that the deceased had left outstanding.[31]

Such stories obviously exploit deep-seated anxieties about the infringement of taboos connected with death. Within the context of the 1830s, this is frequently situated within the context of a debate between materialist science (considered to be a product of the eighteenth-century) and contemporary spiritual values.

In Chapter XVI of *L'Ane Mort,* Janin describes the extremely unpleasant treatment Henrietta undergoes for venereal disease. Such treatment, it is implied, amounts to a punishment for the transgression of sexual taboos. This medical theme is picked up again by Balzac in his short pastiche of the novel. The act of female dissection has itself, however, been seen by some feminist commentators as an act of misogyny. After all, the body on the slab is always feminine — never masculine. This is how Elaine Showalter presents the case:[32]

Men do not think of themselves as cases to be opened up. Instead, they open up a woman as a substitute for self-knowledge, both maintaining the illusion of their own invulnerability and destroying the terrifying female reminder of their own impotence and uncertainty. They gain control over an elusive and threatening femininity by turning the woman into a "case" to be opened or shut. The criminal slashes with his knife. The scientist and doctor open the woman up with the scalpel or pierce her with the stake.

Showalter goes on to point out that one of the standard images in the realistic novel at the *fin-de-siècle* was that of the "anatomist dissecting the cadaver" — an image commonly encountered in relation to Flaubert and Zola. In this respect, it is significant to note not only the manner in which Balzac leads us into the dissection-room, but also how many times Janin himself uses the term dissection in a metaphorical sense throughout the novel.

One of the most atrocious passages in *L'Ane Mort et la femme guillotinée* — the one in which Charlot is savaged to death by a pack of dogs — occurs in the opening chapter of the novel. Animal fights had been imported to France from England in the years following the battle of Waterloo. They took place on Sunday and Bank Holiday evenings after nightfall and tended to attract an extremely socially mixed audience, including fashionable members of society such as the narrator of Janin's novel. These fights were publicized by posters which were to be seen all over Paris. Some showed engravings of a bull throwing half a dozen dogs into the air, their stomachs ripped open; others featured a champion bulldog by the name of Maroquin, "famous for the force of his jaws", suspended in the air by his teeth. Beneath this would follow the time, date and place of the combat, and then, like a list of toreadors, the names of butchers's apprentices responsible for baiting the animals and, no doubt, cutting them up afterwards. The spectators would take their place on a crudely-constructed grandstands made of wooden planks to watch ferocious battles between dogs, bears, wolves and wild boars. One of the most popular such spectacles was that of a pack of dogs setting on a donkey with a monkey attached to his back.[33]

Théophile Gautier attended one such combat. This is how he describes the opening spectacle:

The evening began with a fight between two monstrously ugly and extraordinarily ferocious bulldogs. As soon as they had been set down on the ground, they set off like arrows and howling in the most furious and fearful manner sank their teeth into each other without a moment's hesitation. They grappled in this manner for some time, taking it in turn to grip their opponent's enormous head in their enormous jaws, and ripping their muzzles with gleaming teeth. Innumerable streaks of bright blood streamed down their bodies, and they would probably have remained on the field of battle until the last bone in their tails was broken if the audience, moved by their heroic performance, had not began to clamour: "Enough! Enough!" All efforts to drag them apart were in vain, so that it was necessary to burn their tails with a hot poker in order to separate them!

For Janin, however, such spectacles recalled nothing so much as the behaviour of the public at official executions — especially those conducted in 1789. "We have not yet a circus, where, as among the Romans, we can devour one another," he remarks, "but, alas! we have already the *barrière du Combat.*" This connection between the idea of circuses and Republican excess is specifically made in Janin's *Barnave* of 1831, a novel dealing with the ambiguous revolutionary leader of the same name: "The power of Augustus provided Rome with security. Liberty was traded for a cleverly provided material happiness. In exchange for their rights, the people had bread and circuses."[34] Between *L'Ane Mort* and *Barnave*, France changed kings — adopting by force of revolution a constitutional monarch in place of an absolutist monarch. In 1831, Janin (politically, a legitimist) clearly anticipated Louis-Philippe's reign to deteriorate into a populist regime dominated by bread and circuses. In this he was proved wrong. By 1835, animal combats such as the one recounted in *L'Ane mort* had been outlawed.

As always, in *L'Ane Mort* it is the narrator's cold detachment from suffering which is the most remarkable feature of the text (and let us not forget that, having gone to see an animal combat on the wrong day, it is he who pays for Charlot to be torn to pieces). The revolutionaries of 1789 who, like him, had elevated themselves to the highest *philosophie*, regarded human life with similar indifference. One member of the revolutionary tribunal would throw a ball the evening after executions had taken place. The executioner sat at his table, and *parler guillotine* was the species of wit in which the guests vied with each other. Another member of the same tribunal refused to allow the cart in which the victims were brought back from the guillotine to be lined with tin because he thought it was better that a trail of blood was to be clearly seen.

Since Hugo was one of the leading writers to incorporate horror motifs into his novels, it is hardly surprising that we should find a number of allusions to these works in *L'Ane Mort*. The stories, for example, told by

[158]

the three men who claim to have been hanged, impaled, or drowned — and which conclude with the offended Capucin monk remarking that he has just had a narrow escape from death by indigestion — cock a transparent snook at *Le Dernier jour d'un condamné*.[35] Janin cites in extenso an article published in *Le Globe* of January 3, 1828 entitled *Dernières sensations d'un homme condamné a mort* which is considered to have inspired Hugo's novel of similar title. Certain parallels with *Han d'Islande* may also be detected, particularly with respect to the morgue episode.

Janin's ambiguous attitude towards Hugo has itself been presented as being indicative of his own intellectual confusion towards this time Although the two writers would later become close friends (united in their opposition to Louis Napoleon), in 1829, Janin — as his articles in *La Quotidienne* clearly demonstrate — was far from accepting without question the tenets of romanticism and the liberal ideology which was beginning to be associated with it. Thus, despite his own preferences for monarchism and classicism, he nonetheless reviewed Hugo's *Odes et Ballades* favourably. On the other hand, he was also responsible for an extremely unflattering review of *Le Dernier jour d'un condamné* — a review in which, at the same time as refusing to participate in any sort of debate over the issues raise by the work concerning the evils of capital punishment, he reproaches the author for entering into so many of the gruesome details surrounding the convict's slow agony as the day of his execution approaches. "This book [...] can only kill any emotions which remain in us [...]" — he complains — "just imagine a death agony of three hundred pages."[37]

Hugo's intellectual realignment towards the left is often considered to date from the publication of *Le Dernier jour*. Janin, more problematically, towards the same period not only wrote for the *Figaro*, an opposition newspaper, but also (from August, 1828) for the pro-government *La Quotidienne*. His seeming political inconsistency towards this time remained a subject for personal attacks for the rest of Janin's life. As late as 1854, the matter resulted in a libel action brought against the *Figaro*.

Given his political ambivalence at this time, it is perhaps hardly surprising that recent commentators have tended to identify Janin himself with his narrator in *L'Ane Mort*. It could be equally argued that Janin occupied a political middle ground, eschewing radical solutions of any kind. This is what Janin (in reply to an attack in a Belgian review) had to say on the matter: "*La Confession*, written at the height of the power of the Jesuits during the Restoration, is a book which is every bit as independent as *Barnave*, published six months after the July Revolution."[38] Despite certain reservations, Janin would seem to have maintained a reasonably moderate Royalist stance throughout the period in question (even briefly switching allegiance in 1830 from the Bourbon cause to that of Louis-Philippe). His over-riding concern, however, as with many right-wing intellectuals, was the threat of increasing social disorder.

As with Pétrus Borel, Janin's career as a *frénétique* novelist culminated with a novel of the French Revolution: *Barnave* (1831). Since this novel con-

Afterword

tains a lengthy account of events leading up to the execution of Marie-Antoinette, climaxing in a description of a women being crucified, it has an obvious bearing on the central image of *L'Ane Mort*.

One recent historian has written, "For the past two hundred years the French Revolution has been the sole heritage of French public life."[39] It is, therefore, hardly surprising that images of revolution are extremely prevalent in *frénétique* fiction, especially after the Revolution of 1830. The latter, of course, was a relatively minor affair: a few days of street fighting, a (legitimate) Bourbon king replaced by a ("constitutional") Orleanist one. Passions ran high, however, and for the next few years every political shade of opinion from that of the radical left (which, arguably, wanted to take off from where Saint-Just and Robespierre had left off in 1794 in their attempts to impose a Republic of Virtue by use of the guillotine) to that of the ultra-royalists (for whom the idea of a constitutional monarch was a self-contradiction in terms) was given expression. The Revolution of 1789, moreover, provided many novelists which a convenient set of historical analogies of relevance, or so they thought, to contemporary politics.

As we have already suggested, a number of writers in the late eighteenth-century made great capital out of the supposed sexual scandals surrounding the royal court. That Marie-Antoinette (amongst others) was the victim of a sustained campaign of vilification of a pornographic nature during the eighteenth-century has long been known. More recently, however, such attempts at vilification have come to be seen not so much as erotic in essence as political.

Thus, the focus of attention has shifted from the extent of her actual involvement in various public scandals to the symbolic meaning underlying the literature dealing with such matters. Sarah Maza, for example, discussing the notorious Diamond Necklace Affair, has drawn attention to the "emblematic status" that the queen attained "in a growing body of revolutionary literature denouncing the political ambitions of female rulers and consorts";[40] Lynn Hunt likewise sees behind the explosion of vitriolic pornographic pamphlets against Marie-Antoinette a "fundamental anxiety about queenship as the most extreme form of women invading the public sphere" coupled with a mounting fear of disintegrating gender boundaries.[41]

Typical of the kind of publication Hunt draws attention to are the *Essai historique sur la vie de Marie-Antoinette* (1781), *Le Godemiché royal* [i.e. "The Royal Dildo"] (1789) and the "more elaborately pornographic" *Fureurs utérines de Marie-Antoinette, femme de Louis XVI* (1791) [i.e "The Uterine Furies of Marie-Antoinette, wife of Louis XVI"].[42] The latter contained coloured engravings depicting an impotent Louis XVI being replaced by d'Artois and Polignac in the act of sexual intercourse with the queen.

Though not in itself licentious, this brand of revolutionary literature culminated with Louise de Keralio's five-hundred-page *Les Crimes des reines de France depuis le commencement de la monarchie jusqu'à Marie-Antoinette* (1791) — a work which begins with a discussion of the crimes of early queens during the dark ages such as Fredegond and Brunehaut, lingers over the vices of Catherine and Marie de Médicis, and concludes, predictably enough, with a protracted exposure of the alleged misconduct of the greatest monster of them all, Marie-Antoinette herself. The entire volume serves to illustrate the simple thesis, advanced in the introduction, that a woman who has been granted absolute power is capable of any excess: "Drunkenness on wine produces more vices in women than in men; the craving for power and the taste for domination has even more unfortunate effects on the former than the latter. A woman who can do anything is capable of anything; a woman who becomes a queen changes her sex [...]."[43] The introduction itself goes on to adduce biblical proofs in support of this statement. Although this work was reprinted at least twice during the 1790s, it is especially significant for present purposes that there was a new edition published in 1830.

The youthful narrator of *Barnave*, Frédéric de Wulfenbuttel, raised in the court of Frédéric II, is trapped between the conflicting desire to be "the disciple of Voltaire" and the knowledge that he is in his heart of hearts "a true feudal baron." Consequently, he is in the paradoxical situation of being relatively unable to take political sides. Nonetheless, almost on his arrival on French soil he notices that abuses have become institutionalised under the *ancien régime*: "As hour by we approached Paris, already I sensed that we were in France due to all the misery I witnessed on the main highway. At every step on our way, we met with fatigue parties, tax-collectors, salt merchants, customs officers, monasteries, feudal castles, corps of constabulary, chain gangs on their way to prison. . . We were obviously approaching Paris. I felt my heart falter with every step that we made towards that abyss without shape and without name." Throughout the novel there are continual reminders of the decadence and degeneration of the country, both of which are seen as the product of misrule. At one end of Paris he finds the gambling-houses and dens of prostitution of the Palais-Royal, at the other end the Bastille. "What was the real cause of all those signs of decadence?" he is forced to ask himself.

The answer is to be found, as we might by now expect, in the debauchery of the monarchy and the aristocracy of the mid-eighteenth century. This finds allegorical expression in a story (told by Cagliostro) concerning Cleopatra and the decline of the Roman Empire. "In the Orient of those times, it was exactly the same as in France before the Revolution of 1789," concludes the narrator. "Sophisms and pleasure spilled out everywhere across the land of the Pharaohs et the Pyramids; the ancient Orient itself was subject to social decomposition. That begins and ends with women and debauchery, just as in the Paris of Louis XV."

Janin's narrator provides a long catalogue of the extent of the corruption from a performance of *Figaro* which so disgusts his mother through to rumours of royal sexual misconduct and diatribes against women's attire at the opera. Finally, the author is driven to biblical comparisons: death hovers over Paris "just as it had weighed over the cities of the sulphurous lakes of holy writ."

All of this, of course, is perfectly consistent with the image of Paris presented in *L'Ane Mort*. Against such descriptions, however, it is significant to note that Marie-Antoinette, unlike Henrietta, is portrayed as extraordinarily chaste. Indeed, Marie-Antoinette alone of all the central protagonists is depicted as passing her nights innocently. It is this innocence, no doubt, which is the cause of the pact between Mirabeau, Barnave and the narrator to protect her at all costs from revolutionary fury. Their concern does not seem to extend to Louis XVI, who is hardly mentioned. This rejection of the male figure of authority is extremely curious, but whatever the reason behind it the political compromise that the author would seem to wish to establish — between the despotic past and the demands of the future — are focused on a matriarchal image.

In the event, the novel does not describe Marie-Antoinette's execution in detail. Instead, there is substituted an horrific description of a girl being crucified that the narrator accidentally witnesses shortly after the failed flight to Varennes.

Suddenly, through the windows of the house opposite, at the moment of our greatest discouragement, a strange apparition attracted our attention. A bright light appeared at this window, and inside the apartment we could see a number of people enter, each with a sad and thoughtful countenance, who stationed themselves on their knees against the walls [...] men and women, priests in their cassocks, young girls in white dresses who struck their stomachs as they prayed. Finally, a side door opened, and we saw an old priest come in dragging a wooden cross [...]. When everything was ready, the same door opened again, and this time the victim came in [...]. She was a young girl with haggard eyes. Two older women directed her step, holding her arms. A supernatural force took hold of her senses when she saw the cross and the nails. At the sight of these things, she started up with a convulsive movement, and took a few steps forward unassisted [...], she lay down on the cross, raising her head and, crossing her feet, stretched out her arms, and opened her hands, two hands covered in blood. . . and in this position she waited, patiently and resigned, she too. — *I will save the world by my suffering*.

[...] The victim was ready. The old priest approached her, he kissed her feet and hands with the respect that a dying man kisses the seven wounds of Christ. At the same time, the child presented him an iron hammer on a silver platter. The hammer drove a large nail through her feet, then another through the victim's hands. . . And the nail parted the flesh, parted the tendons, broke the bone, blood trickled over her chest! And the crucified girl was joined to the cross. . . Her eyes swollen, her cheeks hanging, her breast beating, her neck lined with blue veins, almost fainting. . .

This 'black' passion of Christ would again seem to resume many of the themes we discussed in relation to *L'Ane Mort*. The voyeuristic nature of the event is clearly in evidence, though the narrator is now accompanied by his mother, with whom he exchanges a look of comprehension, and his fiancée. They themselves, moreover, are being watched in turn by an "motionless spy". The victim, who is once again feminine, is also being both punished and deified.

In political terms, however, the strongest reference is perhaps to Joseph de Maistre's conservative doctrine of salvation through blood. During the first half of the nineteenth-century, the blood of innumerable saints, the working class, and Louis XVI were all ascribed by various groups with such powers of atonement. Here the victim atones through her purity not only for the political crimes of her epoch but for the crimes of her sex. Janin alone would seem to have extended the category of those with redemptive powers, if only symbolically, to the much-hated Marie-Antoinette. In contrast with, for example, Borel whose hatred of the monarchy is strongly developed in *Madame Putiphar*, Janin articulates a mystical love story centred upon a dead queen.

The satirical elements of *L'Ane Mort* are displaced in *Barnave* by an attempt to mythologize the events of 1793. The key to both this crucifixion scene and the guillotining of Henrietta is provided perhaps by *le fou de Marie-Antoinette*: "Tell me, though, I beg you, have you never thought of the consequences of all this revolution? Have you never thought of the executioner who dispatches, even as he adores her, the victim who has been thrown to him? What an abominable crime! What exquisite torture!"

In this manner are the figures of the prostitute and the former queen of France, united through a belief in their ungovernable sexuality or incredible chastity, redeemed by their symbolic deaths. If this remark seems fanciful, let us recall that in October 1793 Chaumette, *procureur* of the commune, mooted the idea of bringing two prostitutes to trial with Marie-Antoinette. The true horror of these works is, thus, perhaps the manner in which they reveal the full extent of French Romantic misogyny.

— *Terry Hale*

Notes

Although it would have preferable to cite the original French text beside English translations, this has been precluded for reasons of space. All translations, except of *L'Ane Mort*, are by the present writer unless otherwise specified.

1. *Maxime du Camp*, Souvenirs littéraires, Paris, Hachette, 1892, Vol. II, p. 284.
2. *Arsène Houssaye*, Confessions. Souvenirs d'un demi-siècle, Paris, Dentu, 1885, Vol IV, p. 339.
3. *Mario Praz*, The Romantic Agony, Tr. Angus Davidson, 2nd. edition, London, Oxford University Press, pp. 124-130. *The link between Janin and Sade was perhaps first forged by an article in the* Journal de Liége *in 1834 à propos Janin's* Le Piédestal. Cf. Le journaliste franco-belge (anon.), Revue de Paris, Oct., 1834, pp. 56-75.
4. *Joseph-Marc Bailbé*, Préambule to L'Ane Mort et la femme guillotinée, Paris, Flammarion, 1973, p. 14.
5. *Jacques Landin*, Jules Janin. Conteur et romancier, Paris, Société Les belles Lettres, 1978, p. 104.
6. *Lewis S. Feuer*, The Conflict of Generations. The Character and Significance of Student Movements, London, Heinemann, 1969, p. 11. *See also Anthony Esler, "Youth in Revolt: The French Generation of 1830", in* Modern European Social History, Robert J. Bezucha (ed.), Lexington, D. C. Heath, 1972, pp. 301-334; James Smith Allen, Popular French Romanticsm. Authors, Readers, and Books in the 19th. Century, Syracuse, Syracuse University Press, 1981, pp. 74-101.
7. *Feuer*, op. cit., p. 264. *The youthful Frédéric Soulié, later to become a major author of frénétique works such as* Les Deux Cadavres *(1832), for example, would seem to have been involved to some extent with the Charbonnnerie.*
8. *Daniel Arasse*, The Guillotine and the Terror, London, Penguin, 1989, p. 2.
9. *Adèle Hugo*, Victor Hugo raconté, Paris, Plon, 1985, p. 418.
10. Cf. *Adèle Hugo*, op. cit., p. 417; Gérard de Nerval, "Le Cabaret de la mère Saguet" (1830), now in Oeuvres complètes, Paris, Gallimard, 1952, Vol. 1, pp. 475 - 476.
11. *Adèle Hugo*, op. cit., p. 418.
12. *Though, as we shall see, it would be unfair to directly equate Janin with his narrator, it is perhaps worth pointing out that the former's own domestic arrangements towards this time were to say the least somewhat curious. In 1829, he entered into relations with Mlle George, the actress, who was also the mistress of Paul Harel, director of the Odéon, who was married to her sister. All four lived together in a house on rue Madame — a house, in Alexandre Dumas's words, "d'une composition bien originale". Mlle George, moreover, was Janin's elder by seventeen years.*
13. La Confession, p. 211. *Page references are to the Flammarion edition of 1973. Janin's epithet for this chapter, appropriately enough, is drawn from Hamlet, thus associating Anatole's behaviour with the revenger's madness.*
14. *The remainder of the novel is taken up with Anatole's attempt to gain absolution for his crime. When, after a period of temporary insanity, he finally manages to achieve this goal, it is by accepting permanent emasculation: he becomes a priest.* (p. 310) La Confession did not, of course, introduce the theme of male impotency into Romantic fiction. Indeed, Madame de Duras would seem to have originally suggested the idea, an idea rapidly taken up by Latouche in Olivier (1826) and shortly afterwards by Stendhal in Armance (1827). Cf. Denise Virieux, Introduction to Mme de Duras's Olivier ou le secret, Paris, Corti, 1971, pp. 31-39.

15. René Girard, Violence and the Sacred, Tr. Patrick Gregory, Baltimore, Johns Hopkins University Press, 1977, pp. 139-142. More traditionally, Jacques Revel considers that the motifs associated with the confusion of the genders probably date from the 1750s and the threat of the invasion of the public sphere by women during the reign of Louis XV: "Marie-Antoinette in Her Fictions: The Staging of Hated", in Bernadette Fort (ed.), Fictions of the French Revolution, Evanston, Northwestern University Press, 1991, pp. 111-130 at pp. 112-113. With respect to Janin, see especially his highly unflattering portrait of the Chevalier d'Eon (Barnave, pp. 182-183). Likewise, one of the reproaches he makes of the Mariage de Figaro is sexual in nature: "Etre double et dangereux hermaphrodite, il peuplait la ville de Chérubins de quinze ans [...]." (Barnave, p. 78.) All page references to Barnave are to the 1860 edition published by Michel Lévy. This differs in some respects to the original edition of 1831.

16. See Stallybrass and White, The Politics and Poetics of Transgression, London, Methuen, 1986, especially pp. 149 - 170.

17. Sigmund Freud, 'From the history of an infantile neurosis (the "Wolf Man")' (1918), cited by Stallybrass and White, op. cit., p. 153.

18. For a number of less frénétique (though nonetheless slightly obsessional) accounts of a young man's fascination for working girls, see Janin's "Elle et l'Ane" (1829); "Encore elle!" and "La Grisette". All these pieces, according to Janin's Petits Mélanges (Paris, Librairie des bibliophiles, 1881) in which they are reprinted, date from 1829.

19. Hunt, op cit., p. 126. (See preface, Note 12.)

20. Peter Brooks, "The Revolutionary Body", in Bernadette Fort (ed.), Fictions of the French Revolution, op. cit., pp. 35-54 at p. 38.

21. Cited by Linda Kelly, Women of the French Revolution, London, Hamish Hamilton, 1989, p. 102.

22. Arasse, op. cit., p. 4.

23. On the trial of Marie-Antoinette, see particularly: Hunt, op. cit.; Revel, op. cit.; and Brooks, op. cit..

24. e.g. Parent-Duchâtelet's La Prostitution dans la Ville de Paris (1836). Such reformers were not necessarily particularly enlightened in moral outlook. Parent-Duchâtelet, for example, described the prostitutes as "the woman-sewer." Cited by Elaine Showalter, Sexual Anarchy, London, Virago, 1991, p. 193.

25. Sarah Maza, "The Diamond Necklace Affair Revisited (1785-1786): The Case of the Missing Queen", in Lynn Hunt (ed.) Eroticism and the Body Politic, Baltimore, Johns Hopkins Press, 1991, pp. 63-98 at p. 68.

26. Hunt, op. cit., p. 112.

27. Cited by Brooks, op. cit., p. 36.

28. Reprinted in Contes fantastiques et littéraires, Genève, Slatkine Ressources, 1979, p. 61. The word vertu occurs frequently in L'Ane Mort, even providing the title for Ch. VII in which the narrator seeks a definition of the term. Significantly, the only ones he discovers prove to be be farcical.

29. Russell C. Maulitz, Morbid Appearances. The Anatomy of Pathology in the Early Nineteenth Century, Cambridge University Press, 1987, pp. 140-141.

30. Anon. "A Bill for preventing the unlawful Disinterment of Human Bodies, and for regulating Schools of Anatomy. 1829." The Quarterly Review, Vol. XLII, Jan. 1830, p. 9.

31. "La Fille du Chirugien", in Louis Couailhac's Les Septs contes noirs (Paris, Bohaine, 1832); "Fain, Vengence et Justice" and "Rien" in Arago and Kermel's Insomnies (Paris, Guillaumin, 1833).

32. Elaine Showalter, op. cit., p. 134. Significantly, Sade describes as early as 1787 a failed

attempt at the dissection of a young girl in The Misfortunes of Virtue (O.U.P., 1992, pp. 58-61).

33. *Much of the information here is derived from Jules Bertaut's essay on "Les anciens combats d'animaux à Paris"*, in Visages Romantiques, *Paris, Ferenczi, 1947, pp. 125-130.*

34. *This passage, to be found in a chapter entitled "Les deux Filles de Séjan", was omitted from the 1860 edition. It is to be found in the first edition of* Barnave *(Paris, Levavasseur, 4 vol., 1831), Vol. II, p. 235.*

35. *Geoff Woollen's new translation of this work,* The Last Day of a Condemned Man *(O.U.P., 1992) is to be highly recommended.*

36. *Cf. Landrin, op. cit., pp. 63-68.*

37. *La Quotidienne, Feb. 3, 1829.*

38. *Le journaliste franco-belge, op cit., pp. 65-66.*

39. *François Furet, "The Tyranny of Revolutionary Memory", in Bernadette Fort (ed.),* Fictions of the French Revolution, *op. cit., 1991, pp. 151-160, at p. 151.*

40. *Maza, op. cit., p. 82.*

41. *Hunt, op. cit., p. 123.*

42. *Ibid, pp. 118-119.*

43. *Les Crimes des reines de France, Paris, au bureau des Révolutions, an II [1793], pp. vi - vii. There are a number of doubts about about the authorship of this work. Formerly attributed to Prudhomme, it was attributed to Louise de Kéralio by Quérard on the basis of the article on her in the* Biographie universelle. *Quérard's view would seem to have prevailed. Wife of Pierre Robert (an influential deputy in the National Convention), Mme de Kéralio herself also helped edit the* Mercure national *(1790-1791), a journal which reflected the advanced views of the Cordeliers Club (which was open to women) of which Danton and Marat were the leading lights. Given her own political inclinations, it is doubly ironic that such an anti-feminist work as* Les Crimes des reines de France *should have been the product of her pen.*